Blood Rain

by Chloe Cocking

Filidh Publishing

ISBN 978-1-927848-31-9
Second Soft Cover Edition
Filidh Publishing, Victoria, British Columbia

For Rob, always

Table of Contents

Chapter One

I slid into the tub. The water was hot, and the frothy bubbles felt creamy against my skin. My fluffy grey cat, Bluebell, was curled up in the bathroom sink. Only the tips of her ears were visible from my position in the tub, but I could hear her purring. I felt my shoulders start to unknot in the warm water. In movies, this is when the doorbell rings.

The doorbell rang. I sighed. Clenching my eyes shut, I remained motionless in the bathtub. Surely whoever it was would get tired of ringing and go away? No such luck. Nope. They were leaning on the bell and pounding on the door at the same time. With a resigned sigh, I stood up in the bath, grabbed my robe, and wrapped it around my sudsy body.

As I walked into the living room, I could hear Dougherty on the other side of the door, shouting "Goddammit, Suzanne, come on, I know you're in there!"

I shouted back, "I'm coming, I'm coming, keep your pants on!"

I swung the apartment door open. Dougherty stood there with a woman I'd never seen before. They both grinned at me and each other. Dougherty's blue eyes twinkled, and he started to chuckle.

"Nice face, Suzanne," Dougherty said.

My hand flew to my cheek. Oh. The facial mask.

"What now, rehearsing for the Blue Man group?" he continued. I frowned at him. I shivered inside my damp robe.

"Come in, it's freezing, and I'm wet," I said.

I moved back to allow them to enter. Dougherty and the woman with him stepped inside, carefully avoiding the puddle I had made on the laminate. As usual, Dougherty was clad in what I think of as 'detective chic' clothes: a collared shirt, grey sports coat, relaxed fit jeans, running shoes, a black leather belt holding his gun and Seattle PD badge. His salt-and-pepper hair was cut close to his head. Dougherty was tall, and his broad shoulders and thick torso allowed him to fill the doorway.

I looked at the woman accompanying Dougherty. She also was tall, maybe five-foot ten or eleven—even in her flat, sensible shoes. She was the kind of woman that other women in less enlightened eras loved to hate—leggy, slender, and drop-dead gorgeous. She wasn't even wearing any makeup. She looked about thirty, maybe thirty-five. Her deep green suede blazer matched her eyes. Her long red hair was gathered into a tidy bun at the nape of her neck. I faux-hated her already.

Dougherty saw the question in my eyes and said "Suzanne, this is Wendy McCabe, she's in Vice, usually, but she's also spooky. She's been loaned to us to work on something. We're going to need your help, too. What's going on is . . ."

I held up a hand. "Stop right there. I'm dripping everywhere. Give me ten minutes to de-blue my face, dry off, and get some clothes on—I'm so cold my teeth are starting to chatter. There's Diet Coke in the fridge, help yourself to that or whatever you want, I'll be back."

I returned to the bathroom and had the world's quickest, hottest shower. I managed to get all the facial mask off without a mirror while I was under the water and keep most of my hair dry at the same time. Talented, huh? I very carefully avoided thinking about what it might be that Dougherty wanted. I am always apprehensive at the start of a case. It had been a couple of months since I had last consulted with Seattle's informal Spook Squad. I had enjoyed the peace and quiet.

In my bedroom, I stood in a towel in front of the closet trying to decide what to put on. I looked regretfully at the flannel pajamas I had laid out on my bed. They were my favorites—they were hot pink and had grinning polar bears on them that glowed in the dark. No way was I going to see the inside of those for at least a couple more hours

"Ok, something warm," I said to myself, rubbing the goosebumps on my arms. I drew my long black skirt out of the closet and tossed it on the end of the bed. I added my fuzzy peacock blue sweater to the skirt and searched my dresser for some clean underwear. Unsuccessful, so commando tonight. I put on warm knee socks and my hot pink Chuck Taylors.

I quickly looked at myself in the mirror. "Well, it's as good as they are going to get at 8 o'clock on a Sunday night," I muttered, running my fingers through my curly hair.

Back in the living room, Dougherty and McCabe were seated on my couch, each with a cup of coffee in hand. Another cup sat at the elbow of the nearby chair.

"I took the liberty of making a pot of coffee," Dougherty said.

McCabe looked at me over the rim of her cup. She seemed still and humorless. Maybe that was what working Vice did to you. It was unnerving.

"So, what do you know about vampires?" asked Dougherty.

"You mean, beyond the allergic-to-garlic, no suntan, "I never drink wine" stuff? Nothing except for what I've seen on the late show."

"So, don't know any of Those Who Live Between?" McCabe asked.

"What's that?" I looked at her quizzically.

"Not "what," "who," Suzanne," McCabe replied. "Those Who Live Between" is how organized, civilized vampires refer to themselves. They see themselves as existing between life and death, between the human and supernatural communities, really even between "good" and "evil." You could hear the air quotes in her voice.

"Supernatural communities?"

McCabe glanced at Dougherty with irritation. Sliding her gaze back to me, she said, "Let me start at the beginning: Suzanne, I am told you are a powerful psychic, particularly attuned to death and death magick. Many would consider you part of the supernatural community. You don't have any experience with other super-people?"

My right temple began to throb. All the tension the shower had melted out of my neck returned.

"No, I don't, because Batgirl and Aquaman had me drummed out of the union for non-payment of dues."

McCabe frowned and opened her mouth to reply. I interrupted her.

"So, you're telling me that the things that go bump in the night have organized themselves into bowling leagues and Mah Jong clubs?" I asked sharply.

"Not all the things," McCabe said, quietly. She sighed. "I hadn't expected you'd be this hard to convince, or—no offense—this green," she said, glancing at me before looking reproachfully at Dougherty. "Paul, maybe she's not the one to help us."

Dougherty shook his head. "She's the real deal, Wendy, she just needs education, she's in the supe-closet, even to herself."

"Err, uh, guys? I'm still here, sitting in the room with you—can you kindly just tell me what's going on and why you got me out of my bath on a Sunday night?"

McCabe smiled at me. "I think sometimes I forget that most people aren't steeped in vampire lore."

"And you are?" I said, trying to keep the sneer from my voice.

"I am," she said evenly. "My Master's degree is in anthropology; my dissertation was on vampire secret societies."

"Huh," I said. "So, you are an expert in this stuff. Goody. I am not, I've only done a couple of cases with Paul . . ."

Dougherty broke in. "Hand to God, Wendy, she is not an expert, but she gets shit done. She's doing this work because I wouldn't leave her alone until she did."

I smiled and shook my head ruefully. "It's true. He recruited me through a friend of my uncle. So far I've only done a couple of jobs with the SPD."

"So, you didn't apply through the usual channels for psychics?" McCabe asked.

"Nope," I said.

Dougherty said, "I was working the Padelecki murder about six months ago. We were in the weeds, and it looked like it might go cold case. One of my poker buddies mentioned to me that his friend had a niece that was some kind of psychic and who could talk to the dead. I pestered him until he introduced us."

"Then he pestered me until I helped him out," I said, smirking.

Dougherty grinned. "I'm charming like that."

McCabe frowned. "Is it safe to say then that you are reluctant to use your abilities?"

"Yes, usually I am. I'd rather not be a death psychic. In fact, I don't even want very many people to know about my abilities. But in the few months, since I've been helping Paul out, I notice that working with my abilities is easier. I think I need an outlet. I'm learning aspects of ritual magick to help with management, too."

McCabe took a thoughtful sip from her coffee mug. "I wish you had more experience with this. But there is no way a standard psychic can do it; they can only read the living." She sighed.

Dougherty cleared his throat. "What about this, Wendy? Let's tell lil' Suzi-Q here the details, see what she thinks."

McCabe nodded.

He continued. "It breaks down like this, Suzanne—the local vampire poo-bah contacted the network of spooky cops. The vamps have a problem on their hands. They need us to help them solve it."

I took a breath and let it out slowly. I didn't know much about vampires, not beyond the usual stuff everybody knows. I had not actually ever met a vampire; they were pretty rare on the West Coast. They were more established in Europe and the Eastern seaboard. Truly I think I'd spent more time learning about Turkish Kurds or Ashkenazi Jews that I had vampires and their culture. The two societies were pretty segregated. Right or wrong, I think that probably came as a relief to both sides.

Dougherty walked over to the kitchenette and poured himself a warm-up for his coffee. He said, "Here's the deal, the vampires in the Seattle area are charter members of Those Who Walk Between. That means they have an appointed Coven of more senior vamps that basically keep vamp law and order," Dougherty continued. "They make sure that younger vamps learn self-control, that any older vamps who go mad are kept contained, and they do their damnedest to prevent much association between vampires and human beings."

I glanced over at McCabe. She was nodding in agreement as Dougherty spoke. The lamplight made her porcelain skin glow and illuminated dark pomegranate highlights in her hair. *Wow, she's really beautiful.* I felt a pang of envy. I know I'm not supposed to feel envious of other women, twenty-first-century sisterhood is powerful and all that. But I sometimes did anyway. I wished I was beautiful.

I looked at the pale but intensely freckled skin on my forearms. I didn't gleam like bone china in the lamplight; my skin looked merely pasty underneath the freckles. My dishwater blond curly hair gets dry and brittle if I try to straighten it. My eyes are an unremarkable grey. I'm short, round, and pudgy, not lithe and long-limbed. Against my will, my eyes flicked back to McCabe, admiring the elegant way she had crossed her ankles as she sipped her coffee.

"Suze?" asked Dougherty.

"Wha? Huh?"

"Looks we lost you for a sec there. . ."

"Yeah, sorry, lost in thought for a minute. I'm paying attention now," I said.

"Ok," McCabe said, then sipped her coffee. "Someone has been making revenants out of children. Those Who Walk Between don't know who's behind it. Making revenants is against vampire law—you have to get permission to sire any kind of vampire. And no one is permitted to transport children to The World Between. In fact, the vampire we want you to interrogate, Leopold Von Ursler was imprisoned for that crime."

"Um, hold the phone: 'revenants'? Also, how do you manage to lock up a vampire?" I asked, raising an eyebrow.

"Revenants are people who've received non-lethal vampire bites but have not been given any of their Master's blood in return. They have some of the usual vampire powers, but not all of them. Their will is essentially slaved to their Master's. Revenants are used as serfs or slaves. Only vampires of the highest rank are permitted to make revenants."

I took a swig of my rapidly-cooling coffee and shifted in my seat. "So, let me get this straight—normally vamps either kill you with a lethal bite, or they give you a non-lethal bite, and then open a vein for you—it's the bite plus their blood that makes a new vamp?"

"Yes, precisely," said McCabe, nodding.

"And the revenants get bit but not fed, so they are kind of like mindless robots with no will of their own?"

McCabe leaned forward and placed her empty coffee mug on the coffee table. "Not exactly robots, but close enough," she said.

"And they locked up this Leopold guy for doing this? How do they keep him under wraps? How do they know he wasn't the one who did it before they locked him up? Maybe he made other revenants they don't know about."

McCabe cleared her throat. "They locked Leopold up in 1910. He didn't make a revenant; he turned a teenager into a regular vampire so that Leopold and his boyfriend could have a companion and lover."

"But how do they know he didn't also make some revenants?" I asked.

""The revenants we are talking about were all twenty-first-century kids," Dougherty interjected.

McCabe shifted in her seat. "Yes, that's true, we know these are modern crimes. Von Ursler's been imprisoned for over a hundred years."

I leant back in my chair and pushed some of my still-damp hair out of my eyes. "Ok, so how do the vampires manage that? Is there any way he could be slipping out and making revenants?"

"No. He's trapped in the Den of the Forsaken," McCabe said.

"What's that?" I interrupted.

"It's what they call jail."

"Ok," I said, nodding.

"Getting out of the Den is nearly impossible. Each individual coffin has a unique magickal ward, and once a vampire has been in there for a while, they are very weak, very sick . . ."

"You seem pretty certain."

"I'm as certain about that as I am about anything," she said flatly.

I let out the breath I hadn't realized I'd been holding. "Ok, so we're confident Leopold is not behind this. But the big-bad vamp council . . ."

"Not "council," "Coven"" interrupted McCabe.

"Ok, the vampire Coven has asked for help because they think Leopold knows something that will help find some vampire creep who is running around biting kids and turning them into his slaves."

McCabe looked at Dougherty, then back at me. Her eyebrows beetled together over the bridge of her nose. She sighed. "Biting kids, turning them into his slaves, and using them in the sex trade, to be more specific."

I felt winded like I'd been punched. "You've got to be kidding me!"

The throbbing in my temple felt like someone banging on the hot metal doors of Hell. I looked at her in disbelief, then at Dougherty for confirmation of what I'd heard.

"It's true, Suzanne, Vice found out about it because they were investigating some leads around non-supernatural child sexual exploitation, and it got passed to McCabe, one of the only spooky cops in Vice. She's leading the investigation, and has unofficially tapped me for help, knowing I have a psychic necromancer on retainer."

I looked at the cold coffee at the bottom of my cup. I felt nauseated. "Why me? I know you have regular psychics working for you," I asked.

McCabe uncrossed her ankles as she shifted on the couch. "Suzanne, your particular set of psychic abilities is very useful for interviewing vampires. Vamps are immune to most psychic intrusions or readings—except when the psychic in question is a death psychic, a necromancer. You have powers over the dead. That's why you have the type of visions you have—of people about to die, the newly dead, and spirits who are trapped or defiant. You have a connection with the dead. Since vamps are essentially the spirits of dead people anchored to a body re-animated through viral infection and magick, you have an affinity for them. That's why I was so surprised that you said you didn't know anything of Those Who Live Between. Usually, necromancers have encountered vampires by the time they've reached adulthood; there is a psychic draw between the two groups."

My right temple throbbed, and the pain made me squint. "Does she always talk like fucking Wikipedia?" I growled in Dougherty's direction. It came out even sharper than I had intended. McCabe's cheeks flushed red, and her green eyes flashed in anger. Dougherty looked from my face to hers, and back again.

"I don't know what bug's gotten up your ass, Suzanne, but that was uncalled for," Dougherty said quietly.

I rubbed the knotted muscles in my neck.

"You're right. McCabe, I'm sorry. You were just trying to fill me in, and I snapped at you. It was mean. I'm tired and grumpy, and I just want to go to bed. Please, forgive me and forget it happened."

I sighed. Dougherty and McCabe sat silently, waiting.

I looked at them. They both sipped their coffees, their gazes nonchalant.

Ok, well, fuck it. I said, "Fine, if we are going to do an interrogation tonight, let's just go do it, alright?"

Dougherty nodded. "First we interrogate, then we report back to 'Juliet, Acolyte of the Western Lands'," said Dougherty.

I could hear the air quotes in his tone of voice. I sighed.

McCabe and Dougherty smiled. They waited for me while I turned off the coffee pot and grabbed my messenger bag with my 'go' kit.

On our way down to the parking lot, I asked, "Ok, anything special I need to know about interrogating this Leopold guy or meeting vampire royalty?"

"She's not royalty, just an Acolyte. That said, there's a fair bit you need a briefing on; they are sticklers for etiquette and protocol, and there are a lot of details about the Den of the Forsaken, too. I'll explain it in the car on the way. We've got about a forty-minute drive ahead of us, plus the time it takes to get from the Den to Juliet's home."

Great, just great. Quality time in the car with Encyclopedia Brown. This was going to be one long night.

Chapter Two

The metal door protested as we slid it open. The warehouse was lit, barely, by dim, buzzing fluorescent lights. The long side walls were lined with heavy industrial shelving from floor to ceiling. The shelving held hundreds, maybe even thousands, of coffins. It was reminiscent of those catacombs you see in photographs, where the walls of the cave have had recesses carved deep and long enough to hold a coffin. This was definitely the place. Either that or something had gone seriously wrong at Costco.

Some of the coffins were the cheap pine boxes of paupers, others ornate polished mahogany with decorative carvings and brass detailing. A few appeared to be made from some kind of concrete or other stone slab material. Every coffin was bound with chains and old-fashioned iron padlocks. Beyond that, I wasn't going to investigate too closely; I needed to get the circle of protection cast and operational. Even though I interrogate dead people for part of my living, I still get creeped out.

That's a relatively new way for me to earn some money. Gods know, my high school guidance counsellor never pulled a pamphlet out of his desk describing the fun-filled world of talking to the spirits of murdered children. I would have screamed and run away if he had.

My friend Star tells me that the proper word for my type of magick is "necromancy" and that I'm a "necromancer." Apparently, the word "necromancer" means "one who interrogates the dead." I prefer "death psychic" or just "psychic" myself. The word "necromancer" has connotations of raising the dead, reanimating zombies and the like. I don't know how to do those things. I wouldn't want to. Icky dead bodies, gross.

If I had any real options in the matter, I wouldn't have anything to do with the supernatural. Having tried ignoring my powers when they first manifested, over time I've come to see pretending to be a mundane is not an option. In some ways, being a psychic is like having a compulsion— you know how some people just have to check to make sure the iron is turned off, or that they double-bolted the door? I can't seem to stop talking to the dead. These days, I was opting to work with this ability, not against it.

I moved closer to the shelving on my right and looked more closely at the padlock. It was a crude iron padlock, but it had delicate engraving on it. Several symbols I didn't recognize were engraved in a circle.

Dougherty cleared his throat nervously. "The chains, those symbols on the lock, what are they for?"

"The chains are just for show; it's the magick in the locks that keep the vamps trapped. I haven't seen the runes around this name before, though. I'm not sure what they mean. Could be the personal magickal symbology of whoever warded this particular coffin?" McCabe said.

Dougherty cleared his throat again. His hand went to the gun at his waist. He didn't like that she didn't know.

I put my messenger bag down on the floor and started to rummage through it for supplies. The sooner I laid the circle, the sooner we could get out of here. I took out a Mason jar full of sea salt and lavender.

"Paul, Wendy, you're ready?" I asked. I knew Dougherty knew what to do next, and since McCabe was some kind of expert in all things magick-y, I figured she also knew the score. They came and stood near me. I paced out a circle nine feet in diameter, pouring salt and lavender as I went.

"What's the lavender for?" asked McCabe.

Without looking up from my task, I replied, "Angry or scary spirits smell really bad to me. Sometimes the smell is hard to get out of my nose. It's like I can taste it at the back of my throat for days after the interview. The lavender helps a bit."

"You told us you didn't really know anything about vamps – how do you know they'll have a psychic smell like spirits do?"

"I don't. I'm guessing they will. Probably "creepy" and "pissed off" stink no matter where they come from."

I closed the circle and put the lid back on the Mason jar. There is always a moment, once I'm in the sacred circle, but before I've opened the channels, that feels a bit like being underwater. Sound is muffled, and I can hear my blood throb in my head better than I can hear anything outside me. It's a moment outside time, pregnant with expectation. Star told me that's because the universe is holding its breath, waiting for me to open myself. Grandiose as that sounds, it does feel something like that. I think it may be that even without the channels open, I can feel the eagerness of the spirits.

McCabe had a funny look on her face. Maybe she was a Sensitive? I'd have to ask her later. She looked disturbed.

Dougherty just looked scared and like he was trying to cover it with cop-face, but not doing a great job. This was going to be a big one; I think we could all feel it. *Oh shit— I'm about to open myself to maybe a thousand trapped and most likely deranged vampires. Fuck! What a Sunday night I'm having.*

At first, I felt nothing, like some part of me has switched off. The world had shrunk down to just me, standing in stillness, trying to create a space for the voices of the dead. Then the bubble of silence burst and my ears roared with voices. The force of the sound made me stumble inside the circle. McCabe looked at me with surprise, and Dougherty grabbed me under the arm to keep me from sliding to the floor.

"Hold on there, Suzi-Q, don't punk out on us now, we need you." He sounded like he was far away or inside a tin can. I could see the worry in his eyes.

The voices hit me again, throbbing in my ears like a hammer to my brain. I felt my knees buckle again, and Dougherty's ham-sized hand gripping my upper arm, mashing the soft fibers of my sweater against my flesh.

I took a deep breath, and blew it out slowly, feeling some strength return to my legs. I centered myself and focused my attention on the feeling of breath in my body. The wall of sound that enclosed me dulled somewhat. It became more like the sound of staticky radio turned to top volume rather than a pulsing tsunami.

I shrugged off Dougherty's hand, squared my shoulders and said, "I am here to speak to Leopold von Ursler. Leopold von Ursler, you must answer my questions. You are compelled, for I am the fulcrum of darkness and light, a point of balance in the cosmos, and I will be obeyed."

Dramatic, I know, but spirits seemed to respond better to that sort of language than sentences like "Hi guys, Suzanne the necromancer here. Can I speak to Aunt Petunia, please?" At least, the spirits of regular dead people responded to it well. For all I knew, vampires responded best to invocations in pig Latin. If this didn't work, maybe I'd try that next.

"Leopold von Ursler, appear before my sacred circle and reveal your secrets to me—NOW!"

I spoke the last word with force. I could feel the magick behind that word drop from my lips and snake away from me. In my mind's eye, I could see it, a luminous red thread weaving among the stacks of coffins in the warehouse. The thread started to throb and pulse. I was getting close to Leopold's coffin. Then the thread made contact with Leopold's spirit.

With an unseen pull like that of a magnet, my magick drew his spirit from his imprisoned body, like a thick milkshake drawn up through a straw. In my mind's eye, I watched the red thread pull his spirit through the magickal wards surrounding his coffin. His spirit was a wisp of light mist, silver, softly glowing.

My magick pulled him slowly and inexorably to me. His spirit would stand before me. He was compelled. When Leopold's spirit came to rest at the edge of the sacred circle, my nostrils filled with the scent of rotten fruit and sulphur, strong enough to overpower the lavender mixed with the salt. I gagged and fought back nausea. This was no time to throw up; I had to interview this creep and find out what he knew.

"Leopold von Ursler – I compel you to answer my questions, in the name of light and dark, the left-hand path and the right. You stand before me, and you must speak," I intoned.

The static radio sound grew softer and clearer. Somehow my magick knew how to twist the dials on the cosmic radio to just the right place. It had dialed in on Leopold.

~What do you desire, necromancer?~ asked Leopold, inside my mind. His voice dripped with disdain.

"Juliet, Acolyte of the Western Lands, has bid me question you about your crimes. Who was your accomplice? Who turned some of your child victims into slaves?"

Leopold laughed, bitter and mocking. ~Is this the best she can do? Imprisoned for years, and she sends the likes of you to simply ask me? You may have power, girl, but you do not yet fully know how to wield it. I will tell you nothing.~

"You will tell me of your accomplice. I command it!"

Leopold's spirit moaned as if in pain.

~Juliet tortured me for weeks with fire and silver knives, and I did not yield to her the name. I will not yield to you.~

I took another deep breath and fought back my gag reflex at the stench. I centered myself, feeling the earth under the concrete floor. I felt steadier, but grounding also drew my attention to the other spirits in the warehouse. They were aware of me. They were waiting. I shuddered.

I placed my right hand over my heart and breathed deeply again. "Leopold, who helped you with your crimes? You are bound to me until you speak. Speak now!"

Leopold screamed, high and horrible. His scream was high-pitched and terrified, like that of a baby rabbit in a wild dog's jaws. For a moment, I wondered if he would ever stop.

I felt myself open my mouth. *Was I going to scream, too?* A bass tone rumbled at the bottom of my throat. I could feel my body vibrate with . . . something . . . a musical note, I guess? I opened my mouth and sang. Not words, just tones. I was singing a rich, resonant wordless melody. Me, who always lip syncs "happy birthday" at parties! Whatever was going on, there was no time to think about it, not with a shrieking spirit just outside my magick circle. *Focus, Suzanne, get curious later.* I directed my attention to Leopold's spirit. I could feel his spirit start to vibrate. Leopold's spirit started to resonate with my song.

My song seemed to envelop his spirit, quieting him. The stench died away, too. He stopped screaming.

In my mind, I could hear Leopold's voice break. He sobbed. ~Enough! No more, Necromancer! Do not make that sound again, and I will tell you something. My friend left when I was captured. Went to South America. You will know my accomplice by the mark. But I will tell you no more.~

I drew a deep breath in, as though my torso was filling with air from the bottom up. My lips shaped themselves into an "O" shape, and suddenly I was singing again, a different note this time, one with more urgency to it.

Leopold's spirit made terrified yipping sounds, like an animal with a paw caught in a car door. ~I-I-I-I- will not tell you the name. You will never catch all of them.~ Leopold's voice broke again, devolving into incoherent sounds of pain and rage.

I closed my mouth and was silent. I probed his spirit once more with my magick. It felt like stabbing a chopstick into warm gelatin. Leopold had managed to resist my will partially, but he had paid the price. He was now just babbling nonsense in what I think was German, punctuated with outraged, frustrated screams.

My stomach clenched. I couldn't help feeling that what I'd just done to Leopold's spirit was akin to an old-fashioned beat-down with a sack of doorknobs. *That's me, necromancer and spiritual bully. Ugh.*

"Leopold von Ursler, I return you to your prison. Return there at once, and remain there according to the magick that binds you. I have no more need of you this night. I am the fulcrum of light and dark, a point of balance in the cosmos, and my will commands you." My voice sounded weirdly resonant.

In my mind's eye, I saw the red thread of my magick draw Leopold's spirit back to his coffin. Is it possible for someone's spirit to look bedraggled and spent? If so, Leopold's did. I shuddered inside myself to see that, then pushed the thought away. No guilt about that now, ask McCabe later about what was happening exactly. The rotten fruit and sulphur stench, which had reappeared when I stopped singing, slowly started to dissipate. I breathed in the lavender scent of the sacred circle, trying to clear the bad odor from my nose.

Another deep breath and I started to close the metaphysical opening I had created in myself. The radio static grew fainter and fainter. I opened my eyes and looked at McCabe and Dougherty. They were both staring fixedly at my face, wearing matching worried expressions.

McCabe said "Suzanne, are you ok? Are you back with us?" Her voice sounded very small and far away, tinny. The sound of her voice was out of sync with the movement of her lips. Then the bubble popped. I could hear normally again.

I nodded at McCabe. "I'm ok. I'm not sure I got us enough from him, but I got the beginnings of something. It's like you said in the car, it is a contest of wills between his spirit and me. It's not like interrogating a regular spirit at all."

"Have you used the polyphonic singing technique before in spirit interviews? I've heard of people doing that, but I've never actually seen it done before now," she said.

I shrugged. "I have no idea where that came from. It felt . . . right . . . somehow. I went with it to see where it would lead."

McCabe raised her eyebrows. "You've never done that before?" she asked.

"Nope," I replied, "I'm kinda making this up as I go along."

McCabe opened her mouth, then closed it. She pursed her lips together into a flat line.

"It wasn't like any of the other spirit interviews I've done," I said. "I think I hurt him."

Dougherty made a scoffing sound. "Never mind that, Suzanne. He deserves it. No point in being sympathetic to some perverted vampire bastard so rotten even his own kind wants to lock him up."

McCabe's eyes flashed angrily; she opened her mouth to reply. I interrupted her. "Look, just help me pack up my ritual shit and get out of here. This place is Sam's Club cross-bred with the country seat of the Dracula clan. It gives me the willies. Let's go argue about vampires over grilled cheese sandwiches, ok?"

Dougherty shrugged. "Sure," he said. We both looked at McCabe.

"Yes, I imagine you have questions for me, and I certainly have some for you," said McCabe.

I nodded and said, "Issaquah must have a twenty-four-hour Denny's, right?"

Chapter Three

Issaquah did have a Denny's. Seated at a plastic and vinyl booth colored in a nauseating shade of yellow, we ordered food and drinks. Our waitress repeated our orders back to us ("two orders of *Moons Over My Hammy*, an order of deep-fried cheese sticks with extra marinara dip, a tea, a coffee, and a Coke"). She brought our drinks almost immediately.

"What did you two notice? Did you see or smell or hear anything during the ritual?" I asked as I stirred the third sugar into my coffee. After talking to the dead, I always craved sweet things.

Wendy added milk to her tea, and said, "I didn't notice anything like that, did you, Paul?

Dougherty shook his head and took a sip of his Coke.

"Interesting. But you did, Suzanne? What do you think that means?' queried Wendy.

"You got me there. I have no idea. Usually, when I contact spirits, they have an odor of some kind, though it varies in intensity and pleasantness. When spirits are angry or out to hurt someone they usually smell pretty bad. But tonight, the vamps with Leopold at the warehouse— the smells were stronger than I've experienced before."

"Do you think it's possible that Those Who Walk Between smell more because their spirits have a corporeal anchor?" she wondered aloud.

"You mean, maybe their spirits smell more because their spirits are connected to sort-of living bodies?" I asked.

She nodded.

"Sure, that sounds plausible. It makes me wish that I knew another necromancer. I've only got a sample of two interviews for comparison. The other psychics that help the spook squad have tried to school me, but there's only so much overlap. I'm flying blind a lot of the time in this work."

"Way more than two, if I remember right," Dougherty put in.

"How so?" I asked, fiddling with the empty paper sugar packets on the tabletop.

"Well, Suzi-Q, you've said to me many times that if you don't practice magick and formally speak to the dead, the spirits of the dead bother you and make your life miserable," he said.

"You can't compare that to this," I objected. "Why not?" he asked.

"Well, for one thing, informal contact with spirits is on their terms – it could be that they can mask some aspects of themselves if they want to–I dunno. When I've used a sacred circle to speak to spirits, it's on my terms, so maybe they have less power to manipulate if I call them up?"

"That's certainly a debate in the literature on the subject, there is actually a research team headed by Jackson and McGovern who . . ." added McCabe.

I stopped listening. Dougherty looked amused, but I was feeling a little irritated with Ms. Professor McSpooky-Pants. I drank some more of my sweet coffee. *Where were my damn cheese sticks?* I looked around for our waitress.

". . . and that's why I suspect Suzanne is actually "blinder" than usual, "McCabe said, eyeing me over the rim of her mug of tea.

I raised my eyebrows.

She took a sip and explained, "Because you are new to phageology."

"What's that?" I asked.

"The study of vampires."

The waitress emerged from the back of the restaurant with a tray loaded with food. My cheese sticks were molten-hot. I picked one up and blew on it. I value the roof of my mouth.

McCabe took a bite of her sandwich, chewed, swallowed, and continued to speak. "See, that's the part I find kind of hard to understand, Suzanne. Since you have helped out on only a couple of other supernaturally-orientated cases before, it makes sense to me that you'd only have so much expertise in your specific area. But the fact you didn't know any vampires seems odd to me, given the natural affinity between your kind and Those Who Walk Between."

I furrowed my brow as I chewed a cheese stick, trying to think of how to explain it.

"It's not that I didn't know about them, it's that I've never met a vampire and have never really thought much about it. The whole topic of vampires is just way out of my experience."

Dougherty swallowed a mouthful of sandwich and said, "Think of it this way, Wendy. Consider sumo wrestlers."

"Ok, I'll bite. Sumo wrestlers?" she said, raising an eyebrow.

"So, you are aware of sumo wrestlers, right?"

"Yes," she said.

"But what do you really know about them, beyond the fact they are big Japanese guys in fancy underwear who wrestle each other?" he asked.

Wendy nodded and added some ketchup to her fries. "So, what you are saying is that Suzanne's life is so far removed from vampire culture, she hasn't given it much thought, and can't see why she should."

"More or less," Dougherty said, nodding.

I considered this. "Actually, to be honest, it's more than that, guys. I grew up being kinda scared of supernatural things. I'd say I've actively avoided knowing anything about vampires." *As they say, denial is more than just a river in Egypt.*

Dougherty wiped a sheen of grease from his lips with a paper napkin. "Don't forget that until recently Suzi-Q spent most of her time with the normies, cossetted away in the freaking libraries and bookstores, she's only dipped a toe into our world. I think she'd like to keep it that way."

McCabe ate a French fry, chewing thoughtfully. "I think that's what surprises me. You obviously have a lot of power behind your necromancy, but you've said yourself that you are primarily making it up on the spot, no offence meant, of course."

I felt my cheeks flame, and I considered a tart answer in response. But she was right. I practiced just enough Wicca to give me some control over talking to the dead. I had a bit of empathy that guided me in terms of what questions might be the right things to ask of the newly dead. Beyond that, I am flying blind. So, rather than tossing McCabe some sass-mouth, I nodded and dipped another cheese stick in marinara sauce.

McCabe's zeal lit up her face. "Don't get me wrong; I'm not criticizing you. I know you are needed on this case. The rarity of necromancers notwithstanding, I think you are a good choice because of the sheer power you wield. But let me be frank with you: the fact you still surprise yourself with your abilities worries me. The fact you are a novice in phageology worries me even more."

Dougherty broke in, "You and I have already been through this with the squad, Wendy. There are no other necros in Seattle. Believe me, if we could go to someone other than Suzanne, we'd be doing it."

"What's that supposed to mean?" I snapped at him. Sometimes he's just rude.

"I just want to protect you, Suzi-Q. I'm the reason you're involved in this, and I have enough on my conscience already," Dougherty said.

Great! So, Dougherty thinks I'm an idjit. I felt my face flush.

"Hey," said McCabe, soothingly, "I think we can all agree that more experienced staff would also be the first pick for any challenging and politically-sensitive case . . ."

"Exactly!" said Dougherty. "If there were a necro with ten years' experience we could turn to, we would, no offence to anyone. But ever since the Amazing Rolando died, Seattle's had no one. If I hadn't found Suzanne a few months ago, we'd be doing all this mundane-style, and watching every lead go stone friggin' cold."

I sighed. "So, if I'm so terrible, why not borrow one from another police department?"

Dougherty swigged the last of the liquid from his can of Coke. "It's not like every police force has a necro on speed dial—as far as I know, New York City has two, New Orleans has one, and Los Angeles say they have one, but the rumor is their guy is just a con-man, not the real thing."

"Don't they loan their guys?" I asked.

"After Rolando died, Seattle PD tried to borrow Madame Mogaba from New Orleans— they wanted four hundred thousand dollars just to send her here, more if she solved it."

"Wow," I said.

"Wow, like 'I can't believe police departments would be so money-grubbing with other police departments when after all they are pledged to the public safety'?" asked McCabe, frowning.

"No, more like: wow, I should be asking for a raise," I said, grinning.

McCabe rolled her eyes, and Dougherty chuckled. We ate for a few moments in silence.

Dougherty finished his meal first. He wiped his fingers on another paper napkin, then cracked his knuckles.

"You know," he said reflectively, "I think we're missing the most obvious point about the smell of vampires."

I raised my eyebrows.

"In your other interviews, the spirits smelled a bit musty and unpleasant, right?" he asked.

"Yes, that's accurate," I said.

"Well, both of those cases involved kids who were murdered. Their spirits were mad about being murdered, and wanted to tell their stories so that the guilty were punished."

McCabe and I nodded.

"So, maybe a somewhat unpleasant odor is a function of the spirits being angry and vengeful. But with Leopold, maybe his smell is so much worse because he's more than angry, he's straight-up evil. We know that this Leopold asswipe was some kind of pervert when he was running around loose. It seems to me that if spirits stink, then they are baaaad news."

I considered Dougherty's theory. "I'm not sure that's accurate," I said.

"Too small a sample to make any extrapolations," said McCabe.

Dougherty smiled. "Well, I know one thing for sure."

"What's that?" I asked.

"If we don't get over to Juliet's with a report on this Leopold dink, we're up the creek," Dougherty said.

We paid the bill and left.

Chapter Four

We had to drive through Issaquah and beyond so we could report back to the Vampire Big Cheese. ("Don't call her that," McCabe had warned).

The rain had not let up—if anything, it was heavier. It hit the windows on the car like the powerful water jets in a car wash. I'd enjoyed a brief second wind in the Denny's, but now I was tired and just wanted to get home to bed. I've never been interested in getting involved with vampires and their politics. Vampire culture was as unknown to me as the menu-planning strategies of gluten-sensitive vegans with nut allergies.

We'd left Issaquah behind, and were headed north, towards the mountains. The velvet forest inched close to the edges of the road. There were no streetlights or even light pollution this far from the town center. The headlights on the Crown Vic didn't illuminate the road in front of us so much as puncture the dark.

McCabe turned around in the front passenger seat so she could make eye contact with me.

"Since Dougherty and I didn't have much opportunity to brief you before your interview with Leopold, I'd like to fill you in on some details before you meet Juliet," she said.

"Ok," I said.

"You should be humble and polite when you meet with the Coven, and you should not make eye contact with any vampires."

"How come?"

"They can mesmerize many people with their gazes. You being psychically gifted may provide you with some resistance, but it's likely to be unpredictable."

"All right, so I should make nice but not make eye contact."

"Yes. One last thing, this is the most important thing: you should only give your word if you are certain you can keep it," said McCabe.

"Why's that?"

"Older vamps come from times when a person's word was their bond. For them breaking one's word is a terrible dishonor. Even though younger vampires may not see it that way, the culture of the older, most powerful ones predominates."

The car was no longer climbing a steep road. We'd levelled off to a small plateau, and the trees had thinned. We got peek-a-boo flashes of the whole Issaquah Valley. The lights looked dim and sad through their veil of rain.

There were just a few houses on the plateau before the ground rose and became a mountain again. They were too spread out to be a real community. They all had long gated driveways. It didn't look like the folks here were big on block parties or neighborliness.

Dougherty turned the car onto a gravel drive, stopping at the ornate wrought-iron gate. Was it my imagination, or were there bats worked into the design? *Someone had a sense of humor.*

McCabe got out of the car and walked over to the intercom mounted on the fence. A motion sensor switched on a light, illuminating the area around the car. A blinking red light on the security camera told me that the camera was motion sensitive too. McCabe dialed a number on the intercom keypad, spoke, and tilted her face upwards—it gave a better view for the camera, I guess.

The gate clanked as it unlocked. It slowly swung inward. Dougherty inched the Crown Vic forward.

"Any last questions?" McCabe asked.

"Umm, are they going to eat me?" I joked. My voice had more quaver in it than it should have, though.

McCabe looked at me sympathetically. "Hey, everyone is nervous the first time they meet a vampire. That's perfectly understandable."

Maybe, maybe not. Since I'm spooky, maybe I should be more blasé about meeting up with vampires, but I'm not. I had enough creepy arcane shit going on just by being me. I didn't need any extra added to the pile. It didn't look like I was going to have much luck with that tonight.

Dougherty steered the car slowly along the narrow gravel drive.

"We're closer to the house than you think, it's just ahead, around a bend," said McCabe.

Dougherty eased the car around the hairpin curve, and the forest parted like theatre draperies to reveal the house.

It was a three-storey split-level structure straddling a ravine, its back against an inky old-growth forest. Beyond the back of the house, the mountain continued to rise. The subtly illuminated balconies on the second level of the house had sleek rounded lines. Most of the exterior of the house was taken up by large floor-to-ceiling windows. What remained of the exterior was faced with flat pieces of slate. It was not what I expected.

I couldn't see any lights on through the windows, but the flicker and glow behind the glass suggested someone had lit candles.

Dougherty parked the car near the three other vehicles in the gravel clearing.

"So here we are in the secret lair of the head vampire, and there is not a decaying castle or creepy Victorian gingerbread mansion to be found. What gives?" I asked.

Dougherty smirked. The same thought must have crossed his mind. McCabe ignored us.

We got out of the car and started to walk toward the house. As we approached, I could hear rushing water. *Was there a stream nearby?* The path to the front door took us over a small arched footbridge. The sound of water was louder now. I looked over the side of the bridge. A stream swollen with rain rushed rapidly under the bridge.

"Does the stream run under the house?" I asked McCabe.

"The house was built over the ravine, so yes, the stream runs under the house. You can even hear the water from certain rooms in the house," she replied.

The front entry area was dimly lit from a source I couldn't see, just enough light to allow us to see the iron knocker. It, too, was shaped like a bat. I smiled in spite of the tension in my neck and shoulders.

McCabe knocked on the door, and it was opened almost immediately by the palest person I had ever seen. He wasn't pale in the way of some white folks in the Pacific Northwest. People like me were pasty-pale because we didn't see the sun ten months a year.

This man was not human-pale. He was pale as paper, pale like things that lived underground and never saw the sun, ever. His carrot-colored hair was so close-cropped his scalp shone through it, like a polished eggshell. His eyes were the soft, sherry brown of a faithful dog. His oval, even-featured face was unremarkable except for his pallor. He was tall, perhaps six-foot two or three, but painfully thin in the way of young men who think too much and eat too little.

His face lit up at seeing McCabe.

He greeted her enthusiastically, "Wendy! Hello!"

He stepped forward quickly and embraced her. The look on his face as he held her was one of pure, unadulterated bliss. McCabe stood stiff and embarrassed in his arms.

McCabe stammered, "Jack, th–this is a business call, not a social one."

She stepped back from his embrace. Her face had gone red. He let her go, his crestfallen expression as dismayed as that of a boy who'd accidentally stepped on his puppy's tail.

His voice subdued, he said, "Follow me, Juliet and the others are waiting."

Jack led us in through the small entry hall and into a large living room dominated by a fireplace made of natural stone. The walls were painted a creamy yellow color, enhanced by the many flickering candles placed throughout the room. The furnishings were spare and simple—a low chocolate suede sectional couch, some bright pillows on the floor, a large, tweed-covered square ottoman in place of a coffee table. A built-in shelving unit next to the fireplace held an Ipod docking station and many books. Uncurtained floor-to-ceiling windows covered two of the walls. During the day, the windows would have made the trees on the lot seem a part of the room. Now in the evening, the windows were walls of ink.

A small, plump white woman with long wavy brown hair was seated cross-legged on the floor in front of the fireplace, one elbow on the large ottoman. She appeared to be about thirty, with the beginnings of laugh lines around her eyes. She was clad in faded jeans and a peasant top embroidered with psychedelic butterflies. Her tiny feet were bare. Her toenails sported green glitter nail polish. Humor twinkled in her blue eyes and played at the dimple near the corner of her mouth. She looked like a Vermeer milkmaid dolled up for a Jimi Hendrix concert. She watched us expectantly.

"Ah, Miss Wendy, finally, this is the necromancer of which we spoke? And another human, a policeman, perhaps?" Her voice rippled through the air like the music of tinkling bells.

McCabe cleared her throat and spoke, keeping her eyes on the floor, "Mistress Juliet, may I present to you Suzanne Murphy, psychic consultant, and Paul Dougherty, police officer."

Juliet gave us each an appraising look. I struggled against the impulse to look at her eyes. Eye contact is such a normal part of conversation; it's difficult to break the habit.

"Welcome to my home, Suzanne and Paul. I am pleased you came so promptly. Soon we will have this unpleasant business behind us."

I felt Dougherty relax somewhat beside me, an almost imperceptible level of tension released.

Juliet looked past us to Jack, standing at the threshold of the room. "Go get the others, and bring something for our guests to drink."

Jack crossed the room and disappeared down a hallway the led off from one side of the fireplace.

Juliet stayed put but motioned us to the suede couch.

"Please be seated; we shall begin before the others come in, they have heard what I am going to say before."

McCabe, Dougherty and I moved to the couch and sat down.

Juliet began, "I am certain that you have been partially briefed by your companions, Suzanne, but possibly more explanation is due."

"Well, ma'am sort of . . ." I said, looking at my hands folded in my lap.

"Over a hundred years ago, two vampires in this territory went rogue and did things that are forbidden. Among their many crimes, they attacked children and brought them over. To use a child this way is dangerous to us all. Child vampires create too much attention from curious humans. 'Why is this so-helpless child prowling the night?'"

Jack re-entered the room, carrying a highly polished wooden tray. It contained several small, stemmed liqueur glasses and a cut crystal decanter filled with a golden liquid. He was followed into the room by two people and a terrible smell. At first, I thought the smell was the beverage he was carrying, but it was too powerful: a mixture of acrid fear, moldy garlic and stale blood. I swallowed and tried to breathe shallowly. Both Dougherty and McCabe were either too polite to give any outward sign they smelled it, or they actually didn't smell it.

The people accompanying Jack looked out of place in this casual and modern home. The woman, in particular, had a Late-Late-Show appearance. Her long black velvet dress did little to conceal her ample cleavage—the pale mounds of her breasts pushed voluptuously against the edge of her low-cut bodice. Under her impressive bosom, her belly swelled prodigiously. *Was she pregnant?* If so, she was at least eight months gone. Her mouth was sensual—wide, red, moist. But her blue-green eyes flashed like shards of jagged glass, and her severe features were arranged in a coldly contemptuous expression. The way she had styled her straight dark brown hair did nothing to soften her face. It was simply parted in the middle, and fell to her hips, unadorned.

The man, also clad in black, was of average height and slender build. He moved with fluid athleticism. His bearing suggested training in dance or martial arts. In the human part of his life, I imagine he would have had the rich golden skin tone common to people in south-east Asia. Now, as a vampire, his skin had faded to a delicate pale champagne. When the light hit his long silken hair, the highlights in it gleamed blue.

"Ah, Yvonne, Bao, you came more quickly than I thought you would. Please, be seated. Our Wendy has brought us what we need—Suzanne, a necromancer, and a policeman, Paul. Jack, please, give our guests some Frangelico."

Vampires can drink alcohol? Who knew?

Wordlessly, Jack placed the tray on the large footstool and bending at the waist, started to pour the syrupy liqueur into the stemmed glasses. He handed the glasses around. I gratefully held mine under my nose. Hazelnut liqueur was an infinite improvement over garlic, blood and anxious sweat. *Do vampires sweat? Ask McCabe later and focus, Suzanne.*

Glass in hand, Juliet continued, "We were speaking of the crimes committed before—it is important that no one gives the Shadow Gift without permission; eternal life should not be bestowed lightly. How is it children say it now? Not to "randos"?"

Dougherty looked puzzled, and I smiled at my hands. *I wonder if Mistress Juliet has a Twitter account.*

Juliet continued, "If we are to maintain our freedom in a world dominated by humans, Those Who Walk Between must be adults with self-discipline. If we do not control ourselves, the humans will do it for us, as in days of old."

I raised my eyes from the floor, unable to stop myself from the habit of making eye contact when speaking to someone. I quickly glanced down to the glass in my hands as I realized what I had done. Not making direct eye contact was hard.

"You have a question, Suzanne?" asked Juliet.

"Yes, ma'am, I do. If Leopold has been under lock and key for the last hundred years, what could he know about the recent crimes?" I asked.

"You surprise me. Wendy told us you were known for being, how did she phrase it? 'A smart ass'? Either Wendy

warned you about our ways, or you are secretly Canadian."
Juliet chuckled at her own joke.

Yvonne emitted a low hiss from her corner of the sofa.

"Be quiet, Yvonne, a simple joke at your expense, it's
the least you should expect," growled Juliet. There was a
deeper note in her voice, one that raised the hair on my
arms, like the growling of a wild beast.

"Yvonne is Canadian, and yet is not as famously polite
as her countrymen. What is the joke, so nice they say you're
welcome when the ATM screen reads thank you?"

Yvonne made another sound of displeasure.

From the corner of my eye, I saw a blur of motion.
Somehow Juliet had moved faster than my eye could catch
it. She loomed over the seated Yvonne, her hand on the
other woman's face. She cupped Yvonne's chin and forced
her head back. Juliet's pretty face was a mask of cold rage.

"Lady, make no mistake, I tolerate your insolence
because it amuses me. When my patience wears thin, you
will not enjoy it."

Juliet released Yvonne's chin. Without warning, she
struck Yvonne across the face with the back of her heavily-
ringed hand. It sounded like a ping-pong paddle smacking a
vinyl couch. I heard the blow but did not see it, Juliet was
that fast. Just as quickly, she returned to her seated position
on the floor.

Quietly, she said, "I trust you understand me, Yvonne."

I glanced at Yvonne. Her face was frozen in fright and anger as mahogany-colored blood trickled from the corner of her mouth.

"Yes, Mistress, I understand you." Yvonne's voice was remarkable: like sticky bourbon poured over sandpaper, a sensuous, rich purr even in this situation. She had dropped her gaze. Her body quivered with suppressed emotion-fear, rage, and embarrassment. Bao was absolutely still and silent like he was carved from travertine. His dark brown eyes glittered with hatred as he looked at Juliet.

I was mildly shocked. I don't know what was more unsettling: how fast Juliet could move, or someone striking a pregnant woman. Yeah, I know, she's likely a satanic hellspawn with a dozen dastardly plans tucked in her brassiere, but still, it bothered me.

No hero am I; I kept my mouth shut and my eyes on the floor. Interestingly, so did Dougherty and McCabe. I would have expected Dougherty to jump to the lady's defense, him being such an old-school man's man. Apparently not in this circumstance. Juliet sipped her liqueur placidly, her tiny bare feet tucked underneath her.

"Returning to your question, Suzanne. How it is that Leopold has valuable information when he's been imprisoned for over one hundred years? Leopold had at least one accomplice when he made a vampire. We never caught the accomplice. We assume he left the Western Lands and went elsewhere. A fugitive and a rogue in the territory of another Acolyte is not my concern. Children were no longer being taken in my territory, and the curiosities of your human authorities would no longer be piqued. But now that children are being taken and brought over once again, we must find this accomplice and punish him."

"Madam, with respect, why tell me this now, after I've interviewed Leopold?" I asked.

"I wanted to hear what you could learn from him without you knowing much about the situation. Leopold is very cunning, and will likely need to be interviewed a number of times to get good information. He can be very tiresome that way." Juliet sighed.

She continued, "There was also the concern that if he could deduce what you already knew, he would only tell you what you already knew. He is a master dissembler who requires significant motivation to tell what he knows. Which brings us to what you learned tonight, Suzanne."

"He gave me very little." Looking steadily at Juliet's rounded chin, I said, "I have never interviewed One Who Walks Between. I do not know if I have produced the results you want."

Juliet glanced sternly at McCabe, "But you are a necromancer, yes?"

"Yes, I am."

"Then you will have no difficulties. It may take several tries since you are a novice. You may visit him as much as you need to get results. What cannot be gotten all at once may come in pieces. That is fine."

"Mistress Juliet, another question for you, if I may?"

"You may, Suzanne," she said, inclining her head slightly.

"If I get this information and give it to you, then what happens? Do the police . . ."

"When I have what I need, I will capture the rogue and deal with him according to our customs."

She nodded at Dougherty and continued. "In the Western Lands we have an arrangement with the police about rogues. That does not concern you. He is a vampire, not human."

Dougherty shifted uncomfortably in his seat. Whatever the arrangement was, I was betting he didn't approve.

"And what of the children, if there are survivors?" I asked.

"What of them? They will all be destroyed, as is our way. They are a liability we cannot afford."

"Is there no way they can be . . . changed back? Healed?" I queried.

Juliet chuckled. "Oh my dear, a necromancer with a tender heart. I will indulge you: children who have been turned endanger us all; they cannot be permitted to survive. They will be destroyed. That is better for them, particularly revenants."

Avoiding her gaze still, I pursed my lips in disapproval.

Juliet said, "I can see you do not believe me. If you like, I can show you one of the revenants. I have one downstairs in . . . storage."

Yvonne and Bao exchanged a significant look. They looked worried. Yvonne said nothing, but Bao moved gracefully to one knee, gaze lowered.

He said, "Mistress, that is not advisable, the witch will become too frightened if she sees that . . . child."

Juliet rose to her knees and leant forward, peering at me. I said nothing, but my face must have spoken volumes. Her gaze had weight like a lead mask.

"I am just trying to think of uses for the revenant before it is time to slay her. Rise to your feet, Bao, no need to grovel."

His body stiffened at that characterization, but he said nothing. He regained his position at Yvonne's side.

Juliet heaved a sigh. "Perhaps you are right, no need to scare our valuable witch away."

Our witch? Was I their witch now? I bit the inside of my cheek to stop myself from saying something stupid.

Dougherty cleared his throat, his eyes firmly on the floor. "Mistress Juliet, what role do I have in this?"

"You will support Suzanne in her queries, and protect her as best you can. Wendy will do the same. You will report your activities to your superiors as you always do. Your participation has been authorized by them."

Juliet rose to her feet and stretched in a cat-like way. She continued, "If that is all you need to know, we shall part ways here. I want you to interview Leopold again, tomorrow evening or the next. Yvonne, Bao, you will remain, there is much other business to discuss. Jack, please escort our guests to the door."

Jack looked wistfully at McCabe but did not voice the question on his face: would she return to stay with him this evening? He escorted us from the room, walked us through the foyer to the front door. He watched silently as we, pelted with rain, walked out into the blustery night.

Chapter Five

Dougherty picked me up at my apartment at eight am. Yuck. He managed to lure me out of bed with the promise of coffee and doughnuts on the way to see the supervising social worker. We rode in silence in the Crown Victoria until I had drunk enough of the black elixir that I felt capable of speech.

"So, the mundane police are handling the missing children's cases, what did they discover before the disappearances were kicked over to the spooky squad?" I asked. I bit into a powdered doughnut.

"Well, according to their report, one thing was obvious—all the kids had been in foster care," said Dougherty.

"Suggesting that the vampires behind this are picking kids who might be perceived as unwanted or disposable?" I asked.

Dougherty nodded. He added, "The other feature is that most of them had behavioral problems. They were the kind of kids that are hard to find placements for."

I sipped my coffee. "So, you think he or they is targeting at-risk youth whom no one is going to look too hard for?" I asked.

"Yes, I think our scumbag thinks of it that way, he is looking for the low-hanging fruit," Dougherty said.

He guided the Crown Vic down Heath Street and into the narrow opening of the underground parking lot. We prowled the low-ceilinged lot in search of visitor parking. We finally found something in the back-left corner.

We got out the car and walked through the clouds of stale exhaust fumes to the elevators. The elevators smelled of urine and industrial disinfectant. Dougherty pressed the button for the third floor. Someone had carved various curse words and the sentence "he's the one" into the aluminum panel that housed the elevator buttons. An arrow was also scratched into the metal, connecting the sentence to the third-floor button.

"Look," I said, pointing at the graffiti, "Our work's done for us."

Dougherty smirked. "Sure! Let's just arrest everyone on the third floor, and as sure as Bob's your uncle, the case is solved."

We exited the elevators and turned left down a hallway with stained carpet. The hallway was also scented with urine. At the end of the hall, a frosted glass door read "PIERCE COUNTY DEPARTMENT OF CHILD SERVICES." The reception area contained a desultory collection of armless vinyl chairs. They crouched unhappily along the gouged wall. Some bruised-looking children's toys were heaped in one corner. A couple of limp magazines were splayed over a coffee table scarred with coffee rings and burns from cigarettes. Someone had carved TWISTED SISTER ROOLZ into its surface.

The woman working as the receptionist was ensconced behind a chest-high laminate counter topped with thick Plexiglas. It was rigged with an intercom system. The woman reminded me of a gerbil. Her greying brown hair was cropped close to her head, displaying her prominent rounded ears. Her facial features were slightly pointed. Her eyes were glossy black beads. I half expected to see a circular plastic tube leading from the reception area to another part of the office.

Before Dougherty could press the intercom button on his side of the Plexiglas, she pressed the button on her side.

"Can I help you?" she asked.

The expression on her face suggested that the last thing on this earth she would like to do is help anyone, especially the likes of us. *Maybe if I'd had some sunflower seeds with me? Unkind thoughts "R" us.*

"Detective Dougherty and Suzanne Murphy to see Neil Geruyter, please," said Dougherty.

"One moment," she said. She picked up the receiver of her phone, pressed a few buttons, and then said something we couldn't hear through the Plexiglas. If she'd had whiskers, I am sure they would have been twitching in curiosity.

"Please be seated; he'll be with you in a moment."

Dougherty and I placed ourselves carefully on two of the chairs. At six-feet four inches tall, and the proportionate poundage, Dougherty was skeptical of most plastic furniture. I shared his skepticism—I'm not tall, but I'm thick through the middle. Using my ass to shatter plastic chairs and make a spectacle of myself is not on my bucket list, so I try to sit as gently as any short round woman can. I glimpsed at Dougherty. He had picked up a yellowing copy of *Consumer Report*. The date on it? 1991. The cover article was about the best new VCRs. I sighed to myself. I hoped we weren't going to be waiting long.

After about ten minutes, the steel security door next to the reception area opened. A tall, narrowly-built man with receding sandy hair stood there. His pale blue eyes were piercing. He nursed a small round belly under his beige and blue argyle sweater vest.

"Detective Dougherty and Ms. . . . . Murphy, was it? I'm Neil Geruyter," he said, as he extended his hand to us. We each shook it in turn. I shuddered inwardly as I did so— touching his hand was like gripping a chilly, damp fish.

"Let's go back to my office," he said and led us through the security door.

We followed him down a narrow hall that smelled of scorched coffee. He led us to a small cubby of an office with posters and corkboards covering the walls. Most of the posters depicted various landscape and forest scenes of the Pacific Northwest, but the largest poster was a retro one. It depicted a fluffy marmalade kitten just barely hanging on to a bar by the claws of its front feet. It was captioned "Hang in there baby!" Ugh. This guy was a sap.

Geruyter seated himself on the rolling chair near the desk. The desk was overloaded with papers, files, and an ancient desktop computer. He motioned for us to be seated on the worn blue corduroy couch opposite him. We were separated from him by a coffee table that was a cousin to the one in the waiting room. This table had also clearly had a hard life. Two of its legs were haphazardly reinforced with silver duct tape. A clear glass bowl of dusty Scotch mints adorned the center of the table. The office was so small the coffee table abutted Dougherty's knees. I had a bit more clearance, but hey, I'm only five-foot three.

"So, Detective Dougherty, I assume you are here about the three children in my caseload that have gone missing?"

Dougherty nodded.

Geruyter continued, turning his eyes to me. "But you, Ms. Murphy, in what capacity are you here?"

"I'm consulting with the police on this case," I said simply. No need to tip our hand about the vampire connection.

"You look awfully young to be doing that kind of work," he remarked, his voice unctuous.

I shrugged and said nothing. Dougherty just looked at Geruyter, giving him cop-face.

Geruyter shifted in his chair, uncrossing and re-crossing his ankles. He said, "Of course you both realize that the Missing Person detectives have already been all through my files, and asked me every conceivable question."

Dougherty, nodding, said "Yes sir, we realize that, but follow-up interviews are often conducted by a second team just in case you remember something else in the interim. It's standard practice in situations like this one." Dougherty was a smooth liar.

Geruyter let out a breath and leant back in his office chair. I think he saw that a quick brush off wasn't going to get rid of us.

Dougherty took out his small notepad to check his facts. "Ok, let's see, my understanding is that in the past three weeks, six children in care have gone missing. Three of them were on your caseload, is that right?"

Geruyter nodded.

"So, what can you tell me about the three kids you knew?" Dougherty asked.

Geruyter cleared his throat. "Well, let's see . . . The first to go missing was an eleven-year- old, Taylor Nahanee. He's an American Indian child who has been in care almost his whole life, I think since . . ." Geruyter paused while he thumbed through the thick pile of files on his desk, selected one, then opened it.

Geruyter continued, "Yes, here it is, he started out in voluntary care when he was six months old. Father unknown, the mother was a subsistence sex trade worker who had a crack cocaine problem. She tried to do the right thing, put him in what was supposed to be a short-term placement to give her time to clean up and get her life together. She made it partway through rehab before she found out she was HIV-positive. She dropped out of treatment at that point and went back to street life. No cops on the vice or narcotic beats have seen her on the stroll for a number of years now, no one in her band knows anything. It's been eight years since she had any formal contact with us. I can't say for sure what her outcome has been, but I would imagine she must have either moved on to a different city or she's passed away in an AIDS hospice."

Dougherty nodded and made a few notes in his notebook.

"Any chance Taylor got curious about his mom and ran away from his foster placement to find her? Or maybe he wanted to get in touch with his roots and meet the people on his reserve?" I asked.

"I think it's pretty likely that he's run away, but the leads you mention have already been checked, Taylor wasn't found," Geruyter replied.

Dougherty scribbled something in his notebook.

Geruyter continued, "The thing about Taylor is this: he's got ODD, oppositional defiant disorder. You familiar with that?"

"Go ahead and fill us in," Dougherty said.

"Kids with ODD aren't very people-orientated. They feel thwarted by others a lot of the time and have a hard time understanding that others have rights. They are very challenging to deal with in foster care because of their extreme behaviors. Many young boys diagnosed with ODD end up as psychopaths in later life. That was likely the way Taylor was headed since he already had the Unholy Trinity of behavioral precursors."

"Such as?" I asked.

"Fire-setting, bed-wetting, and hurting animals," Geruyter replied.

"Ok, so this kid was a handful: angry loner, not connected to anyone, a dangerous kid. Not the kind of kid that is typically targeted for stranger abduction," Dougherty said.

"Yes, that's my take on it. I think it's much more likely that Taylor got fed up with his foster parents and decided to strike out on his own. He's already got a mini rap sheet for theft and vandalism, so I think sooner or later he's going to turn up in the juvenile system somewhere," Geruyter said.

"Ok, what about the next one that went missing, uh, the nine-year-old Breanne Rosa Gonzales?"

"Well with Breanne Rosa, it's complicated again. Like Taylor, it was hard for her to maintain a foster placement. That's as much the system's fault as anything," he said sadly.

"What do you mean by that?" I asked

"Breanne Rosa came into care when she was three. Her mother's boyfriend had been molesting her. The mother was unable to protect Breanne Rosa, wouldn't give the guy up to keep her daughter safe. It was the babysitter who called it in initially, and mom denied it. But the med exam and some of Breanne Rosa's behaviors were pretty conclusive." said Geruyter.

"So, what part of that makes her hard to place?" I asked.

"That part came later. There was a problem with her first foster placement. She went to live with a long-time foster family, people we'd placed kids with for fifteen years or so. Everyone thought they were the nicest couple. Breanne Rosa was with them for four years, and from this end, things looked fine. Eventually, Breanne Rosa got some sexual abuse prevention training as part of her school curricula. Based on what she learned, she made a disclosure to her teacher. Sexual abuse was proven, and Breanne Rosa was removed from that couple's care to another placement" Geruyter said.

"Proven how?" Dougherty asked, his eyes on his book as he took notes.

"Breanne Rosa tested positive for syphilis. The same strain was found infecting her foster father. That's pretty open and shut," Geruyter replied.

"I see," murmured Dougherty, still scribbling.

"So, then Breanne Rosa had a series of placements. In the first couple, they were families that had school-age children. In each case, the foster family refused to continue to foster Breanne Rosa. She was having a lot of behavioral problems with the other children."

"Example?" asked Dougherty, scribbling.

"She was acting out sexually with younger children, repeating some of the things that had been done to her on others," he said.

"Why would she do that? I don't understand." I interjected.

"When children have been sexually abused, some of them respond by compulsively repeating the same or similar actions. It's thought to be a way to rework the trauma and gain mastery or control over it." Geruyter said.

"So, Breanne Rosa was trying to assert control in an area where she previously had none?" I asked.

"Yes, exactly," Geruyter replied. "It's also thought that some children act out sexually as a way to manage the stress and anxiety caused by the assaults. Some of them develop compulsive sexual behaviors as a way to soothe themselves."

Dougherty said nothing, his pen moving steadily across his notebook page.

"So, the only problem is that she can't be allowed to treat other children that way, obviously, no matter how well we understand her behavior's origins," Geruyter continued.

Dougherty and I nodded in unison.

"So, after a couple of placements where Breanne Rosa interfered with other children in the family, we placed her with a single foster parent, someone with experience dealing with sexually traumatized children and youth." He paused for a moment. "Would either of you like a glass of water? I'm going to get myself some."

"Yes, please, that'd be great," I said.

"None for me, thanks" Dougherty replied.

"Excuse me, I'll be right back," Geruyter said, then walked out of the office and down the narrow hallway.

"Wow, these kids, messed up lives, messed up situations," I commented.

"Shit, yeah," Dougherty muttered.

"At least this Geruyter guy is forthcoming," I said.

"Yes, he's positively Chatty Cathy," Dougherty smirked. I could tell he thought there was something not quite right with Geruyter.

Geruyter came down the hall holding two glasses of water. He entered the office and handed one to me. I sipped at it. He drank more than half of his down in a single swallow, then placed the glass on the scarred coffee table.

"Eventually even the foster parent with a lot of experience got burned out by Breanne Rosa. I think she was just tired of how hard it was to reach her."

"So, let me guess, she 'cashed Breanne Rosa in' too, so to speak?" I asked.

"Yes, exactly," said Geruyter. His finished his remaining water and set the glass back down on the table again.

"So, next we placed her with a couple fairly new to foster parenting. She'd only been there three weeks at the time she went missing," he said.

"Do you think she ran away, too?" Dougherty asked.

"No, actually given the extremes of Breanne Rosa's sexual acting out, I wouldn't be surprised if a local pedophile had targeted her for abduction. Such a person might be powerfully drawn to a child such as Breanne Rosa," he remarked.

I shuddered despite the fact the room was warm.

"So, you don't think all these disappearances are all necessarily linked?" Dougherty asked.

"No, I don't," Geruyter said. "I think Breanne Rosa may have been abducted, but I find it hard to ignore my gut when it comes to Taylor. Something tells me he just took off and we can't find him."

"What about the last one to disappear from your caseload, the 12-year-old Tiffanii Shaniqua Lombard?" Dougherty asked.

Geruyter reached for a file on his desk, pulling it from the middle of a stack. He opened the file and glanced through it briefly.

"Yes," he said, "Tiffanii with two "i's." She always dots the "i's" with little hearts. Nice girl. I have her and her fifteen-year-old brother Braydon on my caseload. They both got a group home placement. I could have found a family for her, but she really wanted to be with her brother. Trying to find a family for a fifteen-year-old boy is next to impossible. So, they both got placed in the same group home."

Dougherty asked, "How did Tiffanii and her brother Brandon . . ."

"Braydon," corrected Geruyter.

"How did Tiffanii and Braydon come to be in the care of Child Services?"

"They were in a car accident with both their parents. A drunk driver t-boned the family's car on the passenger side. Their mom was killed instantly. Their dad hung on for a few days in the ICU, but he died during one of the follow-up surgeries they gave him. Tiffanii survived with just a broken arm, Braydon just had minor cuts and bruises."

"There was no family to take them in?" I asked.

"Not that could take them. Only one grandparent is still alive, and she's pretty far gone with Alzheimer's. The mother had a brother, but he's unmarried career military stationed in Afghanistan, so there was no one from her side. The rest of the father's side of the family refused to have anything to do with the Lombards because they disapproved of a racially integrated marriage, they wanted nothing to do with their half-black nieces and nephews. The Lombards had never named godparents, and there were no provisions in the will. No will at all, as a matter of fact," Geruyter said.

"So Tiffanii and Braydon's parents both die, the kids are taken into care in a group home setting, and then what?" I asked.

"Well, they had a hard time settling in, as you can imagine. They were in a new environment, both going to new schools. Braydon seemed hard hit, but I wondered about Tiffanii. She seemed like she was coping pretty well, under the circumstances. Maybe too well. It made me think it was just a facade. But I was never able to reach her." Geruyter said.

"What do you think happened to her?" I asked.

Geruyter sighed. "I hate to think it, but I suspect that Tiffanii might have killed herself somehow, and we just haven't turned up a body yet."

I raised an eyebrow at him.

Dougherty said, "What makes you suspect that, Mr. Geruyter?"

"As I said, I think she was probably depressed after her parent's deaths, but covering it up with a thin facade of coping. I kept trying to reach her, but I think she was just too far gone."

"What does that mean?" Dougherty said.

"She wouldn't talk about how she felt about anything; she couldn't connect with anybody, not even her own brother. Though that's as much him as it is her," Geruyter remarked.

"How so?" I asked.

"Braydon is kind of closed down, emotionally speaking. He's not able to be there for Tiffanii emotionally or to ask for the help he needs for himself. He's one of those youths who've aligned themselves with the Goth subculture, black nail polish and spider tattoos; you know what I mean?"

"Got an idea, anyway," said Dougherty.

"So, his way of coping is to draw further and further into a world of Goth music and poetry, leaving his poor sister on the outside looking in. Their relationship isn't what she wanted it to be. It was Tiffanii who wanted them to be placed together. I suspect Braydon may have been indifferent," Geruyter said.

"Hmm, interesting," muttered Dougherty as he made another note in his book. Without looking up, he added, "So when can we interview Braydon Lombard?"

Geruyter frowned. "Well, I don't think there is much he can tell us that hasn't already been said to the first team of investigators."

Dougherty looked up at Geruyter and smiled, the kind that doesn't go all the way up to the eyes. "I know it may be inconvenient for you, but our due diligence requires I go over a few things with him."

Geruyter frowned and let out a sigh of exasperation. "If you must, detective, you must. It can be arranged. I will, however, have to be present when you interview him since I am his legal guardian."

Dougherty smiled unpleasantly at Geruyter's increasingly brusque tone of voice. He could tell he was irritating the social worker. Irritating people, that's one of Dougherty's best things. I'm told we have that in common. *Who me, a brat? Never.*

"That sounds just peachy to me, Mr. Geruyter. Can we arrange for something for later this afternoon, after school is out for the day?" asked Dougherty.

Geruyter continued to frown. It was clear he did not care for us. "Yes, I can arrange for that. Let me make a couple of phone calls. Please excuse me, but can you go ahead and wait at reception for me? I'll let you find your own way back there."

With that, he ushered us out of his office to wend our way back to where the gerbil-faced woman was seated. She buzzed us through the door into the waiting room side of her counter. Dougherty and I each took a seat on one of the sad, precarious chairs.

"That hallway is claustrophobic," Dougherty remarked, "I half expected to get a big piece of cheese when we made it back here."

I smirked. I caught a brief mental image of the rodent-like receptionist hoarding all the reward cheese, but before I could giggle at my own mental process, Geruyter was buzzed through the door into the waiting room with us

"All right, Detective, here is my card. I've put the address of the group home and the time to meet there on the back of it. It's almost nine-thirty now, we'll see each other today at four pm with Braydon in the group home," he said.

Dougherty reached out and took the card from Geruyter, then put it in his pocket.

"Thank you, Mr. Geruyter. We'll be seeing you then," said Dougherty. His smile had still not made it all the way to his eyes.

"No problem, see you later," Geruyter said, his own eyes as cold and insincere. He turned on his heel, and Gerbil Face buzzed him back through the door.

Dougherty and I rode the elevator down to the parking level in silence. When we were both safely belted into the Crown Victoria, I regarded Dougherty.

"You really didn't like that social worker," I observed.

"Yeah there is something not right about that guy, I don't trust him."

"Maybe you're letting the elevator graffiti cloud your judgement," I said, grinning.

"Cute," he said, scowling.

"What's wrong with him? He was forthcoming with everything we wanted to know; he gave us good backgrounds on the missing kids."

"That's just it; he was too cooperative. Here's a social worker who's not at all defensive that three kids in his caseload, his legal wards, are missing? I don't buy it. Why wasn't he trying to cover his own ass? I don't get him admitting his department's SNAFU in some of these kids' histories, either. Usually, with government types it's cover your ass with one hand, pass the buck with the other. I am not buying the nice guy act."

I digested this is silence for a few moments. I'm strictly the supernatural talent, so it was easy for me to defer to Dougherty's investigative experience. As I pondered the meeting we had just had, I had a brief flash of something, the mental equivalent of seeing something out of the corner of your eye. But as quickly as it was there, it was gone. I couldn't catch it. Damn. Sometimes I can't stay abreast of my own mental processes. Add a bit of the magickal into the mix, and often I was confused by the thoughts in my head as other people were when I tried to discuss them.

"So, what do you want to do until it's time to go to the group home?" Dougherty asked.

"If it's all the same to you, I'd like to stop at the Emporium and take care of a few things," I said.

"Sure, I can drop you off and swing back later to get you . . . but didn't you take a vacation week?"

"I emailed Star about that last night when I got in, but I want to check my work email and see how things are around there, it didn't give her much notice."

"You not only can't take the bookstore out of the girl, you cannot even pry the girl out of the bookstore," he quipped.

"Funny," I said, without enthusiasm.

He grinned and said, "Quick Sonic drive-through on the way? You need to keep your strength up with all the book shelving you'll be doing."

Chapter Six

Dougherty pulled up in front of the bookstore and honked. He was an hour earlier than I thought he'd be. I grabbed my coat and bag, left the store, and got into his car. I managed to avoid the water rushing through the gutter. In Seattle, dry feet are a priority. Sure, those of us born and raised here could wear rubber boots like the tourists do, but why? I had yet to find rubber boots I liked as much as my hot pink Chucks.

"Hi there," I said, as I got into the car and buckled up. "You are early and idling your engine pollutes the environment and wastes fuel."

"Yes, I am early, it is part of the plan. And yes, so I've heard, from you, about five thousand times," he replied, grinning. He glanced at me out of the corner of his eye as he maneuvered the Crown Vic away from the curb and back into traffic.

"It's a case of old dog, new tricks. I'm too stubborn to change," he said. He chuckled to himself, amused by his own obstinacy.

We've been having conversations like this one the entire time I've known him. My nagging and his resistance were a game at this point.

"So, what's the plan for our interview with Braydon?" I asked.

"Get there well before Geruyter does, see if we can talk to the kid alone. Plus, whatever we can get him to talk about in front of that dink Geruyter," he grumbled.

"Yeah, I guess that is our basic problem," I agreed.

"Any excitement at the bookstore today, Suzie-Q?" he asked.

"I started to research the polyphonic techniques necromancers have used historically, I'm trying to understand it. Plus, Star and Sarah invited me to watch Josh's basketball game at Evergreen school tonight," I said.

Star was my friend, my boss, and the owner of Goddess Grove Bookstore and Metaphysickal Emporium. Sarah was her wife. Josh was Sarah's teen son from a previous relationship.

"Evergreen High, huh? The group home is close to the school, I think. Can you check the file? It's in the back seat."

I turned and saw a battered manila file folder resting in the middle third of the Crown Vic's back seat. I grabbed it and started flipping through it.

"Why do you still use all this paper, couldn't you have this stuff on your smartphone or a tablet or something?"

Dougherty snorted. "Right, the department has money for that. May I also remind you: old dog, new tricks?"

"C'mon, you're not that old, I've seen you use a computer."

"It's not the years, Suzi-Q, it's the mileage." I glanced at his profile as he drove. *Was Dougherty actually looking tired?*

He cleared his throat abruptly and changed the subject. "You love hanging out with Star and her crew. Josh is what, tenth or eleventh grade now?" Dougherty asked.

"Yep, he's in grade eleven now."

We passed the rest of the trip to the group home in idle chat. Just a few minutes before three, Dougherty pulled his Crown Victoria up to the curb in front of a squat bungalow with peeling yellow paint. The untended yard was a rowdy jumble—the leftovers from a drunk giant's game of Pick-Up Sticks.

We walked up the cracked concrete pathway to the front door. Dougherty's meaty knuckles rapped sharply on it. I was grateful for the portico that gave us a little shelter us from the pounding rain. In true Seattle style, half the time the rain came at us sideways rather than from above. *What was it now? Twenty-eight or twenty-nine days of rain in a row?* It was the first week of October, and I think it had been raining non-stop since Labor Day.

As I was pulling my damp hair into a low ponytail, a heavily tattooed woman with a prominent lip ring opened the door. Her soft brown eyes regarded us calmly.

"Yes?" she said.

Dougherty said "We're with the police. I'm Detective Sergeant Dougherty, and this is Suzanne Murphy. We are supposed to talk to Neil Geruyter and Braydon today."

"Yes, Neil called about that, come in please," she replied and pulled the door open.

It opened into a shabby living room furnished with stuff that had first seen the light of day in the mid-eighties. Lots of powder blue and dusty rose floral patterns.

"Please take a seat while you wait," she said, gesturing to the couch. "I'm Megan, one of the staff here. Would you like water or coffee or something like that? "

"Nothing for me thanks, Miss," said Dougherty.

"A glass of water would be great," I said.

Megan smiled and walked toward the kitchen. When she passed a door that presumably hid stairs that went to the basement, she opened it. She shouted down the stairs, "Braydon, people to see you, come upstairs please."

Megan continued into the kitchen and returned a moment later with a glass of water for me.

As she handed me the water, she remarked "You guys are quite early, and Neil may be a bit late, he had a case conference this afternoon, sometimes those run overtime. But Braydon should be upstairs in a moment. I'll be right back."

As she padded into the kitchen in bare feet, I noticed that her toenails had glittery silver skulls painted on them. She sported a snake toe ring on one foot. All that was a match for her camo pants and faded NIN t-shirt.

Dougherty whispered, "Did you check out her tats, and the bolt through her lip?" and winked.

Before I could respond, Megan came back in the room and observed, "Hmm, no Braydon yet, huh? I'll go dig him out of his room." She ran lightly down the stairs.

A few moments later, a slender boy of about fifteen slouched sullenly into the living room. Though most of his head was shaved, he sported tightly curled forelocks that flopped forward over his eyes. His black jeans, black hoody, and studded leather cuffs and collar all announced his goth affiliation. He had chipped black nail polish on his fingernails. His demeanor and facial expression communicated his reluctance to be in the room with us.

Megan said, "Dude, just sit on the couch and chill for a bit. You're not in any trouble. Hey, do you want that pop I owe you?"

Braydon dropped his bony frame onto the faded floral couch and nodded at Megan. He swung one leg over the arm of the furniture and slouched in our general direction. He crossed his arms over his chest and stared hard at a spot on the carpet. It's hard to know for certain what he was looking at with his sheepdog bangs falling over his eyes.

Megan returned with an opened can of root beer. She handed it to Braydon. "Root beer is your poison, right, dude?"

Braydon graced her with a grunt and started to drink his pop.

"Thank you, Megan, for getting me a pop," said Megan theatrically, looking pointedly at Braydon.

"Thanks, Megan," Braydon said softly. Megan grinned at him and walked into the kitchen.

Braydon's voice was deeper than I expected based on how skinny the kid was. Under the guise of tilting his head back to take a long swallow of root beer, Braydon peered at Dougherty and me from underneath his curled thatch of bangs. His eyes flicked over Dougherty quickly, and I thought I saw Braydon's assessment of 'cop' flit over his face. He seemed a bit uncertain of what to make of me, however.

"So, Detective Dougherty and I are here today to ask you a bit about Tiffanii."

Braydon said nothing, but he tossed his bangs out of his eyes with a quick shake of his head. He looked at me directly, anguish welling up in his eyes.

"What do you want to know?"

"Well, we know you've been through all this before, but we've been brought in to help the other cops look for

Tiffanii. Anything you can tell us about her would be helpful," I said.

"Do you guys work with Neil?" asked Braydon.

Dougherty frowned. He said, "We've talked to him, we don't work with him."

Braydon absorbed that and regarded Dougherty closely. He took another sip of his root beer.

"What do you think happened to her?" I asked.

"Somebody took her," Braydon said, flatly.

"What makes you say that?" Dougherty asked.

"'Cuz," Braydon said, digging the toe of his sneaker into the carpet. He sighed sadness in his exhalation. "She never would have left me. We were all we had left, ever since Mom and Dad . . . you know."

His voice cracked, and he rubbed his eyes with his thumb and forefinger, shaking his Bieber-bangs over his face for privacy.

This was not what I expected from Braydon, based on what Geruyter said this morning. "Braydon, I know this is awful to talk about. But we want to help; we want to find her and bring her back," I said.

Braydon sniffed and rubbed the back of his hand over his eyes. He looked at me intently. "I think if she hasn't come back by now, she won't be coming back at all. If she could get free from some pedo who took her, she would, she would fight and try to run away. I think she's prob'ly dead or locked up somewhere and can't get away."

"Can you think of anyone who might do that to her?" I asked.

He shrugged.

Dougherty said, "Anyone at all, even the first person who pops in your head, even if it seems crazy to say . . ."

Braydon muttered something inaudible.

Dougherty said, "Help us bring her home, Braydon." Braydon sighed.

Very quietly, he said, "No one would believe me even if I did say."

The doorbell rang. I had been so focused on Braydon; the sound made me jump. Megan walked through the living room and answered the door.

"Hi Neil, the cops are . . ."

Geruyter shouldered past Megan into the house, his face red. He glared at her. Braydon shrank back into the couch and dropped his gaze to the floor.

Geruyter's face was splotchy and red. Voice too loud, he asked, "What are they doing talking to Braydon without me?"

"Is that a problem? I mean, I knew you are on your way, and Braydon's not in any trouble, so I thought. . ."

"You thought? You thought? I doubt you thought at all, Megan. I'll be talking to your supervisor about this. Now take Braydon out of here, this interview is over."

"But Neil, they're trying to help find Tiffanii . . ."

He interrupted her again, holding up a hand. "Enough! I'm his guardian, and I say it's over. And if you want to keep your job, you better do what I say, when I say it."

Megan's face flushed pink, but she nodded. Braydon kept his head bowed. He was very still.

Megan looked as if she was about to speak to Geruyter. She took a breath instead. She looked at Braydon and said, "C'mon, we gots to bounce. Air hockey?"

Braydon nodded, closely inspecting the pull tab on his can of root beer. They went downstairs, closing the door behind them.

"Detective Dougherty, what is the meaning of this?" Geruyter demanded.

"What do you mean?" asked Dougherty, calmly.

"We agreed that you would not speak with Braydon until I was present as his legal guardian."

Dougherty's tone was amiable. More cop-face, though.

Dougherty said, "Is that what we agreed?"

He looked at me and asked, "Suzanne, is that what you remember from this morning?"

"Not that I recall," I said. See, I catch on fast. I could get used to having some official outlets for all the sass-mouth built up inside me. It was actually fun to watch Geruyter get a bit frustrated.

Geruyter slapped his forehead with his palm.

"Great, ok, go ahead and get cute with me and try to circumvent the rules. See where it gets you. Because I'm Braydon's legal guardian and I am now denying any informal access to him. You want to interview him further, you'll have to go through channels with cause, with both me and a lawyer present."

Dougherty smiled his unpleasant three-quarters-of-the-face smile. "Suits me, Mr. Geruyter."

Geruyter scowled. He half-turned and pulled the front door open sharply.

"You know what to do next," he growled.

Dougherty and I walked out of the house while Geruyter glared at us.

I opened my mouth to say something as we walked down the pathway. Dougherty shook his head. I closed my mouth.

When we were a block away in the Crown Vic, Dougherty said, "Yes."

"Huh?"

"Yes, he's suspicious. Yes, I think he knows way more than he's letting on about these disappearances. Yes, it's time to dig into that sonofabitch."

"Ok," I said, "What about tonight?" I asked.

"What about it?"

"We gonna go try again with Leopold in the warehouse?"

"You're the witch, you tell me," he said, smirking.

"Well, Juliet said we should go tonight or tomorrow night."

Dougherty thought about it for a moment. "Not sure McCabe is free, do you need her there, too?"

"It can't hurt, but she's not essential," I said.

"I can pick you up at Evergreen school, if you want, the game's probably done at around 9 or so, right?"

"Yeah, that works."

"And yes, I'll drop you at the Emporium so you can get back to your research. See, I'm psychic, too."

Chapter Seven

The floor of Star's ancient Toyota Tercel was thin; you could almost feel the road under your feet. Star's driving habits left a little to be desired in the paying attention to the road department. I was grateful I was in the back seat. Riding shotgun with Star always felt like I was taking my life into my hands. I was happy to leave the front passenger seat to Sarah, Star's wife. I shared the back seat with Sarah's son, Josh.

The other concern I had when riding in a car with Star was auditory in nature. She was fond of turning the music up really loud. She sang along, mostly off-key. Her musical taste was entirely questionable. Her collection of MP3's ran mostly to hits from the eighties, with tracks by Yanni and whale sounds music thrown in for good measure. Sarah's devotion to Star was such that she never once complained about the volume, the singing, or the dreadful music. Instead, Sarah held Star's hand while Star drove, letting go periodically so Star could shift gears. Wisely, Josh had opted for musical self-defense and was listening to his own tunes via his phone and ear buds.

I was still quite lost in my thoughts when we pulled up to the back of the school. Rather than try to find parking near the front of Evergreen, Star had opted to slink in the back way. She parked near one of the dumpsters out behind the gymnasium. Grabbing a sharpie from her purse, she wrote "emergency plumbing work, girl's bathroom in gym" on the back of a Chinese food take-out menu she had tucked behind the driver's seat visor. She placed the note on the dashboard and said, "Ok, we're good to go."

Sarah rolled her eyes at Star and smiled. Josh popped out an ear bud and said, "Is that even going to work? They will tow you."

Star smiled at Josh. "It always works. Tell people you have a tool belt and you can go anywhere, park anywhere. It's like magick."

Star looked at me for moral support. "No comment," I said.

Our feet crunched on the back-lot gravel as we wended our way around rain-filled potholes to the side of the gym.

"Can't we go in through the back door?" asked Sarah.

"Nope," said Josh, "They always keep them locked during games so if kids sneak out to smoke weed, they can't get back in."

Sarah and Josh walked ahead of Star and me, their long legs quickly surpassing our sedate pace. "You are quiet, Susie-Q."

I looked at her.

"Even during dinner, you didn't have a lot to say. Rough day on the case?"

I nodded. Almost everything about my day today had been awful so far. No—scratch that; it wasn't my day that had been horrible. It had been a day punctuated with hearing about horrible things happening to other people, with a sprinkling of Geruyter behaving badly. Plus, I had a nagging sense of mental distraction, my mind wandering to unfocused thoughts.

"I spent some time with a social worker who was a real asshole."

"Like a smarmy 'drugs-are-bad-hmm-kay' social worker?" she asked.

"No, like 'I'm the fucking boss of you, do what I say or else' type of guy. That and the fact that some of the kids might still be, if not alive, maybe somewhat save-able."

Star raised an eyebrow at me as we rounded the front corner of the school. Josh and Sarah were walking quickly to the back of the line to get into the gym. We paused so they could draw even further ahead of us.

"Save-able how? You always come in after everybody is dead."

"Yes, usually, but not this time. I'm not sure how much I should say about it. Probably nothing." I thought for a minute, considering my options. "What I can tell you is that the fact there might be people who can be rescued stresses me out. There is no urgency if everybody is dead. It's just a question of getting the bad guy. But in this case, there might be victims who are running out of time. I feel like I should just work and work and not stop."

Star nodded, brows knitted together in concern. "Like if you stop to say, I dunno, have dinner and go to a basketball game, that bit of time might have made a difference to saving people?" she asked.

"Yeah, exactly. I also feel shitty because I'm still not exactly sure what I can add to this case. I feel like Dougherty and McCabe are carrying things by themselves."

"Have they said that?"

"No, not yet, anyway."

"Well, I don't know about this McCabe, but Paul's not exactly a guy who will pull his punches. If he thought you were slacking, he'd tell you to pick up your game."

I considered what Star was saying as we started for the back of the line. Josh spotted us and waved his arm. We stood next to them in line.

"Ok, I gotta go in and get changed, get the last-minute pep talk from the coach," Josh said.

"Good luck, Josh," I said.

"Yep, break a leg, kiddo," said Star.

"Ice cream after, but only if you win," Sarah's eyes twinkled when she said it.

"Really?" he asked, believing her.

"No, you get ice cream either way. But remember, losing sucks, winning is better," she said, grinning. Sarah was a lawyer—a very good one. She nearly always won her cases.

Josh smiled at his mom, and trotted quickly to the front doors, squeezing past the ticket-takers. After a minute or two, the line started to move toward the door. The pre-game show was loud enough that we could hear some of it; that seemed to energize the people taking tickets as well as the people waiting.

You might be good at football
You might be good at track
But when it comes to basketball
You might as well step back
Might as well step back
Say whaaaaaaat?
You might as well step back
Can't hear you
Might as well step back
Go————————————Pinecones!

I snickered. "For real, their team is called the Pinecones?"

Sarah shrugged. "Well, you know; Evergreen school—pine cones—it makes sense, right?" I nodded. "Sure, but it doesn't really strike fear into the other team, though, does it?"

Star put her arm around Sarah. "I'm just glad it's not a stupid racist name like some sports teams have. That's bad karma."

Sarah chuckled. "You tell 'em, baby, turn those sportball racists into newts!"

"Don't tempt me!" said Star, grinning.

We'd reached the front of the line, and Sarah handed over our tickets to the teenager minding the entrance. The girl didn't say anything; she just popped her gum at us.

We walked down the crowded hallway toward the gym, the sound of the cheerleaders' chants and clapping getting louder:

Hey–Hey Hey–Hey
Are you ready?
Are you ready?
To play
Say go team
Go team
Pinecones all the way!

We entered the gym, one side decorated with dark green bunting and posters that announced: "Pinecones all the way!" The cheer squad consisted of five girls moving in almost syncopated rhythm. They were loud, but their movements were not coordinated. They wore Evergreen Pinecones jerseys over black bike shorts, black ankle socks and black running shoes. The dark green of the jerseys had faded to grey.

The competitor's side of the gym was somewhat more high-tech–they had brought a digital projector and laptop with them, and were projecting images of great moments from their previous games on one wall. Their cheer squad was co-ed and had more than twice the number of youth. Their yellow and black spandex uniforms glittered as the cheer team moved. Their squad was just completing a human pyramid as we walked in.

"Jeeze," I whispered to Star, "look at these kids from the other school. They make the Pinecones cheerleaders look like extras from a Nirvana video."

"Yeah, the Panthers come from Capitol Hill Collegiate. Rich kids' school."

The tiny girl at the top of the pyramid jumped from her perch, flipped over once in mid-air, and was caught by two muscular boys. They placed her small feet gently down on the gym floor. She started to dance, and bellowed:

You shoot 'em
You pass 'em
You dribble down the floor
Panthers! Panthers!
Score! Score! Score!

The rest of the cheer squad dismounted and formed a line behind their leader. Their movements were synchronized perfectly.

The overhead lights in the gym switched off. Pools of multi-colored light from disco balls started to sweep the floor and walls of the gym. Loudspeakers thumped with Queen's "We Will Rock You." The cheer squad clapped along to the music, encouraging the crowd to join in. The players for the Panthers ran out onto the court and stood with military attention on their side of the court.

The referee blew his whistle and tossed the ball in the air.

The two teams battled on the basketball court. The Panthers were spectacular—fast, fluid, with lightning reflexes. The Pinecones were demoralized from the very first time a Panther sunk a ball through the Pinecones' hoop. You could see it in the slump of their shoulders.

Ten minutes in, the game still had not improved.

Star leaned over and said, "The Pinecones are getting spanked."

I nodded in agreement.

Sarah said, "Looks like Josh's going to need two scoops tonight as a consolation prize."

From the stands, we could see that Josh looked frustrated as he played—his face was flushed, and he was scowling. He ran as fast as he could, nimble and quick, but it just wasn't enough to keep up with even the slowest member of the Panthers. Josh's teammates looked frustrated, too. The Pinecones' coach was red in the face, and gesturing to someone on the sidelines.

I overheard the people sitting in the bleachers in front of us
". . . Heard a rumor the Panthers coach was giving the team vampire blood to enhance performance."

I nudged Star and jerked my chin at the couple in front of us so she would join me in eavesdropping. I put my hand into my purse, reaching for my cell phone.

"Where'd you hear that?" the young woman asked. She had long dreadlocks like twisted black satin rope and a polka dot top. Her ebony skin was smooth and flawless.

My boy next to her removed his baseball cap and rubbed a hand over his close-cropped blonde hair. He said, "My older brother. He plays ball for U-Dub, and some of the team use it. Apparently, a lot of the high school boys being scouted are doing it too."

"Can't they test for it, like for steroids?" the dreadlocked young woman asked.

"Nope, not yet—they say that maybe a piss test for it could be developed, but right now, there's nothing."

"So basically, everyone is taking advantage of it while they can."

"Yep, pretty much. It's shitty, too. Look at how are these Pinecone guys are trying, and they just have no chance," the boy said.

"I feel bad for the Pinecone cheerleaders, too," said his companion.

I leaned in close to Star's ear and whispered, "Did you catch all that?"

She nodded.

I settled back in my seat.

More loudly than I normally would, I said, "I think I have some parsley in my teeth from dinner, just going to use my phone to check."

Star nodded. She knew me well enough to know what I was thinking.

"Good idea," she said, loudly. "I think you might have some spinach in there, too."

I held my phone up in front of my face like I was using the camera app to check my grooming. Instead, I snapped a couple of pictures of the couple we'd been eavesdropping on.

The couple in front of us noticed nothing. Disinterested in the game in front of them, they were debating the merits of various cheerleading movies, and looking up actor bios on their phones.

I looked back to the game. One of the Pinecones was bent at the waist, hands on his thighs, trying to catch his breath. The tallest member of the Panthers—who was easily closer to seven feet tall than he was to six—had outpaced him with long fluid strides. He nearly floated up to the basket to drop the ball in. The out-of-breath Pinecone frowned and hunched his shoulders.

I can't watch any more of this; it's so depressing.

I leant over and said to Star and Sarah, "I'm going for popcorn, you guys want anything?"

"No thanks, I am ok," said Sarah.

"Me too, I'm going to wait for the ice cream," said Star.

I squeezed my ample behind past the people seated beside us and started to make my way down the steps of the bleachers. I spotted Braydon standing near the edge of the court, talking to one of the Pinecone cheer squad. *What's he doing here?* I thought for a beat. *That's right, his group home is the catchment for Evergreen.*

I quickened my pace, hoping to catch Braydon before he saw me and disappeared into the crowd. This was my chance to talk to him without Geruyter around—if Braydon was still willing.

Just as I reached court level, the half-time whistle blew, and people surged out of the bleachers, hurrying to the concession lines. The girls' bathroom already had a line up out the door, but predictably, in a crowd that was predominantly mothers, sisters, girlfriends and classmates of the basketball team, no one was heading toward the men's room. In the crush of people, I almost lost sight of Braydon but managed to make out that the washroom was where he was headed.

I tried to move more quickly through the crowd, but it wasn't working very well. At five-feet, three inches, the top of my head is well below the line of sight for most people, so people in crowds often don't realize I'm nearby until I am literally right next to them. That, combined with the self-centeredness of humans in crowded spaces, meant it took some time and some effort for me to wedge my way across the crowded gym.

I was about ten feet from the boy's bathroom door when I heard the scream.

It was a primal screech of surprise and fear. It echoed off the tiles in the bathroom and rang out into the gym, audible despite the din of the crowd. A few heads turned in the direction of the scream, but the disorderly crowd was intent on moving toward the concession stand, so it was ignored.

I struggled against the people in my way, but couldn't worm my way through them. I felt dread skulk in the pit of my stomach. Something in my chest clenched. I dug my elbows into people to make them move. People just elbowed me back. I was losing precious seconds. In frustration, I shoved the man in my path out of the way and ran for the boy's washroom door.

The hospital-green tile work was splashed everywhere with blood; arterial spray had even reached the ceiling. The small window high on the far wall had been smashed open, glass shards on the floor.

A gangly, redheaded kid was frozen in place coming out of the bathroom stall. He looked at Braydon's body crumpled on the floor, eyes wide with shock.

Braydon lay on the tile floor in a puddle of blood, his hands gripping the red ruin of his throat. He saw me, and his eyes burned into mine, his lips moving in an inaudible plea for help.

"Hey, Red!" I shouted at the screamer, "Call 911 right now on your cell, then go get the coach!"

I ran toward Braydon as I yelled.

The ginger kid looked at me blankly for a moment. "Do it, now!" I screamed.

He ran from the bathroom fumbling in his pants for his cell. He avoided the floor tiles that were slick with Braydon's blood. I slipped through it and landed awkwardly on my ass next to Braydon.

"Keep your hands on it, Braydon. You are doing well. Help is coming," I said as I pressed my hands against his.

Despite the pressure on the wound, his blood oozed between our fingers. I could feel the fading warmth of the blood pool I was sitting in.

Braydon's eyes started to close.

I nudged him with my right knee and said, "Braydon! Buddy! Stay with me, ok? Help is coming; we're going to get you fixed up. Just hang in here with me."

Even as I said it, I knew I was losing him. The part of me attuned to the dead could feel his life force ebbing away, dwindling down to a shining silver thread. The coppery tang of his blood seemed to stick to the back of my throat as I breathed. I fought my gag reflex.

Tears welled up in my eyes and spilled down my cheeks. "Braydon, please stay here, please, we can fix you, don't go, don't go, honest—someone can help you." *Where the fuck was the coach?*

Braydon made a gurgling sound, more from his shredded throat than from his mouth. His eyes fluttered open, and he looked sadly at me. His eyes closed, and the blood welling from his wound slowed. I felt the silver thread that attached his soul to his body snap.

I felt my usual anchoring—the metaphysical binding that helped me keep the voices of the dead out of my head—start to fade. *Is my necromancy trying to follow him?*

Heedless to the other spirits that may be around, I started to open the part of me that communicated with dead things. I needed to talk to Braydon. In my mind's eye, I could see the frayed end of Braydon's soul receding. With no time or equipment to cast a protective circle or bless the space, I shoved at the spiritual gateway inside me, opening it all the way.

A wall of sound slammed into me. Hundreds of voices pleaded for my attention. I could feel fingers wispy as tattered cobwebs trailing over my skin.

I shivered, and called out "Braydon!"

His silver thread continued to recede. I tried to send some of my own ki—a red tendril—out to touch his silver one. The other spirits clamoring for my attention seemed empowered by my ki, drinking it like nectar. Braydon's soul continued to recede. The spirits standing closest to me seemed to thicken and solidify, their voices getting clearer, their outlines sharper.

"I'm sorry, I have no time for you right now," I said. In my mind's eye, I drew the red tendril back into my own heart. I could feel the spirits trying to keep drawing on my energy like a nursing mother feels her infant's lips reach for her as she pulls her breast away.

I breathed in deeply, the sickly-sweet tang of Braydon's blood clinging to my airways. I blew out the breath and slammed the door on the spiritual gateway.

The red-haired kid ran back into the room, his cell plastered to his ear. The red-faced coach was on his heels. The coach veered around Red and knelt on the other side of Braydon's body. He peeled up one of Braydon's eyelids and looked into his eye.

"Yes, I am standing right next to her . . . She's holding her hands over his throat . . . I'll ask," Red said into his phone.

He pulled it away from his face. "Hey lady, have you been giving CPR at all?"

"No, I don't know how. Just pressure on the bleeding."

"She says no."

The coach started to perform CPR on Braydon's body. Knowing it was pointless, I continued to hold on to his throat anyway.

In the distance, I could hear someone shouting in the gym, "Stay back! Keep the way clear! Boy's room is closed right now for a med emergency."

The coach continued the chest compressions. I could feel the blood on my hands cooling. It was sticky now. Through the broken window, I could hear the wail of approaching sirens echo off the tile walls.

"Yes," the red-headed kid said, "I can hear them, they are close."

The voice outside the bathroom got more urgent. "Clear the way for the firefighters! Stay back! Give them room."

Three large men in yellow firefighting gear ran into the bathroom. The tallest firefighter quickly approached Braydon, shouting, "Sir, Ma'am, back up from the boy so we can help him! Back up now and give us some room!"

The tall firefighter knelt on the tile floor and resumed CPR on Braydon. Clad in full gear, he started to perspire as he worked. His dark skin gleamed almost purple under the fluorescent bathroom lights.

One of the other firefighters, a barrel-chested white man with a droopy grey moustache, drew the Pinecones coach to one side of the bathroom and started questioning him. I stared mutely at Braydon's body and began to shiver. The wet cobweb sensation the spirits had left behind on my skin was cold and creepy.

"Miss, are you ok?"

I continued to stare at Braydon, as though gazing at his waxy features could re-animate him. *Why am I so cold?*

"Miss!" the third firefighter said sharply. "You are going into shock. We need to get you out of here."

I looked at him in wonderment. He had chocolate brown eyes with thick black lashes. I was dimly aware that he looked concerned. Is that why I felt so weird, shock? Or was it something else, because I crossed the gateway without casting a circle?

I looked down at my arm. The firefighter had gently gripped my forearm and was leading me out of the bathroom. I felt weak and spacey. I let him steer me through the crowd in the gymnasium. Some people were holding the curious crowd back from the entrance to the boys' bathroom. They had cleared a path from the bathroom to the gymnasium doors.

A murmur of panic spread through the crowd.

"Is that blood on her?" someone said.

"Oh, my god, it's all over her hands!" exclaimed another person in the crowd.

"What's going on? Is she hurt? Was she the one screaming?"

"Did she just murder someone in the bathroom?"

The crowd surged forward, only to be pressed back by the people holding the clearing. One muscular Asian man in a red polo shirt knew how to project his voice: "Keep back, let the firemen do their jobs! Keep back; everything is ok." *Wow, that dude lifts.* The muscular man continued to preserve a pathway with his body and outstretched arms, casting worried glances over his shoulder.

The firefighter gripped my arm more tightly and quickened his pace. He led me out into the parking lot, where a fire truck, an ambulance, and an SPD patrol car were parked at haphazard angles. The faces of the fair-skinned first responders were stained lollipop red from the flashing lights on the vehicles, their darker skinned co-workers a deep mahogany. The rain had stopped, and at least for now, there were no clouds. I imagined I could see Braydon's silver ki floating into the dark sky. The stars wheeled overhead as though splatter-painted on the inside of an overturned ceramic bowl. There was no moon.

One of the EMTs, a petite, muscular woman with a brown ponytail and smooth olive skin, spotted us and ran over with her kit.

"Wuzzup, Barry?" she said, addressing the firefighter.

"Potential witness, probably unharmed, presents with shock."

"Hey sweetie," she said, flashing her penlight in my eyes. "You come with me, ok? You need a blanket to stay warm."

She took my other arm and gently led me away to the back of the ambulance.

About ten minutes later, I was wrapped in a rough wool blanket and seated on the ambulance bumper. I sipped from a paper cup of steaming over-sweetened coffee. The EMT had checked me out and satisfied herself that I wasn't the source of the blood on my hands and my clothes. She told me to stay warm and sit tight. I was deep inside my own ruminations about what I had experienced, so I didn't notice Dougherty until he was standing right in front of me.

He had his cop-face on, brittle as wax, and less expressive. *Uh oh, that means he's really freaked out.*

He squatted down near me. "Hey Suzi-Q, how are you feeling?"

My mind reeled with potential answers, but I wasn't sure where to start. He looked at me with a raised eyebrow.

"I heard the emerg call on my radio in the car and remembered that you were coming here tonight for Josh's game. I also remembered that this was Braydon's school, too."

I nodded and sipped the weak coffee.

"Here's what the patrol officers told me: the red-headed kid says he was in the stall using the toilet and he could hear Braydon washing his hands at the sink. He heard another person come into the bathroom. Apparently, Braydon said something like "fuck, no, lemme alone, get off me." After that, the kid says he heard only gurgling sounds and the sound of the glass breaking. He says he was so scared, he just froze in the stall and didn't really know what to do."

"Yes," I said quietly.

"Then he says you came running in, yelled at him to call 911, and that you were trying to hold Braydon's throat closed."

I nodded again.

He leant closer to me and lowered his voice. "And I think you did some magick to try to stop him from dying or something, and now you're all fucked up and spaced out."

Tears welled up in my eyes. I blinked them away and nodded. "I opened the gateway without a circle, and there were some spirits who wanted to . . . interfere a bit."

"You've never done that before?"

I shook my head. I wish I had a tissue so I could blow my nose.

"So, we're both in unknown territory right now," Dougherty said.

I started to cry in earnest now; silent tear drops rolling down my cheeks. One splashed into the now-cold coffee.

"Aw, fuck, Suzi, don't do that!" Dougherty exclaimed. "Where the fuck is Star and the rest of them? Have you seen them?" He looked around as he spoke.

I felt my cell vibrate in my pocket. *Perhaps it had been vibrating for a while, and I hadn't noticed?* I pulled it out of my pocket and peered at the small display. Yep. 20 text messages from Star, all some variation of 'where r u?'

"It's her," I said, gesturing with the phone. I pressed 'reply' to her last text.

"Outside nr ambulance"

'Thnx gods! Whts happng?'

'Come find me, I'll tell u then'

A few minutes later Star had located us and been tersely briefed by Dougherty. I was still spaced and numb. I found it hard to look away from the whirling bowl of hard stars in the inky night sky.

"Take her home, please, she did some kind of magick without protection, and now she's all fucked up. The EMTs say she's good to go, so just get her outta here," Dougherty said to Star.

"Okay," Star said, a line forming between her brows.

"Thanks. Suzi, I'll check with you tomorrow morning, ok? I gotta go."

Gasoline rainbows gleamed on the wet asphalt as Dougherty walked back into the school.

Star glanced at her phone and said, "Looks like Josh and Sarah are in the car, I'll just tell them where we are." Her thumbs flew over her phone's tiny on-screen keyboard.

Star sat next to me on the ambulance bumper and put her arm around my shoulders. "You know what you were saying before the game, about maybe feeling obligated to help because people might get hurt?"

I nodded.

She sighed heavily and squeezed my shoulders. "I think you're right."

Chapter Eight

Star dropped Josh and Sarah off at home first. I sat mute in the car. I think Star must have texted Sarah and Josh and told them not to ask any questions. We rode the short distance to their home in without speaking. Even Star's MP3 player was silent.

When Star finally dropped me off at my apartment, I had to tell her a few times I'd be ok on my own. I could tell she didn't believe me, but she also knows me well enough to know that sometimes I just need to be alone.

"You're really sure?" she asked, for the tenth time.

"Yes, I'm sure," I said.

"You're not just saying that?"

"No, I'm too spent for hysterics right now. I want to shower and go to bed."

Suspicion clouded Star's face, but she knew better than to argue more. That just makes me dig in my heels.

Walking up the stairs to my apartment, I knew I hadn't processed what I had seen tonight. I don't think I'd even processed the day before, for that matter. There was no time to sit and think without distractions.

I knew I felt sad. Beyond that, I was bone-weary and calmly, oddly . . . resolved. Witnessing the gruesome spectacle at the high school had exhausted me. It had also made me certain I needed to do something, anything—to make this shit stop. Seeing Braydon's blood spilling out all over the tiles in the boy's bathroom was not something I wanted to re-live, so we needed to pick up the pace on this investigation. I had to figure out a way to get more information from Leopold in my next interview with him.

I dropped my keys and purse on the small table near my front door. My clothes were too filthy to just strip off in the hallway. That would end up smearing blood everywhere. My small grey cat Bluebell came running to the door to investigate my arrival. She could smell the blood and magick on me, I think. Instead of wrapping figure-eights around my ankles as she usually did, she merely sat on her haunches in front of me, twitching her fluffy tail.

I noted the time on the wall clock and sighed. It was 11:14 pm. Too late to go back to Issaquah tonight, even if someone would give me a ride. For perhaps only the tenth time in my life, I cursed my lack of drivers' license. Talking to Leopold was something I could do, but it would have to wait until tomorrow sometime.

I walked to my tiny bathroom and took off my shoes. They were ruined, so they went in the trash. *Fuck, Chuck Taylors aren't friggin' cheap.* I stood fully clothed in the tub, removing my socks, one at a time. I stripped off the rest of my clothes and left them at the bottom of the tub. If I showered, then let the clothes soak in chilly water, maybe the bloodstains would come out? *Worth a shot, anyway.* I pushed all the clothes to the far end of the tub and endured a tepid shower, shielding my clothes from the barely warm water with my body—being a thick girl comes in handy at the strangest moments. I plugged the tub and added a large amount of cold soaking water.

Teeth chattering, I stepped out of the tub and wrapped myself in a towel. Followed by Bluebell, I walked into my chilly bedroom and donned my polar bear pjs. Bluebell lounged in the middle of my bed, stretching and rolling in an invitation-to-pet. I considered brushing my teeth. I couldn't face the mess in bathroom again. I think I've seen enough blood today. I buried myself under the thick duvet and squished my pillow into the correct shape. Bluebell draped herself over the top of my head like a fuzzy cap. Her tail wrapped across my throat, the tip nestled in my left ear. Bluebell purred. Within minutes I was asleep.

I'm not sure how long I slept before I started to dream. It was grotesque. I was in a Victorian parlor with flocked red velvet wallpaper. There was an ornate plaster ceiling medallion from which the gilt chandelier chain emerged. Candle smoke had smudged the perfect white of the medallion. The chandelier was a multi-armed behemoth dripping with crystal teardrops. It held maybe fifty lit candles. The wax had dripped onto some of the crystal drops. You could smell the beeswax.

I was lying down on something . . . correction, I was tied down to something. I was on my back on a table. I tried to move, experimentally. The bonds were tight. As I looked down my body, I noticed two things: I was wearing a dandified green velvet suit, replete with what appeared to be a silk cravat and bejewelled stick pin. Secondly, I wasn't me. I was a man. I had long, lean limbs, narrow chest and hips, and the largest feet I'd ever seen. My toes, clad in square-toed suede boots, stuck straight up in the air.

This may not seem remarkable, but for me it was noteworthy. I haven't seen my feet when I look down my body since before puberty. I'm a curvaceous and shorter than average. Weight-wise, I'm somewhere in the range of plumpish to zaftig. If I lie on my back and stare straight down the length of my body, I can see as far as my boobs, and no further. Somehow being able to see my feet, and having them be so far away from my head, was more of a shock to me than being a man.

A shadow fell over my body. Turing my head slightly, I saw Juliet. This Juliet was not the woman in jeans and a hippie top I had met on Sunday evening. This Juliet was attired in a stiff corseted dress. The pale blue watered silk covered her from her tightly buttoned wrists to her high-collared neck. The fabric color made her blue eyes the more striking. I could hear the folds of fabric rustle against the carpet as she moved toward me.

Her hair was piled on her head in an elaborate upswept style. Wearing her hair that way, with her pale creamy skin and rosebud mouth, she looked like a Gibson girl. Unlike the serene gaze of the women in Gibson's drawings, Juliet's eyes burning with a cold fury. It was only then that I noticed the blade in her hand.

"Leopold," she said calmly, quietly, "Did you think you could flout my authority forever?"

I opened my mouth to speak. Before I could, I heard my dream-self speak with my dream body's voice. My voice had a baritone rumble, heavy with a mid-European accent I could not identify.

"I do not acknowledge your authority over me." The contempt in my voice was withering.

Juliet smirked. "That is a shame since it is you who is tied up and at my mercy. Perhaps I can convince you to respect me."

Without warning, she drove the blade into my left forearm, missing the two bones, but striking so deep that I felt the knife chunk into the wooden surface of the table below me. The pain was incredible. It felt more like a chemical burn than a knife wound. Sharp arrows of pain shot up my arm.

I opened my mouth to scream at her to take it out, that it burns, to please please take it out, but before I could speak, the body's voice spoke again.

"I had no idea that you liked to play so rough, Juliet. The silver is a nice touch. Expecting me to whimper and cry like a mewling pup? You will be disappointed."

Juliet produced another blade and drove it through my left elbow. Again, this strike was deep enough that I felt the silver blade bite into the table. The pain was worse in the joint than it had been in the forearm.

Juliet purred, "We can play all night, my poppet. We will play until you tell me who helped you Turn those children."

Juliet moved to the small table to her left and took a delicate sip of sherry from a small crystal glass. She put the glass down and picked up another knife.

Suzanne, you are dreaming. You are having a dream. You are dreaming that you are Leopold. You are not Leopold; you are asleep and dreaming.

The colors faded from the dream, as though the room had suddenly gone from Technicolor to black and white. I felt very far away from the action of the dream like I had floated up and out of Leopold's body. In the dream, I closed my eyes.

Have a different dream, Suzanne, dream about going to Hawaii. Dream about eating pineapple on a beach in Hawaii. For a moment, I thought I heard the sound of waves crashing on a beach. *Thank the gods it's working!*

A bolt of hot pain rushed from my left ear. My head throbbed with it. I opened my eyes. Juliet's face was mere inches from mine, one wavy lock of her hair straying down to curl against her milk-white neck.

"Still with me?" she whispered. "Good. Don't worry; I won't pierce your other eardrum–you do need to hear my questions if you are to answer them. It might take hours for you to heal both ears, and I don't want to wait that long."

She sighed. "I confess I am perplexed why you are not as . . . motivated . . . by my knives, as others have been."

I flicked my eyes away from her gaze and looked down the length of the Leopold body. Silver knives pinned it to the table at the ankle, through the shin, the knee, at mid-thigh, and the hip joint, the forearm, the elbow, the bicep and the shoulder.

The sight of Leopold's body, our body, pinned to the table, and the feeling of the knife in our ear made me feel dizzy, even though I was lying down. I turned my head away from Juliet. I felt I might throw up. Her small hand gripped me by the hair and roughly turned my head back to face her.

"How is it you still resist, Leopold? There is no reason to protect your accomplice any longer. You can save yourself decades in the Den of the Forsaken if you but tell me his name. Perhaps you like experiencing pain as much as you like inflicting it, is that it?"

She walked idly around the table, twisting the handle of each dagger she passed.

"I did not think you would choose someone like me for such games. You might merely have asked, you know, you have certainly gone to a lot of trouble to arrange it, if that is the case. Not that I would have said yes."

She laughed, a tinkling bell.

"That does give me an idea, however," she murmured.

She stood and thought for a moment, idly tucking the loose lock of hair that curled against her neck back into her hairstyle.

"Don't go anywhere, Leopold," she smirked.

How could Leopold resist the terrible pain she was causing him? I was starting to panic. *Wake up, Suzanne, you are dreaming. Think white sand beaches, pineapples, drinks in coconut shells with umbrellas in them, c'mon get out of here.*

Too late. Juliet re-entered the room; her hand tucked under the armpit of a slight and homely young woman in a dingy grey ruffled cap. She shoved the girl toward to the table.

"Do it!" she commanded the girl.

The girl had tears streaking trails down her smudged face. One cheek bore the bright red print of Juliet's small hand.

"Do it now, as I told you."

The girl stood to the side of the table near the knife sticking out of Leopold's hip. She gripped the handle of the blade and pulled it out clumsily. I felt a scream rise up through the dream-body, but no sound issued from Leopold's lips. The girl reached for the button on the fly of Leopold's trousers.

For a moment, I felt an emotion of Leopold's – he was feeling panic. Unbuttoning him, the girl thrust her hand inside Leopold's velvet trousers and touched his flaccid penis. Her skin was rough, work-chapped. The friction of her hand eventually brought predictable results.

Leopold's panic rose with his erection. I tried to draw myself out of Leopold. I might have to watch this, but I didn't have to feel it. After a couple of tries, I felt myself rise out of Leopold's body into a corner of the room. My spirit floating out of the shared body gave me respite from Leopold's physical sensations. Somehow, I could still feel his emotions and thoughts.

"Juliet," Leopold bluffed, "do you think me so perverse I cannot enjoy the ministrations of your scullery girl?"

Juliet's eyes glittered.

Leopold hissed as the maid's hand started to work him faster.

"Yes, I do, Leopold; that is exactly what I think. I think the fact this is the touch of a female is repulsive to you, and apparently much harder for you to bear than the silver piercing your flesh."

Leopold continued to put a brave face on it.

"Ha! You know nothing, woman!" he barked, but I could feel his panic edging toward a higher. Leopold hated this. *Well, who could blame him, rape sucks.*

I could feel a subtle shift inside Leopold as he tried to will his attention away from the girl's hand on his throbbing penis. This was truly more horrible to him than the pain the knives caused him. There was no way to re-frame this as bravery or nobility. There was nothing to do here but curse the body's vulnerabilities.

Leopold started to pant. The girl's rough hand worked faster as tears rolled down her face.

Juliet, laughed, a deep, honey-coated sound.

"Yes, that's it, she is going to make you spend. Then how much will you hate yourself? We shall see . . . Shall I make her stop? Or perhaps you'd like to beg me to force her to continue?"

Leopold was trying to focus on something, anything, rather than the servant's hand.

"Just tell me the name," Juliet commanded.

"No," Leopold hissed. "I will not spend, and I will not tell you the name."

Leopold's body was tight with tension, trying to avoid the climb toward orgasm. He failed. "No no no no nonononononono" he cried, and then ejaculated all over the girl's hand and his velvet trousers. *Why is his semen black?*

Juliet clapped her hands together and giggled girlishly.

"You see, Leopold?" she purred, "You do like girls. I knew I could convince you. Thank you, Dora, you may go.

I may call upon you and your sister later this evening, so please, be prepared."

Dora scurried out, tears still rolling down her face, her palm full of Leopold's cold dark ejaculate.

Juliet sighed and picked up her glass of sherry. "Tell me the name, or every woman in my service will touch you tonight and every night until you tell me the name. I can guarantee that you will hate every moment of it, until you start to enjoy it. Which is worse for a man of your tastes, I wonder?"

Without warning, Juliet drove the silver knife back into the healing hole in Leopold's hip.

I saw tears well up in Leopold's eyes. He blinked them back. He did not scream. Juliet had correctly assessed his character. Physical pain was not unbearable for him. The sexual humiliation was another matter. Physical pain might be a way to prove and enhance one's strength, but humiliation and loss of control threatened to unman him.

"Leopold, have you never given a woman oral pleasure? You will before this night is through unless you give me something to catch your accomplice."

Leopold's face blanched. I caught the edge of his panic again, but he managed to damp it down. His voice was far stronger than his actual feelings.

"Juliet, you are a whore and weakling," he said, then spat in her face.

Juliet carefully placed her sherry glass back on the marble-topped table. She removed a lace-trimmed handkerchief from her pocket and wiped away Leopold's spittle.

"I see you still have the energy to defy me, Leopold. What shall we try next, I wonder, some fire or Dora and her sister?"

I quailed at the thought. Even though I had managed to slip out of Leopold's body, I didn't want to witness anymore. I felt my own panic rise, and woke up in cold sweat in my own bed; Bluebell curled in my armpit. The clock read 2:14.

I got out of bed. *I need another shower to get that dream off me.* I squeezed out the soaking wet clothes and piled them in the bathroom sink. *Those stains are not coming out.* I think I was focused on mundane things so I wouldn't think about the dream. I did not want to re-enter it.

I took the hottest shower I could tolerate. It didn't do much to help me leave the panic and horror from the dream behind, but it was a start. Maybe this is going to be ok. And it was, more by the minute, until I saw the irreparably stained clothes heaped in my bathroom sink. I started to cry. I sat on the edge of my tub, sobbing over ruined clothes. When I could sob no more, I bagged them and the bathroom trash. I cleaned the tub, the sink, toilet, and all the blood-spattered surfaces with sudsy ammonia. Then I had another shower.

I was no longer interested in sleep. I fantasized briefly about never sleeping again. I don't think I could witness another scene like the one I'd seen in the dream and maintain my emotional balance. I had no doubt that what I had seen was not a dream per se but some kind of psychic sharing of memory. Just what I needed, right?

I sighed. In the past forty-eight hours I'd discovered a magickal ability I didn't know I had, used it to abuse a captive spirit, consorted with vampires, listened to disturbing tales of child abuse, witnessed torture and sexual assault in a dream state, and watched a teenaged boy bleed out on the bathroom floor. *Fuck-when does this stop?*

I shuddered, pulled on sweatpants and a t-shirt, and shoved away my revulsion. *Plenty of time to lose my shit about this later.* Sitting at my kitchen counter, I stirred cream and sugar into a fresh cup of coffee. Using the pencil and pad I always kept on the kitchen counter; I started to make a list. *So, what did I know?* Not much.

My best theory was that interviewing Leopold the other day had made him mentally re-visit what Juliet had done to him before he was consigned to the Den of the Forsaken. As near as I could tell, contacting him via the ritual had connected me to him, and so I could experience his thoughts or memories in my dreams.

Bluebell leapt up onto the counter, sniffed at my coffee cup and lay down across my pad of paper. I stroked her whisper-fluff fur and nibbled on the end of my pencil. It also seemed clear to me that if we were going to crack this case, we had to get more information from Leopold about his historic co-conspirator. I was going to have to figure out something that would help make Leopold talk. *Leopold had said she'd tortured him with knives for seven days, didn't he?* The problem was that it had to be something that would work and that something had to be something I was willing to do. That ruled out torture and rape. Not just because I'm not willing to do those things—I'm not, but even if I were, Leopold seemed to have faced those horrors without breaking. If Leopold had spilled the beans back then, no one would be asking him the same questions now. *What could you do to a person who wouldn't talk after all that?*

The accidental metaphysical beat-down I gave him last night may work—if I could figure out a way to yield it more intentionally–and if I was willing to do that. *When does a beating stop being a beating and start being torture? Does it make sense to lump a spiritual beating in with a physical one? If I'm willing to interview him again and try to compel him, can I really say what I'm doing is somehow not torture?*

Bluebell relocated to my lap, purring. I continued to stroke her fur with my left hand, jotting notes with my right. I was going to have to consult the grimoires at the Emporium to get some ideas on how to proceed. I finished my coffee, evicted Bluebell from my lap, gave her a cat treat in compensation, and called an Uber.

Chapter Nine

The rain bounced off the sidewalk and spattered the display windows of the bookstore as I dug through my messenger bag for my keys. My neck twinged. I rotated my shoulders and dipped my ears to each of my shoulders in turn to release some of the tension. The feelings of violation I'd had since being swept up in Leopold's dream hadn't left me yet. I'd never been inside another person's dream before, let alone had to endure torture from a first-person perspective. Further, I was skeptical this was a new-found psychic ability that had suddenly just appeared. *You messed up when you pursued Braydon without a protective circle.* I pushed the thought away and fumbled more deeply in the depths of my bag. I opened the door to the Emporium and punched in the security code. Whether I had screwed up or whether I hadn't, I was worried about Braydon's spirit, I was uncertain how to get information from Leopold without abusing him, and I needed to figure out what to do about all of it, magickally-speaking.

I was aware of some of the basics: the spirits of the newly dead will usually linger for an hour or so after death, but some spirits lingered longer. How much longer seemed to vary depending on which grimoire or book of shadows you consulted. I'd only worked a couple of cases with SPD so far; both times the spirits had lingered for about three days. Each of those spirits had been a child who had been murdered and who wanted to name her attacker. Once the villain was named and apprehended, the spirits dissipated and went on to whatever comes next.

Based on the little I had read before I took my first case, that was typical for such cases. In the months since then, though, Star had shown me some books that described other patterns.

One adolescent spirit with poltergeist abilities had haunted a church vestry for forty years before she was finally exorcised by the combined efforts of a Shinto priest and Hassidic rabbi. Another spirit, an eighty-year-old man who had killed himself by drinking drain cleaner, had wandered the halls of the Shriner's Hospital in Shreveport for half a decade before a Dianic Wiccan medium contacted him to find out what he might need to move on. Older stories were even stranger. With some of the more incredible tales, I imagined some long-ago monk chuckling to himself as he laid down an outrageous tale on parchment.

Star and I were in the process of digitizing her entire collection of old grimoires and books of shadow, but we hadn't made much headway yet. It had only been a couple of months since Sarah had suggested we create a cloud database of all the old books. I was certainly going to check the small amount of data already loaded into CloudWitch, but I had a feeling what I needed hadn't been digitized. Or hadn't even been written.

The streetlights outside the shop windows provided me with enough light to cross the sales area and walk behind the cashier counter. I opened the door to the back-storage room, snapped on the overhead light, and sat down at the computer workstation tucked into a corner of the room.

The computer booted up quickly and CloudWitch greeted me with the characteristic 'cackle' sound Star had programmed into it. I clicked on the search field on

CloudWitch's landing page and typed: SPIRITS LENGTH OF TIME LINGER AFTER DEATH

CloudWitch showed zero query results.

I tried again: SOULS STAYING AFTER DEATH

CloudWitch showed four query results. I clicked on the first one. It was a treatise on how to banish a soul who hasn't been able to accept its mortal death. Not exactly what I needed right now. Though it might've helped the priestess at that Shriner's hospital back in the day, for sure. I bookmarked the entry.

The next two results were similarly unhelpful, so I clicked away from them quickly. Result number four was intriguing. It was a partial text translated from Aramaic that described a necromancer who attempted to make a spirit linger near the site of its mortal death so that he could interview it. The spirit had been approaching the three-day cut off, and it seems the necromancer was late to the scene due to a problem with his donkey. The family wasn't going to pay the necromancer unless he completed the interview, so he tried to prevent the spirit from entering What-Comes-Next.

He was lucky to have been in his protective circle. The spirit he was trying to compel had some talent as a poltergeist and had toppled a heavy clay vessel. Without the protective circle, the necromancer would have been hurt, maybe even crushed by the large vase. As it was, the family refused to pay him, and he had to compensate them for the broken clay vase. *Wow, I was super lucky Braydon didn't want to hurt me, I'd have been a sitting duck.*

I tried a few more keyword combinations on CloudWitch and got nowhere. I was going to have to search the books and manuscripts themselves. For that, I was going to have to don some white cotton gloves to protect the old pages, and clear the space to make sure nothing could get spilled on them.

The clock read four am. I needed coffee if I was going to go much further with any research. My skin was still crawling from Leopold's dream, and I couldn't shake a sense of foreboding.

I walked over to the small sink and counter in the opposite corner of the storage room and inserted a coffee pod in the brewer. The machine started to wheeze as it heated water from its reservoir. I bent from the waist to retrieve a small carton of cream from the mini-fridge, and a headache struck me like a hammer to the temple. I gasped and fell to my knees, grabbing the counter as I went down.

The hammering on my temple continued. I was starting to get nauseated. In the far distance, I could hear music. It was faint, but if I squeezed my eyes shut and focused, I could make it come in more clearly. Was that "Clair de Lune"?

~Yes.~

"What?" I said out loud.

~It is Clair de Lune, my poppet.~

"What?"

~You are tedious, dear girl. Yes, it is "Clair de Lune." I like Debussy.~

I looked around me, wincing as the pain increased.

~Stop fighting it. It will hurt less. Unless you like that kind of thing, of course. Then, as a gentleman, I shall oblige you.~

"Who . . . ?" I couldn't hear his sigh, but I could feel it vibrate through my own body.

~Oh, do get up off that filthy floor, dear girl. I see that you are very stupid, so I shall try to explain.~

I stood up with the help of the counter.

~Continue to make your beverage, and I shall educate you.~

I got the cream from the mini fridge and poured some into the cup as the coffee machine drizzled the black brew.

~You visited me at my prison yesterday.~

"I did?" I said.

~You don't need to speak for me to hear you, poppet, but by all means, continue if you wish to address the bare walls.~

Ok

~After you visited me, it took me a little while to recover. Before your visit, I was in a great torpor. I no longer railed at my imprisonment. I think I had given up.~

Leopold!

~Ah, as they say, the penny has dropped! Tell me you moderns still have pennies?~

Yes.

~Excellent. Some things never change. At any rate, you stopping by to question me so rudely woke something in me.~

Oops

~Don't apologize, my dear. I, too, have had to do Juliet's bidding. It is sometimes distasteful. But as you have seen, her punishments are much worse.~

I quailed inwardly at the pictures that flashed by my mind's eye—Leopold's joints pierced with silver knives, the tears of the chapped cheeks of Juliet's servant, Leopold's expression of disgust and shame.

~Necromancer! Enough of that, I need no reminding, and neither do you. What's past is past, there is no correcting it.~

I sighed. I stirred my coffee and took a sip.

~Oh, delightful, coffee with cream. I have missed it during my unfortunate incarceration.~

You can . . . ?

~Yes, I can taste what you taste, feel what you feel, just as you can taste and feel through me.~

Why?

~I am not certain, but it seems when you interviewed me and increased your power by vocalizing notes, it somehow bonded us. As you saw in tonight's dream. I have been trying to contact you since then.~

Why did it take me so long to notice?

~Your interview was . . . strenuous. I was weak and, er, indisposed for some hours afterwards. After I recovered, I could feel your mind, but only slightly. However, as the hours went by, I could feel more of your thoughts and experience. I was finally able to touch your experience when you did some magick without a circle.~

You felt that?

~Yes, you were calling after someone named Braydon? That sounds like a horse's name, not the name of a young man. Ridiculous, really.~

Why didn't I know you were there?

~I have no idea. I've never had a psychic link with a necromancer before. I've seen it done, though. Damn fine magick when it can be managed.~

So why do you think I finally noticed you were there?

~I decided to try to reach out. So, I started to dwell on various memories from my human and vampire life.~

Why'd you start with such an awful memory?

I swear I heard him snort with laughter.

~That wasn't the first thing I tried to show you. It was simply the first thing that worked.~

Oh. I paused and slowly sipped the coffee again. *Leopold.*

~Yes?~

What do you want?

~Oh my dear! Perhaps you are not as simple as I thought.~

Just tell me. In frustration, I blew at a strand of my hair that had fallen over my eyes.

~Well, my dear, I have something to offer you.~

What's that?

~I think I can help you discover who the naughty vampires are.~

And?

~And in return, I want you to convince Juliet to free me from my prison.~

How am I supposed to do that?

~Oh I am sure you will think of something before more young people die.~

Forget it.

I walked with my cup of coffee back to the computer workstation and sat down, typing idly at some keys, refreshing the CloudWitch landing page.

~Don't you care about poor, poor Braydon? Don't you want to avenge him?~

I winced at the mention of Braydon's name. *Something like that. But if Juliet lets you out, there's no reason for you to help me further.*

~Indeed?~

So, you have to pony up some support for the investigation. Once we have captured the bad guy, then I'll try to convince Juliet you should be let out. I rotated my shoulders and stretched my stiff neck.

~Fine, I will agree to that, but I have one condition.~

Which is?

~Don't tell anyone about our link just yet.~

Why not?

~I fear if Juliet knew we could speak mind–to–mind she would kill you, or take you as one of her own.~

I felt my eyes narrow with suspicion. *Why would she do that?*

~Well, among other reasons, she went to great trouble to imprison me and doesn't yet have reason to think I'll behave. If we can expose the naughty vampire, this helps Juliet's power base. That, added to the fact I will have had some access to the world but have not challenged her might be enough evidence to convince her to free me.~

Really?

~Yes, I was once a great favorite of hers. I was exceptionally unruly for her to punish me so~

I shuddered to think of what 'unruly' might mean for someone like Leopold. *I can accept this condition, but I have one of my own.*

~Pray tell, dear girl.~

I want you to tell me anything you might know about necromancy, psychic links, and the like.

~I see. A bit out of your depth, it would seem.~

Yes. I'll be blunt: I've only talked to a handful of spirits in my life, and all of them have been willing to speak to me.

They wanted to share their information. So far, nothing on this case is like that.

I slumped over the keyboard and typed: PSYCHIC LINK into the CloudWitch search field.

~So, when you interviewed me the other night, I was your first unwilling subject?~

Yes.

~Dear gods, you have power. It took everything I had to be able to resist, and even then it took hours to recover. Other necromancers do not have that kind of force at their disposal.~

So, we have a deal then, Leopold?

CloudWitch returned over 300 results. I sighed. Sometimes more information was as frustrating as less.

~Yes, for better or worse, my dear girl, you have me, and I have you.~

I hoped I wouldn't regret this. I shuddered again, a goose walking over my grave, as my grandmother would have said.

~What was that about geese? ~

Nothing, just a figure of speech.

~Let us press on then: what do you want to know about necromancy? I will tell all— provided I know it, of course~

As I sat in the desk chair, I bent from the waist to rifle through my messenger bag that lay on the floor. I pulled out my notebook and pen. *Can necromancers contact unwilling spirits?*

~Yes, but how that is achieved depends on a number of factors.~

Such as?

~If the unwilling spirit is newly dead, within the first three days after passing, the necromancer will need to make a ritual blood sacrifice, usually of his own blood. It is more easily achieved in the location the spirit passed from the body.~

The place the person died?

~Yes, the place he died. If the unwilling spirit is more than three days passed over, a blood sacrifice will likely not be enough. The necromancer will have to sacrifice a life to speak with death.~

I shifted uncomfortably in my chair. *Lemme get this straight, I'd have to murder someone to talk to the unwilling dead after three days?*

~Not a person, dear heart, just something that lives, usually an animal.~

Like a chicken?

~Yes, a chicken, a cat, a rabbit, any small animal will do.~

I shuddered. I didn't want to kill animals. *So, the blood sacrifice, or the animal sacrifice, it's done inside a salt circle?*

~Yes, salt, or sometimes ash. I have read of a necromancer that claimed he burned the coffins of any vampires he killed and saved the ashes for his magickal workings.~

Either his magick circles were very tiny, or he killed a hell of a lot of vampires. Or he was bullshitting you.

~'Bullshitting?' You mean misrepresenting himself? ~

Yes.

~It's possible, but at when we first started acquired the Shadow Gift, there were many more of Those Who Walk Between than there are now. By my time, our numbers were quite small, and I cannot imagine much has changed in one hundred years.~

We were taught in school that your numbers were always small.

~Bah! Schoolchildren's lessons. My sire was there at the beginning, and he told me the truth of things.~

I sighed and drained my coffee cup. *Ok, so blood or animal sacrifice, inside a sacred circle.*

~I suspect an interview with Braydon may not tell you everything you want to know, dear girl. Spirits do not think of the world in the same way that you or I do. Released from these bodies of clay, their perspective is changed. It is hard for them to tell us what we want to know in ways that make sense to us. Also, even if they can communicate in ways that make sense to us, they are limited by what they knew in life.~

I'm not sure what you are saying.

~If Braydon didn't know something in life, he can't know it in death.~

Given that, is this worth the bother?

~There is only one way to find out.~

I focused on Leopold again. *Alright, Leopold, let's give this a shot.*

~Right now?~

No time like the present.

~How will you get into the school? It is locked, is it not?~

I won't; I'm going to try it here.

Grabbing my messenger bag, I walked from the backroom onto the sales floor. I rolled back the Persian-type carpet that covered the large open area near the cash desk. Though it was concealed most of the time, Star had painted a five-foot circle in glossy black enamel onto the linoleum tiles. When any of the evening workshops offered by the bookstore used ritual magick, they could use the pre-painted circle. Star said having a ready-made circle contained the mess and stopped the workshoppers from getting out of hand and knocking over displays during their rituals.

I reached into my bag and pulled out my screw-top jar of salt and lavender. I sprinkled salt over the black enamel lines, leaving the circle incomplete for the moment. Behind the cash desk, I rummaged for the ritual athame someone had returned last week. "It's not defective; it's just that the bone handle clashes with the wallpaper in my ritual room," she'd claimed. *Gods save me from fashionable witches.* I heard Leopold chuckle at my thought.

I found the athame, and the Tupperware container we used to store thumbtacks. It would have to serve as a chalice. I dumped the thumb tacks on the counter and returned to the circle with my athame and plastic container.

With the last bit of the salt needed for the circle pinched between my thumb and forefinger, I said aloud, "Leopold?"

~Yes?~

Stay piped down for this part, k? I need my concentration.

~As you wish, madam. I confess I am intrigued, I've never seen this from the inside before.~

I felt a distinct glimmer of excitement I was sure was Leopold's. I completed the circle with the pinch of salt and blessed it. The world shrank. The creaks of the settling building and clicks from the ticking clock: gone.

I stood in this silence, trying to create a space for the voices of the dead. Then the bubble of silence burst and I heard the whispery sounds of the spirits all around us. Their spectral forms pressed like cobwebs against the invisible barrier anchored by the circle.

I took a deep breath and blew it out slowly.

"I am here to speak to Braydon Lombard. Braydon Lombard, you must answer my questions. I offer you the sacred gift of blood as payment."

I slashed at the palm of my left hand with the athame, holding the wound over the Tupperware container I had placed on the floor. "You are compelled, for I am the fulcrum of darkness and light, a point of balance in the cosmos, and I will be obeyed."

Nothing happened.

"Oh shit," I said out loud.

~What is it, my dear?~

Nothing's happening.

~Really?~

Yes, normally I can feel it in the ritual when it starts to work, and right now, there is nothing.

~Peculiar. Perhaps you will need to go to the school for this after all? ~

I don't want to do a B and E, Leopold.

~ Whatever that might be. You will need a chicken because~

I don't want to do animal sacrifices, either. There has got to be another way.

~Perhaps there is. Can you use your psychic sense to probe the room for something that might help? After all, this emporium reeks of magick, surely there is some herb on hand . . .~

Good idea. Shhh.

Leopold quieted, and I closed my eyes and breathed deeply. I gathered energy in my first chakra. I firmly set my intention to find something that would help me power up this spell. I sent it out from the sacred circle, a probing red thread in my mind's eye. I edged it inside the various drawers of Star's huge herbal apothecary cabinet. A few tingles from the rosemary, but nothing strong. I wanted strong. Perhaps an incantation, if not an herb?

I steered the red energy thread toward the shelf with some of the oldest books, but before the thread reached the shelf, I felt a twitch. *What was that?* It felt like pins and needles. I moved the energy thread closer to the prickling sensation. The energy thread was heading behind the cash desk.

The tingle was stronger now, electric and rhythmic, like a Tens machine. I allowed the thread to go where it wanted to. It started to circle an object on the floor next to the recycling box. I focused the view in my mind's eye like a zoom on a camera lens and saw that the thread was drawn to a half-empty can of Red Bull energy drink.

"That can't be right," I said.

~Suzanne, in your experience, which is more often wrong, the magick or your perceptions?~

I sighed. Leopold made a good point.

I withdrew the energy thread quickly back to myself, blessed the circle again, and closed it. Brushing a fingertip's worth of salt from the circle, I stepped out to retrieve the can of Red Bull. Peering at the can in my hand, I muttered: "This stuff better give the spell wings, or I'm going to be pissed off."

~What I take to be an attempt at humor is lost on me in this case, Suzanne.~

Never mind. Also, please pipe down.

I thought I heard him sniff disdainfully. I re-set the circle, and cut my hand a second time. Fresh blood dripped into the Tupperware container. I carefully drizzled some of the room-temperature, flat Red Bull and stirred the mixture with the tip of the athame.

"I am here to speak to Braydon Lombard. Braydon Lombard, you must answer my questions. I offer you the sacred gift of blood as payment."

I raised the Tupperware container over my head in offering. "You are compelled, for I am the fulcrum of darkness and light, a point of balance in the cosmos, and I will be obeyed. Braydon Lombard, appear before my sacred circle and reveal your secrets to me—NOW!"

Braydon's ghostly figure started to materialize just outside the sacred circle. He held his transparent hand up to the invisible barrier demarcated by the circle, his fingertips pressed flat like he was touching glass.

"Braydon," I said.

He nodded.

"You know you're dead, right?"

He nodded, slowly. An almost-tangible miasma of sadness, Braydon's sadness, engulfed me.

"You wanted to tell us something this afternoon, Braydon; what was it?" I asked.

Braydon shook his head. He pointed to his ghostly throat: his throat was so much shredded meat, it looked like bloody pulled pork.

Braydon's not been dead long enough to reconstitute his spiritual self-image. That means he thinks he can't talk. Fuck.

Braydon again pressed his hand to the invisible barrier between us, palm flattening like canned ham. He raised his eyebrows and gestured at his hand with a jerk of his chin.

Stepping toward the invisible barrier, I matched my palm to his. My small hand looked dainty held against Braydon's raw-boned mitt. *He's like a puppy whose paws are fully grown before the rest of him.* My stomach dropped at the thought. Braydon's life had been brief and tragic; it had ended in senseless gory violence. I felt tears well up in my eyes. I hardened my resolve, looked into Braydon's ghostly eyes, and said "Who did this to you, who took Tiffanii? Show me."

I could hear a low electrical hum; my palm started to get warm. In my mind's eye, I saw a flash of golden skin like pale champagne and a flurry of black cloth. I heard screams and felt agony as it felt like the muscles and fibers of my throat shredded. I could feel razored fangs slashing me.

I kept my eye contact with Braydon and breathed through the pain. My hand got hotter.

In my mind's eye, I saw Tiffanii's face. Her soft brown eyes were sparkling; her mouth pursed as she tried to blow out candles on a cake. As she blew, a shadow fell over her. Adjusting the point of view in my mind's eye like a camera lens, I tracked the shadow back to the source. A tall figure, maybe male, wore a light-colored collared shirt, rust corduroy pants, and a black cardboard mask shaped like the infinity symbol. The figure loomed over Tiffanii, the tendrils of the shadow spreading like an oil spill. I followed the shadow's journey in my vision. As the shadow touched Tiffanii's face, it changed. The light left her eyes; they became flat and pitiless as a shark's. Her pursed lips opened wide, mouth cracking drily at the corners as she uttered a shout. I felt Tiffanii's scream reverberate through the fibers of my body like a discordant note.

I swiveled my view back to the figure. A small mouse with grey and variegated brown fur poked its pointed head from the figure's breast pocket. Gaining purchase with its claws in the shirt fabric, the mouse skittered out of the figure's pocket to the shoulder. It reared back on its hind legs, gripped the shirt collar with its front paws, and bit ferociously into the figure's earlobe. Blood started to drip from the earlobe, droplets staining the shirt.

Braydon drew his spectral hand back from the invisible barrier. I was shocked by the loss of the heat.

"That's it?" I said, "Give me more, Braydon, I want to help!"

I heard my voice break with emotion. Braydon shook his head, slowly, sadly. The outline of his spirit started to fade. I considered humming a tone as I had with Leopold to force Braydon's spirit to stay.

~Don't do that, dear girl.~

But I need more; I don't understand. . .

~And I warned you about communication with spirits. If this boy has nothing left, why would he care about justice?~

I paused. Leopold was right. I watched the last of Braydon's spirit dissolve into nothing.

~You do not argue with me?~

You're right. Braydon's orphaned, his sister is missing and probably dead, he has nothing and no one.

I tasted bitter ashes and wiped my wet eyes on the sleeve of my t-shirt. I took a deep breath to center myself.

~You see now what I warned you about in the ways spirits communicate? They are not all righteously angry and wanting to point their fingers.~

Yes, you were right about that. The indignant ones are easy. Braydon was not.

~Are you out of ideas? ~

No. I'm not.

~Really, my dear girl, I am most impressed, since I myself am at an impasse.~

What Braydon showed me was like a dream, the imagery he used...

~And? ~

I am wondering if it can be interpreted, like a dream.

~I don't understand.~

It's ok. Not your fault.

I felt him prickle in irritation. He said nothing.

Leopold, you've been imprisoned since about 1910, 1911?

~Juliet bound and warded me in 1910.~

So, you missed it by at least ten or fifteen years

~Missed what?~

A book called On the Interpretation of Dreams

~What are you talking about?

It's a book about a way of thinking about symbols and dreams and visions. The book had been written before you were warded, but no one paid much attention to it until the nineteen-twenties.

~You are saying that vision made some sense to you?~

Not yet, but it will. I don't think I still have my paper copy from university, but it will be online for sure.

I felt Leopold's pressure on my mind, his psychic presence, start to fade.

Are you leaving?

~Yes, I have no need to observe you search for a book or tap at your machine. Do what work you must with your calculor.~

You mean my computer?

~Yes, computer, calculor, whatever it may be. Do your work.~

Hey Leo, when we get you out of vamp jail, remind me to introduce you to Wikipedia.

~Don't call me Leo. What is this you speak of? ~

It's an online book. Never mind that right now. I'm just noticing that a lot has changed in terms of how people think and behave while you've been indisposed.

~Children always say that. Some things are eternal~

Maybe, but sometimes there is something new under the sun. You might even dig it once you get into it, you never know.

~Bah. I do not dig. Manual labor is for peasants.~

I smiled to myself.

~I heard that~

I laughed out loud.

~When we need to speak again think the music for "Clair de Lune" and I shall know you are calling me.~

Ok, and you'll do the same?

~If you wish, I can announce myself that way.~

I do wish.

I had the impression of Leopold smiling wickedly.

~Protective of your privacy, my dear?~

Something like that.

I shivered involuntarily. The mind-to-mind connection with Leopold was like holding a slimy clot on your tongue without swallowing. The throbbing pressure I had started to associate with his psychic presence in my own mind started to fade even more. I was alone inside my head. I needed to break down the sacred circle and make some notes about the vision and the last few days. Then I needed to talk to Dougherty.

Chapter Ten

I spent some time cleaning up the shop. I made some notes in my journal about the psychic link with Leopold and the visions Braydon's ghost had supplied. I checked some passages in *On the Interpretation of Dreams*, too. By five a.m. it was still too early to call Dougherty. I spent an hour scanning grimoires and books of shadow into CloudWitch. At six I called Dougherty's cell.

"Dougherty," he said, voice rough from sleep.

"It's Suzanne."

"Saw that on the call display." He cleared his throat. "What's up? You ok? You were pretty shocky last night."

"I'm ok now." I bit back my impulse to tell him about the psychic link with Leopold. I had promised. "I just couldn't stay asleep, so I figured I'd come into the store and do some research with Star's old books. I read some things that gave me an idea about reaching Braydon's ghost."

I kept my promise to Leopold and said nothing to Dougherty about sharing Leopold's dream memory or speaking with Leopold via our psychic link. But I did describe last night's magickal workings to Dougherty, and how Braydon's ghost had shown me visions.

"So, you think that he was telling you what he thinks happened to his sister with images and symbols?" asked Dougherty.

"Yes, exactly. Because he couldn't tell, he had to show, and the only way to do that is with pictures, right?"

"Makes sense. But if you went back to the school and cast a circle in the bathroom where he died, maybe he'd have figured out that he could speak?"

"Doubtful. When I last saw him, he was disincorporating."

"What's that?"

"Well, you know how some spirits only hang around on this plane to do a certain job?"

"Riiight, so if Braydon was only sticking around to tell somebody what happened to Tiffanii, once he'd done that, he just starts to . . . what, fade out or something?"

"Yep, they basically drift away to wherever ghosts go when they're ready to leave here."

"So, no point in trying to call him up again," said Dougherty.

"Exactly," I said.

"Ok, well I've got a couple of things for us to run down today."

"All right, what's on the agenda?" I asked.

"McCabe worked her snitches in Vice. Turns out there is a pro in the kink trade that may know something helpful."

"Kink trade?" I asked.

"You know, like a sex worker who does all the whips and chains, tie me up/tie me down stuff."

I didn't know, not in any real detail, but I had a rough idea.

"Maybe this is a stupid question, but isn't that kind of dangerous for her?" I asked.

"She dishes out the spankings, Suzi-Q, not the other way around."

I could hear the amusement in his voice. I felt my face get hot. I bet I was crimson right now. I exhaled, then drew a deep breath.

"What's the other thing?" I asked.

"Well, I noticed those basketball players at the high school last night."

"The rich kids from the private school?"

"Yeah, exactly. I've heard rumors that some athletes have been doping with vampire blood injections instead of steroids. Those kids were too good at basketball to be playing straight. I bet they're doping."

"I overheard something about that last night in the bleachers," I said. "This guy was saying that his brother is on U-dub's basketball team and that a bunch of the players there are using vampire blood."

"What else did this guy say?" Dougherty asked. He was wide awake now.

"Well, just that, and the fact that he was surprised the high school players might have started using, too."

"And he was talking about the team from Collegiate, not the Pinecones, right?" It sounded like Dougherty had started to take notes.

"Yeah, just the players from Collegiate. But based on what I saw last night, I bet their cheer squad is doping, too," I said.

Even over the phone, I could hear his pen scratching at the paper. "What'd this guy look like?" asked Dougherty.

"Hang on," I said, and pulled my phone away from my ear. I clicked past the phone dial screen and into my photo gallery. A few more clicks and I'd emailed the picture I'd taken of the gossiping young couple in the bleachers to Dougherty.

"Ok, I'm back."

"Ok, so what'd he look like?" he asked.

Shifting the phone to my other ear, I said, "White guy, late teens, average build. Short blonde hair, black Wu-Tang Clan t-shirt and jeans. Talking to a girl about the same age, I think maybe she was his girlfriend. She was tall, maybe as tall as him. She was heavy-set and wearing a polka dot shirt. Dark skin, long dark dreadlocks, amber eyes–coulda been mixed race, I think. I took some pictures of them. They are in your email."

"How'd you manage that?"

"Pretended I was using my phone for something else."

For a minute, I wondered if Dougherty was going to say something snide about Millennials and our love of our phones, but he didn't.

"That's good, Suzanne, thanks. I'm going to talk to the coach over at Collegiate, then maybe swing by the university."

"What for?" I asked.

"Policeman's hunch. The child-trafficking ring involves kids and vampire blood being used to turn them into revenants. Athletic doping involves kids and vampire blood being used to turn them into basketball gods. I figure the number of creeps who want feed blood to kids and can actually get a hold of some is probably limited . . . Jesus, at least I hope it is," he said.

I think he'd managed to scare himself for a second. I could hear the tension in his voice in response to his own disquieting thought.

"While I do that, Wendy is going to pick you up so you two can interview the dominatrix."

"When?" I asked.

"She'll pick you up at ten-thirty from wherever. Apparently, Mistress Stephanie doesn't get up before eleven. Where will you be?"

"Still at the Emporium, I've got more books to scan," I said.

"You know you're a witchcraft nerd, right?" Dougherty teased.

"Don't make me turn you into a frog," I said.

*   *   *

The side of my head was pressed against the cool glass of the passenger side window of McCabe's green Mazda 3. Outside, it was raining so hard it was like we were in a car wash.

McCabe drove quickly, oblivious to the possibility of the car hydroplaning off Terry Avenue. If we crashed into one of the Pilates studios or dog accessory stores that populated either side of Terry, the businesses of the area would recover. But I wasn't so sure about McCabe or me, let alone any latte-sucking trophy wives inside the stores.

"Suzanne?" asked McCabe.

"Huh?"

"Did you hear any of what I just said?"

"Um . . ." I said, trying to buy time.

The truth was I found McCabe a bit boring to listen to. Her background as an academic had taught her to talk in paragraphs, not sentences. Sometimes I just couldn't pay attention long enough for her to get to the point. Still, I felt bad for not hearing her out. She was just trying to help by filling me in with details.

I said, "Sorry, I'm a bit out of it, I had a long night and an early morning. Probably it's time for another hit of caffeine. What were you saying?"

McCabe turned her indicator light on, signaling she intended to parallel park on Terry.

"Well, we're here now, so I'll be brief. Mistress Stephanie has worked as a professional dominatrix for about fifteen years. She's at the center of the BDSM community in Seattle and has been a confidential informant for SPD Vice for about ten years. She has her finger on the pulse of the kink scene, so we're talking to her because she may have heard something or seen something that could be helpful," said McCabe.

"Does she talk to you guys so you don't arrest her?" I asked.

McCabe's eyebrows climbed her forehead. "No, what she does is not actually illegal, so we'd have nothing to arrest her for."

"But prostitution is illegal, isn't it?"

"Yes, more or less. There are some complexities to that we don't need to get into right now. But more to the point, what Mistress Stephanie does isn't sex work," she said.

My head felt fuzzy. "I'm not getting you."

"Well, without getting into too much detail, the activities she does with her clients are not, technically speaking, sex acts," McCabe said.

I squinted at McCabe in consternation.

She continued, "Suppose she ties some guy up, spanks him, and stuffs her panties in his mouth," she said.

"Ok, suppose she does," I said. I squirmed a bit in my car seat from embarrassment. Was I really going to have this conversation with McCabe? *Blerg.*

McCabe said, "Under the law, as it is right now, unless people are charging money for genital contact, it's not prostitution."

"That's ridiculous," I said.

McCabe shrugged and unbuckled her seat belt.

"I don't write them; I just enforce them. Besides, you'll like her; she's a very interesting woman. Without her help, we'd have a much harder time with certain cases."

McCabe and I exited her Mazda 3 into the temperate rainforest monsoon and walked in silence to a squat three-storey building made of concrete and milky green glass. I was surprised. This was an affluent-looking urban loft building.

"She lives here?" I asked.

"Yes."

"I guess I must have been expecting something else."

"Really? What'd you expect, the seedy back room of a massage parlor?"

I think I actually had been expecting that. I probably knew as much about sex culture as I did about vampires before this case started. Don't get me wrong. I'm not a nun, nor am I a virgin: I briefly had a boyfriend in high school, and I had a long-term relationship with another guy in college. But I spent so much time in my teens dealing with my necromancy, trying to get control of it, I didn't have much energy or opportunity to be what my mom would have called being boy-crazy.

By the time I went to college, I was happy to pass for normal in the non-magickal sense; I didn't sweat being normal in the "getting drunk and having lots of sex with random frat guys" sense.

Even when I finally did lose my virginity to my college boyfriend, I'd sometimes think that I must be missing the point of it. It seemed like everyone made such a big deal over sex, and somehow, I didn't understand the punchline. That went double for kinky sex. I'd some exposure to kinky things through movies and TV, but I'd never known anyone involved in it and had no desire to be involved myself. I shuddered involuntarily, thinking about the memory Leopold had shown me in my dream last night. I know that what Juliet had done to him was a form of rape, but I couldn't see why you'd do want to do that stuff consensually, either.

We entered the building and pressed the button for the elevator. The lobby was decorated in a striking and unusual color combination, burnt orange and teal. Brushed nickel fixtures gleamed dully under pot lighting.

Standing next to me as we waited, McCabe interrupted my reflections. "You cold?" she asked, "You're shivering."

I felt my cheeks flame, as if McCabe could read my thoughts. "No, just a bit wet from the rain," I lied.

"You should get a jacket with a hood, keep the rain off better."

"You're probably right." Ugh. *Why was everyone so composed about this sex stuff but me?*

The apartment door was halfway down the long, tastefully-appointed hallway. McCabe rapped on it with her knuckles. After a moment, a short, thick white woman with a blonde buzz cut opened the door.

She was wearing leather pants, engineer boots, and a leather harness crisscrossed over her bare upper body. A large stainless steel O-ring rested in between her small breasts. My face felt like it was on fire. I didn't know where to look. I settled on keeping my eyes on her face only. Her eyes were navy blue and amused at my reaction. She sported two lips rings and a Monroe.

"Hi Sam," said McCabe, "Stephanie ready for us?"

"Yup, c'mon in. Who's your friend?" she asked, pointing at me with her chin as she stepped backwards into the apartment to allow us entrance.

As we stepped in, McCabe said, "This is Suzanne Murphy, she consults with SPD. She's helping with this case."

Sam looked me up and down, evaluating me. I squirmed under her gaze.

"Too bad she's a consultant and not regular SPD. She'd look great in the uniform," she said, then winked at me.

Honestly, if more blood rushes to my face, I'm going to pass out.

"Sam!" came a voice from the far end of the loft apartment. "What have I told you about teasing the guests?"

A tall, slender woman with long auburn hair was descending the spiral metal staircase at the far corner of the loft. Even though she was clad in frayed sweatpants and a faded Ramones t-shirt, she had royal bearing. She was scowling at Sam.

"I swear, you are the worst house boi I've ever had. They still have their coats on! You haven't offered them anything to drink! Stop freaking the mundanes and do your job!" The words might have been harsh, but there was genuine affection in her tone of voice.

McCabe shrugged off her green suede blazer and handed it to Sam.

"When you're ready Sam, I'd like a peppermint tea, and Suzanne would like black coffee, please," she said.

McCabe strode toward the auburn-haired woman and hugged her. They started to speak with each other, in tones too low for me to hear. Or at least, too hard to hear over the sound of my blood rushing in my ears.

"Your coat, baby doll," said Sam.

"What?" I felt myself blush all over again. *Why are my palms so sweaty?* "Mistress says I'm to take your coat, sweet thang," said Sam.

"Er, ah . . . ok."

She helped me slip out of my hoodless anorak and disappeared into a side room with the coats.

The loft was large, a rectangle maybe fifteen by forty feet. The long wall was floor-to-ceiling windows that overlooked the street. The windows showcased a peek-a-boo view of the Puget Sound. The entire space was decorated in soft neutrals- cream, taupe, dove grey. The color scheme was harmonious with the grey sky and naked, winter-dark trees outside the window. Except for the small side room into which Sam had disappeared, the entire space—living room, kitchen, dining, and computer area— was open-plan.

I walked over to where McCabe and Mistress Stephanie had seated themselves on some tweedy grey couches.

"Suzanne," said McCabe, "This is Stephanie Espinoza, one of my confidential informants."

Stephanie appeared to be about forty years of age. She had smooth golden skin that glowed like it was lit from within by candlelight. Her deep brown eyes were like liquid chocolate.

"Pleased to meet you, Mistress Stephanie," I said, extending my hand. She smiled and took my hand and shook it. Her grip was warm and strong.

"Please, just 'Stephanie'," she said gently, "it's a breach of proper protocol for you to call me "Mistress" unless we have that kind of relationship."

"Oh, um, ok," I said, dropping my gaze to my shoes.

"Please, have a seat," Stephanie said.

I sat down across from her, next to McCabe.

"So, Suzanne, I am guessing that the kink world is all new to you?" Stephanie asked.

"Gods, is it that obvious?" I muttered bitterly.

"Everyone was new to this once," Stephanie said.

Her smile was kind. I took a deep breath and tried to mentally shrug off some of my embarrassment.

McCabe cleared her throat. "I've brought Suzanne here because of a missing kids case. Someone—we think affiliated with vampires—has been kidnapping older children and teens and turning them into revenants . . ."

"And renting them to any rough trade scum that lurks on the edges of the kink community," interrupted Stephanie with a scowl.

"Yes, exactly, how did you know?" asked McCabe.

Stephanie heaved a sigh. "I've heard of this before, at least once when I was living in the Netherlands, and I've heard rumors about it going on in Thailand as well. I think it's the shadow-side of consensual kink."

"I don't understand," I said.

Sam entered the main space of the loft and busied herself making coffee and tea in the kitchen area. She still did not have a shirt on. Stephanie lifted an eyebrow at her companion's mostly naked torso but said nothing. McCabe was seemingly impervious. *Is it 'cause she studied anthropology? Is that why McCabe's so comfortable in this subculture?*

"Look at it this way, Suzanne. You know how in conventional lovemaking, what we kinksters call "vanilla sex," people must consent to the lovemaking; otherwise, it's rape, right?" Stephanie said.

"Right," I said.

"Kink is the same way—whatever activities a person might enjoy, they've got be able to give meaningful consent. If they're too young, or too high on drugs, or too emotionally fragile and dependent, what's going on isn't kinky play, it's sexual assault."

"Ok, but what about bondage and all that? If you've got someone tied up, that's not consent."

"In well-formed, consensual kink, the person playing the submissive role has control over what happens. Usually, the partners work out what's ok and what's not ok before they actually get busy."

"Really? Like with an on-paper contract?" I asked.

Sam walked over from the kitchen area with cups on a tray. She served me a mug of rich black coffee, and McCabe a cup of tea. She handed Stephanie a tumbler full of what looked like carrot juice and knelt submissively at the other woman's feet, eyes downcast. Stephanie placed a proprietary hand on the back of Sam's neck.

"In my work, I always use a paper contract. In my personal life, it varies. Sam and I have a very loose contract because she's been my house boi for a couple of years now, we've gotten to know each other quite well," she said, ruffling Sam's hair affectionately.

"Is it rude for me to ask about Sam being your house boi?" I asked.

McCabe frowned, but Stephanie said, "Under the circumstances, no, I think not. You are trying to understand consensual kink between adults so that you can better understand these criminals you are trying to catch. I am prepared to discuss that. And you, Sam?"

Sam raised her eyes from the carpet and looked at Stephanie. She smiled and said, "As you wish, Madam, I am yours after all."

"That's her way of saying 'fine by me'. If it were not fine, she would have said 'only if you wish it, Madam'," explained Stephanie.

I nodded, "That's a very subtle difference."

"Yes. I agree it is. But I think an ethical dominant is sensitive to the needs of her partner, that's part of the fun of the whole game."

I thought about it for a minute. "So, you're saying that it's an elaborate performance, where the person who looks like they have control is actually being attentive and sensitive, and the person who looks as though they have given up control is actually calling the shots?"

McCabe smiled. "See, Steph, I told you she'd catch on right away."

"Yes, it seems you are right. So, to speak to the issue of my agreement with Sam, it's pretty straightforward. She lives here with me, keeps the house, runs errands, and manages my bookings and the like. When she is unruly, as she was when she greeted you so poorly, I correct her according to her wish-list of preferred discipline. And for the duration of the time she lives with me, I do not seek the kink or vanilla attentions of other women."

I thought about that for a moment, digesting the implications. "What does that mean for your work?" I asked.

"All my clients are men. I don't engage in any vanilla activities with them."

"Doesn't that bother them? Don't they want that as well?"

"Some do, in which case I refer them to another professional dominant. That's simply not in my bag of tricks," she explained, smiling. Her eyes crinkled attractively in the corners when she smiled. Her face looked like it spent more time smiling than it did frowning. She sipped her juice.

McCabe interjected, "Most sex workers don't consider their work to be sex, they consider it work, so it's not unusual for workers to pursue one thing on the job and another off it."

"Hmm, I guess I'd never considered that," I said.

I inhaled the aroma from my still-steaming cup of coffee, then sipped, allowing the rich, dark taste to spread slowly over my tongue. "I guess I must have had a stereotype about sex trade workers . . ."

Stephanie smiled again, "Um, like we're all teen runaways addicted to heroin who get pimped out by some misogynist?"

"Well, frankly, yes."

"I'm not going to lie, that's one level of the sex trade. Certainly, street level workers are in danger a fair amount of the time, and addiction and exploitation are part of that picture. Dealing with that is probably the bulk of your work in Vice, right, Wendy?"

McCabe nodded.

Stephanie continued, "What I do is more white-collar sex trading. I charge a premium for my time. I can afford to pick and choose who I take on as a client and have procedures in place for screening out any problems I can predict ahead of time. I had actually earned my MBA before I made the choice to do some kink for money. Because what I do is not, by law, prostitution I don't need to pay protection money to dirty cops or gangsters. I don't use drugs or alcohol, so addiction doesn't play into it. Truly, I love my work, and I chose it."

"Huh," I said, nodding. There were so many things I had never considered. I looked down at the coffee cup in my hands.

"Ok, what about this: McCabe and I are here to pick your brain about some kind of pedophile ring; if your white collar sex trading is legit, how come we're consulting you?"

Wendy winced at my tone of voice.

Stephanie raised a perfectly groomed brow. "Now I see the consultant and not the shy girl!" she said.

I shrugged.

She continued, "I mentioned that I carefully screen clients before I ever interact with them? The screening process is somewhat lengthy. They must be detailed about the kind of experience they are looking for. At least once per month, I turn down an applicant who wants activities that I will not provide," she said.

"Like what?"

"Well, sometimes harmless things that I find personally distasteful, adult diapers or clown fetishists, that sort of thing. But sometimes their requests are disturbing."

"Such as?"

"Most commonly men who want an underage partner, either someone they bring with them, or someone they want me to procure for them. I won't do that. It's a violation of everything that is important to me about my work. Occasionally I also turn away men who do not seem to understand that this is a game; they're sadists who want to hurt or enslave someone for real, and they want me to help them."

"What do you tell them?"

"The sadists and rapists? That what they want is a crime and I will not participate in that."

"Do you ever refer them on?"

"The adult babies and clown-lovers, yes. Plenty of work to go around, and there are some pros that do good work in those areas. I leave it to them. The pedophiles and sadists, of course not. First of all, I wouldn't be able to live with myself if I did. Second of all, there is no one to refer them to. People who rape and torture and abuse kids don't exactly advertise this."

"So, where do you think we can find these guys, are they organized?" I asked.

Stephanie finished her carrot juice and considered my question.

"Well, the first place I'd try is the Internet, 12Chan would be a likely place to start. If the ringleaders are wise, they don't do any planning through the Internet, but they might do initial recruitment that way."

Wendy shifted in her seat and said, "We've got some officers who go online under various personas, they can start communicating with their online contacts to see what is going on."

"It can't hurt," said Stephanie, "but since this is a group of kinky pedophilic vampire-admirers–a minority within a minority–my guess is that most are going to happen through personal communication in real-life social networks."

"Well, we have some operatives who spend time on 12Chan. That would be a reasonable place to start, hopefully get invited to a get-together or pedophile picnic or something." Wendy said.

The conversation between Stephanie and Wendy continued as I retreated into my thoughts. *12Chan?* I pulled my phone from my pocket and opened a browser tab, and Googled '12Chan'. Urban Dictionary informed me that

> A place for the sophisticated, refined, young pedophile. 12Channers are different from normal pedos regarding the way they think of mentality and children. The older Girl-Lovers and Boy-Lovers just wouldn't understand the way we perceive things today.

Ew. Ok, that question is answered. I slipped my phone back into my pocket. Reading this stuff made me want to take an hour-long shower. I re-focused on the conversation.

"Yes, we do" Wendy was saying.

"I'm glad, because experience has taught me that just barely legal websites and publications are the gateways to the in-person gatherings, and from there, everything becomes possible," Stephanie said.

"Sorry, I needed to look something up, what'd I miss?"

"Stephanie was asking if SPD Vice knew something about a website called Peer Support Exchange; we do, it's on Vice's watch list."

"What goes on there?" I asked.

"See for yourself, just call it up on your phone. Don't bother Googling it; I think it's Darknet so the search engines won't catch it. The URL is prsx.info."

I followed Wendy's directions and opened a poorly-designed page with a fluffy cloud background. The text read:

> A BRIDGE TO NEW FRIENDSHIPS. FACILITATING REAL LIFE CONTACT BETWEEN RESPONSIBLE BOY-ATTRACTED PEDOSEXUAL MALES OF LEGAL AGE.

"So, they use this website to meet like-minded others? How can this even be legal?"

Wendy sighed. "Good question. They walk a pretty fine line. Basically, they believe in what they call 'responsible boy love' and the website is designed to facilitate meeting other adult men who have the same beliefs."

"How can men molesting boys be freakin' responsible?!" I felt my shoulders start to creep up to my ears.

Wendy leant over to look at the screen on my phone. "Just click on the hyperlink, they say what they think it is."

I clicked, and a new tab opened: "The Philosophy of Responsible Boylove" read the title. The text read:

> Responsible boylove is the premise that in any relationship between a boy and an older male, whether sexually expressed or not, the

> legitimate interests of the boy must take
> precedence over the interests of his older
> friend. . . Responsible boylove does not
> include, support, nor in any way condone non-
> consensual sexual activity.

My shoulders clenched tighter, and the coffee in my stomach was starting to burn. "They're just playing word games. Kids aren't capable of meaningful consent. How can this be legal, Wendy? Can't Vice shut it down?"

Wendy opened her mouth to speak, but Stephanie interjected, "They are free to think these thoughts, and they can't be arrested for thought crimes or for expressing thoughts."

I glanced at Stephanie. Her golden skin glowed, but her expression was impassive. "Sure, yes, I get that, but obviously once people meet like-minded others, they encourage each other and turn thoughts into actions. This site just normalizes and perpetuates abuse."

Stephanie nodded. "Yes, I suspect you are right. But do you really want to give the police and government more power to control speech and thought?" She raised her perfectly arched brows.

I didn't know what to say to her. *I can see her point, but . . .*

Before I could finish my thought, Wendy said, "I feel you on this, Suzanne. Anyone looking at the site can imagine what these 'discreet meetings' can lead to. But Stephanie is right, there are a bunch of constitutional protections for this, so Vice can't get the website shut down or anything like that. What we can do is use the site for our surveillance."

I breathed out to release some tension, then took a deep breath in. My shoulders felt like rocks, and my hands were clammy. "Like what?" I asked.

"Well, you see how you can register on the site to meet another man who shares your views and lives in or near your zip code? We have technical operatives who set up profiles and arrange meetings between site users and undercover officers. That was we can gather information on these guys, keep tabs on them, get to know who's-who. We do the electronic version of that with 12Chan, other similar sites, and the various chat rooms too.

"It's a dance," said Stephanie.

"Huh?" I said.

"People, governments, organizations of all kind, they do a delicate dance between security and freedom, pleasure and danger. It has been ever the case."

Stephanie stood up and smoothed her t-shirt and sweatpants as though she was clad in velvet. Sam stood up as well.

"Madam, shall I remind you of the time?" she asked quietly.

"You may."

"It is ten minutes past twelve noon, Madam."

"Thank you, Sam." Stephanie stroked Sam's cheek with the back of her hand, tenderly. With a graceful, languid movement, Stephanie ran her hand down Sam's long throat and over her right breast. Her thumb came to rest on Sam's nipple. I felt my face flush crimson. Wendy said nothing.

Without breaking her eye contact with Sam, Stephanie said, "Ladies, I am glad if I was of service to you today. I have appointments scheduled for this afternoon, and I must prepare. Sam will show you out."

She retreated to the far side of the room and climbed the staircase without a backwards glance.

McCabe and I walked in silence out of the apartment building and out into the torrential rain. Climbing into the Mazda 3, I said: "Is she always like that?"

"Like what?" replied McCabe, as she turned the key in the ignition.

"So, um . . . overt, I guess is a good word," I said.

"You mean the kink part or the girl-on-girl part or what?"

"The PDA part," I said.

"Yes, it did seem like you were uncomfortable with it," she said, glancing at me as she steered the car into the flow of traffic down the street.

"You're not?" I asked, incredulously.

"I don't worry about other people's business."

"Doesn't it seem . . . rude that they would carry on like that?"

McCabe shrugged her narrow shoulders.

"It really doesn't bug you?" I continued.

McCabe stopped the car at the red light and turned her head to look me full in the face. Her emerald-green eyes flashed with anger.

"No. It doesn't bug me. I don't give a shit what consenting adults do to, with, or for each other. My personal value is that if adults consent and they aren't being forced by violence, poverty, or drug addiction to engage in an activity, it's none of my business. I work in Vice because I'm trying to do something about crime, not sex."

"Ok," I said.

She turned her head to face front again and pressed the gas pedal when the light changed.

"Ok, what?" she asked.

"Ok, I take your point. I acknowledge that I'm shy about sex stuff and not used to that level of PDA and nudity and whatnot."

We drove in silence for a few moments, the only sound the sizzling of the car's tires on wet pavement, and the rain pocking on the windshield. McCabe glanced at me from the corner of her eye; her mouth quirked.

"You surprise me," she said.

"How so?"

"I think I expected a death psychic to be, I dunno, more worldly than you seem. You very much come on like the sweet girl next door. Plus, your appearance . . . You're little, and round, and pink-cheeked, and blonde."

"Did you expect Anjelica Huston in a black evening gown?"

"Actually, I think I kinda did. I guess that's a stereotype, huh?"

"I guess so; I certainly get it often enough. Honestly, I think it's 'cos I'm short and look younger than I am. I think if I were tall, people would take me more seriously."

"Well, people misjudging based on appearances is something I know about."

"In your work, I bet you do," I said.

McCabe grinned.

"It's not just that, tho', Suzanne. You're not usually defensive like some people can be if they feel criticized."

I digested this for a moment, then said, "Is it that unusual?"

"Yes, I think so. You're what, about twenty-three or twenty-four?"

"Twenty-six."

"Ok, so in your middle twenties; I think most people are still pretty immature at that point in life, they don't necessarily know how to handle disagreement or perceived criticism. So how come you seem to?"

I considered her question for a moment. *Why do I?*

"I hadn't really noticed that it's so unusual. But maybe it is. Here's what I know: ritual magick is only going to work so well if I'm lying to myself. Necromancy is only going to work so well under those circumstances, too. If I'm walking around with a head full of self-delusion, I am probably taking unnecessary mystical risks. Plus, I feel less 'crazy' if I'm honest with at least myself."

"Sounds like all the death psychic stuff you went through growing up wasn't very easy."

I grimaced. "You're right; it wasn't."

She glanced at me again from the side of her eye, waiting for me to speak. I did not. Moments passed. My cell phone started to buzz. I looked at the screen: Dougherty calling. I pressed the answer button.

"Where are you?" he said.

"With McCabe in the car."

"You guys want lunch?"

"Hold on a sec," I said. I looked at McCabe. "Lunch with Dougherty?" I asked.

"Sure," she said.

I held the phone to my cheek again. "Yes, lunch sounds good."

"Where?"

I thought for a moment. "Flannigan's next door to the Emporium?" McCabe nodded.

"Ok, see you there in thirty," said Dougherty.

We had arrived at Flannigan's before Dougherty did. The host, at our request, sat us in the empty back room, behind the beaded curtain.

Flannigan's was paneled in dark wood and smelled of cigarettes even though it had been many years since people could smoke inside. The back room had no windows, faded green floral table cloths, a dart board, and posters from ancient boxing matches pinned to the walls. The lighting overhead was fluorescent and emitted a low buzzing sound. I liked the place because it was cheap, the food was simple, and it hadn't yet been gentrified into a gastropub. I think Dougherty liked it for the same reasons.

The server had just taken our drink order when Dougherty pulled the beaded curtain aside and strode over to our table. There was a certain bounce in his step. He smiled.

"Hi Suzi-Q, Hi Wendy," he said, as he sat down.

"You're cheerful," I said, raising my eyebrows.

"He's always cheerful when he has a hot lead," McCabe said, the corner of her mouth quirking.

"True, true," he replied, "So tell me about your snitch, Ms. Fifty Shades of Grey." He ignored the menu and pulled his notebook and pen from his shirt pocket.

"She suggested that while the first contact between conspirators might be online, divulging too much that way is risky for them. So, they are likely to use the Internet to make contact and then initiate real-life meetings to further screen and, if necessary, groom their contacts," McCabe said.

Dougherty's eyes flicked to the archway. The server passed through the beaded curtain with our beverages and took our lunch orders. Chef salad, chicken fingers and fries, and a Reuben sandwich.

When she had retreated back through the archway, I asked, "Are we certain that it's a ring and not a single offender?"

"I guess it's possible that it's one guy acting alone, but there are a lot of moving parts to manage. I think we're looking at an organized ring," Dougherty said.

McCabe nodded and said, "Mistress Stephanie also gave us the URL for a website they might be using to make connections with other pedophiles. Off the top of my head, the name of the site isn't familiar, but I'll check back with Vice techs. I bet they already have it on their radar. They may already have some connections through that site. If we really luck out, they might have some names on the creep list that look good for this kind of crime."

"What about you, Suzi-Q?" asked Dougherty.

"What she said. I'm just noticing how freakin' green I am. The whole kink thing is a WTF for me. Also, I feel like murders with sexual motives are—I dunno—grosser than the other cases I've worked."

"Really?" he said, "I'm surprised. The victims in your other two cases were really young, and they were both killed by family members. That didn't bother you?"

"Yeah, sure it bothered me. It's just this case—they're not just killed, it's also that a bunch of sick shit happens to them before they die, and then that death isn't even a release for them, they're kept alive to suffer more." I shuddered involuntarily.

McCabe frowned, her delicate auburn brows bunching together. "For what it's worth, whoever those kids were is mostly gone now," she said.

"What do you mean?" I asked.

"Well, regular vampires retain their personalities and temperaments after they Cross the Divide. It's said that some of the really old ones, the plague survivors, started to change after they'd been alive for a couple of hundred years, but I think that's a function of a really long lifespan changing their perspective on things, outliving your peers, more than anything brought on by vampirism. Revenants aren't like that."

"You're saying the revenants aren't really people anymore?" I asked.

"As far as anyone knows, they're not. They've only partially Crossed Over. People theorize that's part of why they are so easily mind-controlled and enslaved is that the personality and the soul are essentially gone. The revenant's body is just a preserved husk filled with the will of their particular sire."

"So, while it looks like a kid, it's not really a kid anymore?"

"Yeah, that's what people think."

I considered this for a moment. *Creepy for us, but better for those poor kids.* I said, "I'm relieved to hear you say that."

Dougherty put down his pen and picked up a menu. "You want my advice, don't think about it too much. Focus on what's right in front of you, step by step. Worry about the implications when it's all over."

The beaded curtain clacked unmusically as the wait staff came through with a large oval tray loaded with food. She passed out the plates like a blackjack dealer does cards.

We ate the first few bites in silence, but then I remembered something I wanted to ask McCabe.

"I have a question for you, Wendy," I said.

"Oh?" Her left eyebrow arched perfectly.

"Yvonne's pregnancy," I said.

"What about it?"

"I assume she must have been pregnant when she was Turned?"

She nodded. "That's right. Becoming vampire makes people infertile. Life can't come from death."

"So, here she is massively pregnant for decades—why have they not tried a C-section to relieve her of her burden. Could she actually birth it?"

"Good question," McCabe said.

Dougherty snorted. "Do you want to be the one to ask her?" he said.

I shrugged. "Nope. I do not," I said smiling.

Wendy pushed some of her salad around on her plate with her fork, considering. "Just speculating, but my guess is that since vampire bodies 'freeze' into whatever state they were in when they were Turned, she is physically incapable of going into labor. And if she had a C-section, it might grow back."

"Ah, jeez, that's awful," I said. *So many gross things I had never considered.*

We ate a few more bites in silence, then McCabe spoke, changing the subject.

"What about you, Paul?" McCabe asked, taking a sip from her iced tea. "What'd you get at the school and the campus?"

He interlaced his fingers together and cracked his knuckles. "'Most everyone on the U-dub campus thinks the athletic teams are doping with vampire blood. Couldn't get anyone with actual firsthand knowledge to talk, but the rumor is widespread and persistent. Plus, in the last eighteen months every U-dub team has been undefeated: swim team, basketball, football, everything."

I asked, "So what happened eighteen months ago?"

Dougherty smiled a cold, nasty smile. "That's when Jonathon LeFarge was hired as Manager of Athletics for the University. People say he's single-handedly transformed U-dub's athletics programming."

"I bet," said McCabe, scowling.

"The receptionist in the Athletics department told me that LeFarge is on the road with the basketball team at an away game in Coeur D'Alene. Apparently, he's back day after next. I'll be paying him a visit and checking him out." Dougherty said, taking a bite of his sandwich.

We all focused on our food for a couple of minutes. I love chicken fingers and fries, but they're gross when they're cold.

Dougherty popped the last bite of his Reuben into his mouth, chewed, and wiped his lips with a napkin.

"After that, I went over to Collegiate, the private school, they wouldn't let me on the grounds without a warrant. Lots of rich-guy fake nice bullshit to get me to fuck off and leave them alone. Tried to give me a donation to the SPD widows and orphans fund."

I smirked, "That doesn't make them look guilty as sin, not at all."

McCabe rolled her eyes.

Dougherty said, "This afternoon I'm going to run some checks on this LeFarge guy, and see if I can find out more about Collegiate, maybe scare up enough to get a sympathetic judge to give me a warrant."

"Sounds good," McCabe said. "I've got to have a briefing with the techs in Vice, get them stirring the pot to see what floats to the surface."

I dipped my last fry in ketchup and popped it in my mouth. After I had chewed and swallowed, I said, "Sounds like you guys don't need me this afternoon."

McCabe shook her head, and Dougherty asked, "Got something you want to do?"

"Nothing special, I just feel like I should put in a few hours at the Emporium. I've been working on some old grimoires, scanning them into CloudWitch. There's interesting stuff in some of those books and scrolls."

Dougherty said, "Keep your phone on, though. If another newly-dead body turns up, we'll need you to try to make contact with the spirit."

"Of course," I said. *Am I really that calm about remarks like that, already?* I shook my head to clear that thought. Dougherty was right: move forward, think about it later.

McCabe signaled the waiter for the check, paying for the three of us. We walked outside into the rain. I waved as they each headed toward their respective cars, then ducked into the Emporium.

Chapter Eleven

I leant my forehead against the trim around the front door to my apartment as I fumbled in my purse for my keys. After not much sleep two nights in a row and eight hours at the Emporium, I was looking forward to some food, then bed. I unlocked the door and went inside, allowing my purse, shoes, and coat to drop in a trail behind me as I walked down the hall toward the kitchen. Before I fed me, I needed to give Bluebell her dinner.

"Here kitty, kitty!" I said as I strode into the kitchen. I had already shrugged off my cardigan and was in the process of pulling off my long-sleeved t-shirt when I stepped in something warm and sticky. It soaked through my sock. *Oh dammit, has she barfed again?* I yanked my head free of the t-shirt with one hand and fumbled for the light switch with the other. I flicked the kitchen light on.

It took a moment for my eyes to adjust to the light; it took another moment for the brain to register what my eyes reported. Bluebell lay in a large puddle of blood on the kitchen floor, her soft grey fur matted with clots. His throat was torn so ferociously her head was almost severed from her body. Her abdomen was split open, meaty chunks spilling from the cavity. Her once–glorious plumed tail had been ripped off and lay a few feet from the rest of her remains.

I drew a breath, but before I could scream, nausea overtook me. My stomach heaved, and I quickly brought the back of my hand to my mouth. I took a slow, steadying breath and started to back up away from Bluebell's remains. I need to call Dougherty. I had only backed up a couple of steps when something struck my knees. It knocked my legs out from under me. I sprawled across the threshold between hallway and kitchen, sliding in the puddle of Bluebell's blood.

I looked around quickly for what had knocked me over. A girl, maybe nine or ten years of age, squatted over Bluebell's body. Her long dark hair was matted and stringy; her face a pale brown vacant moon. Her pink t-shirt and purple track pants were dirty and tattered. She was motionless and observed me with eyes that were flat black disks, like a shark's. Overgrown incisors protruded from under her upper lip. The tips of her fangs pressed against her lower lip, a plump cushion.

"Oh fuck!" I shouted, scrambling on the blood-slick floor. I couldn't get purchase and ended up making blood-angels rather than getting a hand- or foothold.

"Yessss, fuck," the vampire child said, her voice oddly sibilant. She started to gnash her teeth, making a guttural sound at the back of her throat, "Gnung gnung gnung."

She sprang from her crouch, and landed on top of me, winding me. She brought the stench of the grave with her, as well as over-ripe fruit and–*dear gods, was that semen I smelled in her hair?* My stomach turned again.

The vampire child lunged for my left breast where it swelled over the cup of my bra. Her hands, like steel claws, pinned my arms to the floor. Her ragged nails bit into the skin of my upper arms as her teeth pierced the flesh of my breast. I screamed, but couldn't wiggle free from her. Despite her small size, the metaphysical boosts of vampirism had made her arms strong as steel bands. She kept making that noise, even as she tore at my flesh: "Gnung gnung gnung."

Dear gods, what had they done to this child? Straddling my right leg, the vampire girl wrapped her thin legs around my thigh. She reared her head back, mouth dripping blood and gobbets of gore.

"Yessss, fuck, that's what Daddy says," she whispered, then spat bits of torn skin and breast fat in my face.

She struck again in my left breast, worrying the flesh like a terrier with a rat. She started to rub her crotch against my thigh, "Gnung gnung gnung."

I screamed, high pitched and mindless. No matter how much I struggled, the tiny monster held me fast.

She continued grinding her crotch against my thigh, her small body pumping like a machine. Her blade-sharp fangs continued to tear at my breast, her throat working as she drank my blood down. I felt myself start to retreat mentally from what was happening to my body.

~Panic is better than absence, Suzanne~

Leopold!

~If you leave your body, the revenant will continue to eat you, to use you. You must defend yourself~

DONT YOU THINK I WOULD IF I COULD?!

~But you can, my dear. Do as you did in our first meeting~

What did I do? I cast the circle; I probed for your essence . . .

~And when I resisted you, you made that unbearable sound.~

I'm not even sure what I did! It was by accident!

~If you do not, this little one will eat you and fuck you until you are dead. Maybe even after you are dead. She seems ravenous.~

I started to cry. It seemed so impossible. But Leopold was right. If I didn't save me, I wasn't going to be saved. I relaxed my body, breathing deeply. The revenant girl felt me relax. She stopped rocking her hips against me and reared back from my ruined breast, fangs dripping. I think she was checking to see if I was still conscious or not. Her face was smeared with blood and chunks of flesh. Her eyes were pitiless. I focused on them to muster my determination. *Her or me, it's her or me.* She lunged forward and sank them into the muscle-meat of my left shoulder and tightened her legs around my thigh.

I breathed deeply again, then slowly let it out. I visualized my necromancy as a cellar door opening. Because there was no sacred circle to muffle the sound, the cacophony of the dead was overwhelming. Hundreds of voices babbled at me, in dozens of languages. I ignored them, even when they crept closer and I could feel their fingers on my skin like damp cobwebs. I visualized my spirit, an angry red thread.

~Not a thread, girl. Thicker! More dangerous.~

I blew breath into the red thread. Closing my eyes, I imagined holding it in my right hand: heavy, thick as my wrist. I imagined a hot iron arrowhead on its tip.

I took yet another deep breath, centering myself in my sacrum. A low tone rumbled at the bottom of my throat, my body starting to vibrate with a musical note. As I released the sound from my throat, I visualized my right hand driving the arrowhead into the revenant's ear.

The vampire child froze.

~You have her, my dear~

Now what?

~Give her orders~.

"Get off me!" I commanded.

The revenant delicately withdrew her teeth from my shoulder and released my arms. She rocked back on her heels, releasing my thigh from the grip of her legs.

"Stand up and walk over to the window!" The revenant did as she was bid. Her face was blank. Even the feral hunger and lust writ there before were wiped away.

This is a sick version of Simon Says.

~A children's game involving giving orders, I take it?~

Something like that. Now what?

~You must destroy her~

I flinched. *Shouldn't I just tie her up so she can be questioned or turned back?*

~Revenants cannot be healed, Suzanne. What she is now, she will ever be. You could no more gain information from this one than you could from a rabid dog.~

I shuddered. The movement brought my awareness to my torn breast and shoulder. They didn't hurt much now, but they would once the adrenaline was no longer coursing through my body.

~Do it now, Suzanne, while you still have control. You will not be able to hold her forever. The crowd of ghosts that are flocking to your spiritual beacon will only get denser. ~

He was right. I felt the edge of panic start to rise again. There was no way I wanted to have uncontained, activated necromancy any longer than absolutely necessary. Or at all, really.

~Yes, we both agree, you need to do this. So do it.~

I sighed and felt a few ghostly fingers probing the wound on my shoulder. *Curious dead people, great.*

"Enough. I am not here for you," I said.

I walked over the kitchen counter and opened a drawer.

What should I use?

~Do you have a cleaver or a butchering knife? It's best if you cut off her head.~

Sweet gods! I can't do that!

~The next best thing is something wooden through the heart.~

There were some wooden spoons in the drawer, a wooden rolling pin. Too blunt, too big.

~It doesn't have to be big, just enough to pierce the heart.~

There were a pad and pencil on the counter. I looked intently at the pencil.

~Yes, that will do, at least until she can be decapitated.~

I picked up the pencil and walking over to the motionless revenant. Even her eyes were frozen, they did not follow my movement, or register my presence at all.

So, what do I do?

~Place it over her heart and drive it in with all your might.~

I shivered at the thought. My shoulder and breast hurt, and the wounds had not stopped bleeding yet.

~ Her saliva thins the blood. Do this before you faint, Suzanne!~

I gripped the pencil firmly in my right hand, resting the tip over where the revenant's heart. I took a deep breath, then lunged forward with all my body weight.

The revenant was motionless, frozen. Her eyes blinked from time to time; I pressed the pencil through the child vampire's thin body. She stood there, motionless, an unloved doll. Unlike a human body, it was easy to pierce her chest.

~Yes, it is a weakness of ours. It can be hard work to pierce a human's chest unless you have super strength. With We Who Walk Between, it is much easier. Gives your kind a fighting chance, I suppose~

This is no time for jokes!

~Now that she is pinned, close your necromancy.~

I imagined the cellar door slamming shut. The moist spider web touch and whispering voices of the dead disappeared abruptly. I felt a wave of emotions–panic, fear, rage start to well up from my first chakra. *Not now, not now.* I vomited on the floor instead.

With shaking hands, I took my phone out of the back pocket of my jeans, pressed Dougherty's number. I fainted.

Chapter Twelve

I'm not sure how I'd got from my kitchen floor to the hospital; my memories of it are all quick cuts, like a badly-edited YouTube video. I had a flash of Dougherty bending over me, picking me up off the linoleum. I had a memory of rain falling on my face as he carried me across the parking lot to a car. I remember hearing him say to someone, "Seattle General, balls out and Mars flashing on top. She's going to bleed out. I'll meet you there. We've gotta get the head off that thing in there."

I recall McCabe and an officer in uniform half-lifting, half-dragging me into the ER; I felt like I was spinning, and that I could fly. I could hear the sound of my own laughter—manic, edging closer to a scream. Then Dougherty arguing with the ER admitting nurse. The nurse's dark brown skin looked healthy under the fluorescent lights, but Dougherty's pale Irish complexion looked blotchy and slightly greenish. I felt like I was floating. McCabe sat beside me, pressing a wadded-up cloth into the flesh void in my shoulder. McCabe looked gorgeous, even with a divot of concern between her knitted brows. I had yet to see her with a hair out of place. *I'm not even sure if she sweats.* I knew I was in shock because my mind was busying itself with irrelevancies like that. Plus, McCabe applying pressure to the wound on my shoulder should hurt. It didn't.

The nurse picked up a clipboard with a form and a pen attached to it. She walked briskly past us, down the hall, away from the admitting desk.

"This way!" she yelled.

McCabe and the uniformed officer followed the nurse, dragging me to one of the examination bays. I don't know what happened next because my eyes rolled back in my head, and the world started spinning again. I heard someone say "We need a coagulant! She's lost too much blood!" Then dark quiet took me.

*   *   *

Eventually, I started to hear and feel things. I heard Leopold speaking to me—heard the sound of his cultured voice, anyway. Either I never heard his exact words clearly, or I have forgotten them. I could hear the TV or the radio on very low, people talking in hushed voices. At first, it sounded like people whispering in the next room. Over time, their voices got closer and closer. When it sounded like people were in the room with me whispering to each other, I tried moving my arms and legs a little. I could feel the friction of the coarse hospital sheets on my skin. My left shoulder and breast throbbed. *Why was that again?* It took a moment for my head to clear enough to remember the revenant. Coming back to awareness is like swimming up to the surface of a pool of pudding. My head crested the surface.

With heroic effort, I opened my eyes. Blinking, I looked around the room—standard hospital green. The wall-mounted TV was on, the volume low, tuned to some reality show about ballroom dancing. McCabe sat in a chair next to the bed, reading something on her phone.

"Wendy," I said hoarsely. My mouth was parched.

She startled. She looked at me and smiled. "Hey. You're awake."

I nodded. It hurt my shoulder to nod.

"You thirsty?" she asked, holding up a cup with an elbow straw.

"Yes."

She raised the head of the bed with a button on the side of the bedframe, then maneuvered the tip of the straw between my dry lips. *Water*.

"What's the last thing you remember?" McCabe asked.

I cleared my throat. Still a bit of a tickle, despite the water. "I remember coming here with you and some cop. I think I fainted in the exam bay before a doctor could look at me."

McCabe nodded. "Yep, that's about the size of it. Do you want to know what's happened since then?"

"Yes."

"Well, for starters, it's a good thing we got you here as fast as we did—you'd be dead if we didn't. Apparently, revenants have even more anticoagulant enzyme in their saliva than full-fledged vampires do. You'd gotten a good dose from her because she'd done more damage than just a couple of puncture wounds."

I cringed. "I remember."

"You were close to bleeding out by the time we got you here, that's why you passed out so many times. They ended up putting you in a medically-induced coma for ten days so they could stabilize you."

"Ten days? Holy shit! Stabilize me how?"

Her face momentarily fell, then she recovered her composure. "They needed to give you some surgery on your shoulder and on your breast."

I looked down at my chest covered in a pale blue hospital gown. I could feel that I was bandaged.

"Help me slip off the shoulder of the gown, I want to see it," I said, as I pulled at the left shoulder of the hospital gown with my right hand. McCabe laid her hand gently on my forearm. Her eyes were glossy.

"Don't do that yet," she said.

I felt annoyed. I wanted to see what the revenant had done to me.

"I want to see it," I said quietly.

"You will," said McCabe. "The nurses will change your bandages, and you can see it then. It's pretty bad, so you don't want to mess with it with unwashed hands."

Exhaustion hit me like a cresting wave. I felt too weak to argue with her. "Ok," I said, closing my eyes.

"They started reducing the meds for the coma just a few hours ago; you've come out of it a bit sooner than they said you would," said McCabe. "I'll go let them know and get a nurse to do your dressings, ok? Here, take this" She walked around to the other side of the bed and put the medication pump in my hand. "Just push the button on the end of this if you have pain, I'll be back in a sec."

"Ok," I said, nodding. *Ouch.* Even through the morphine buzz, I could feel the damage. *It looks like I'm still in pretty bad shape.* I pressed the button.

I'd dozed off on a fluffy opiate cloud, deeply enough that I didn't wake until the nurse started to peel off the dressing. Even though her hands were gentle, even with the warm, soft morphine making my head float and my skin tingle, it hurt.

"Your friend told us that you were awake," said the nurse. She was an older, larger woman with caramel skin, friendly grey eyes, and tight ringlet curls streaked with grey, caught up in a top knot.

"Starting to be," I said. I smiled weakly.

"If it hurts, use the morphine pump again, it won't let you take too much," she said. I pressed the button.

"Did your friend talk to you about the surgeries?" she asked.

"Yes, a little."

I could feel the cold air on the injured shoulder. Before I could look at it, the nurse said, "Lay still, let me get all the bandages off before you start to look."

I held still, and she started to remove the bandages on my breast as well.

"I have a hand mirror for you if you wish to watch. Don't touch any part of it, though; you're not out of the woods yet in terms of infection," she said, retrieving a plastic mirror from a rolling nurses' cart.

I held the mirror up so I could view my shoulder and breast. Most of the skin on my shoulder was gone; just a few dried black flakes clung to the edges of the wound. The flakes looked like charcoaled pork cracklings. Two fist-sized chunks were missing from the exposed trapezius muscle. The muscle fibers themselves were stained black.

Looking at the damage made me feel lightheaded. I took a deep, steadying breath and angled the mirror so I could see as much of my left breast as I could. I looked down at my chest. More large bite marks. It looked like most of the pectoralis muscle was gone, too. Same crispy black flakes ringing the wound. Same black staining of the muscle fibers. I adjusted the mirror. Two big bites taken from my breast. One of the bites had taken most of my nipple. The wounds were ragged, black, and ringed with greasy black flakes. Tears welled up in my eyes. I blinked them away.

The nurse put her hand on my uninjured shoulder and said, "Don't forget to breathe. Take it slow. My name's Rosemary, by the way."

She turned back to the rolling cart with nursing supplies, getting things together for wound care. I felt like she was purposefully giving me a moment to compose myself.

I sniffed and wiped my eyes with the back of my right hand. I didn't want to drip tears on the injuries.

Though I sat calmly in my hospital bed, my mind was racing. How my body looked disgusted me. My heart was pounding faster than it ever had, and I started to feel light-headed. I squeezed my eyes shut. The sense of, I dunno, loss was profound. I know it sounds stupid to say that I felt loss because part of my body was gone, but I did. I've never been beautiful, and I knew I never would be, but until now at least I'd been whole. The tears threatened to start again. I gulped back a sob so big that holding it made my throat hurt.

When I opened my eyes, I saw that Rosemary was waiting patiently with tweezers in hand. "You need to be ready for this," she said.

"What are you going to do?"

She paused. "I have to peel as many of the black flakes away from the edge of the wound as I can. If that doesn't work, we'll have to put you under and do a debridement."

"What's that?"

"We scrub at the wound and grind off anything that isn't healthy tissue," she said.

Fuck.

"I don't want that," I said quietly, managing my rising panic.

"Ok then," she said. "You are tougher than you give yourself credit for. Most people would already be dead from what you want through. This is nothing compared to that. The worst part is already over."

I let out the breath I didn't realize I had been holding. *To the sticking place.* "Ok, do it," I said.

She went to work with her tweezers, and I tried to ignore what she was doing and watch the dancing show on the TV. It wasn't as bad as I thought it was going to be. I guess I had enough nerve damage that I didn't have too much sensation left.

After Rosemary had been peeling the charcoaled skin from the edges of the wounds for about half an hour, I could actually watch she was doing with a kind of morbid fascination. About half of the greasy-crisp black skin flakes had been removed. My breast was completely flake-free; only the shoulder wound still needed work. With the flakes removed, I could see that the intact skin around the wound edges was starting to fade to navy blue and indigo.

"What's the black stuff?" I asked her.

"From the lunar caustic they used for the infection, it stains the tissues black. You can see it's starting to fade out to blue. That's your body metabolizing the silver."

"The silver?" I asked.

"Lunar caustic is the old-school name for it; it's also called silver nitrate. Silver is a powerful antibiotic," she said.

"It that why the edges are flaking, too?"

"No," she said, as she continued to worry greasy flecks with the tweezers. "The flaking comes from the cauterization."

"Why did they have to cauterize my injuries? Couldn't they stop the bleeding with surgery?" I asked.

She hesitated for a moment. "You'll have to talk to the doctor about that. He can answer all those kinds of questions."

I thought for a minute. It was obvious there was something she wasn't telling me. She continued to pick at the charcoaled flakes on my shoulder. I stared out the window, considering my next remark carefully.

Outside, the rain pelted the trees and the building I could see from my hospital bed. Uncloaked branches of trees scratched at the bellies of the dark clouds, heavy with rain. I sighed.

"Ms. Murphy, it's not that I don't want to tell you, I'm just not sure what to say."

I met her eyes with mine. "How so?"

"No one who's participated in your care has ever seen something like this before. Revenant bites themselves are rare. I was a nurse for five years before I ever saw one. Revenant bites on a necromancer? I've never seen that before. I don't even think it's mentioned in the nursing textbooks, to tell the truth."

I nodded as I thought about what she said.

"So, it sounds like you're afraid that if you tell me too much about how you guys helped me, I might get mad, or maybe sue because maybe you don't know what you're doing?" I asked, as gently as I could.

"I really can't discuss that," she said quietly. She started irrigating my shoulder wound with some kind of distilled water solution, patting the excess away with gauze squares.

"Can anyone?"

"As I said, the best I can do is send one of the surgeons to speak with you about it; you can ask him questions. I know he wants to talk to you about a waiver or release of some kind," she said, as she peeled the white paper backing off of a clear micropore burn bandage. She gently settled one corner of the bandage on some undamaged skin, and slowly lay the transparent sheet over my injury. Despite her discomfort with the conversation, her hands were steady, featherlight. She was a good nurse.

She continued, "His rounds start in a little while, I'll make sure he comes to see you first."

She started collecting the used gauze pads and bandage backings.

"I'm not mad, Rosemary, I understand why you can't say anything," I said.

She nodded, gathering the other supplies she had used in tending to my injuries, placing them in her rolling cart.

"Thank you," she said as she left.

Moving carefully, I pulled my cell phone from the drawer in the bedside table. It took a while to do it without hurting myself. Once I was settled against the pillows, I opened the browser app on the phone. The app loaded my Google search homepage. I thumb-typed "lunar caustic" and selected one of the returned pages. It read:

LUNAR CAUSTIC refers back to SILVER NITRATE.

Fucking disambiguation pages. I clicked the hyperlink.

SILVER NITRATE: Applied to the skin and mucous membranes, silver nitrate is used either in stick form as lunar caustic (or caustic pencil) or in solutions of 0.01 percent to 10 percent silver nitrate in water. 10 percent solutions are astringent and highly antiseptic.

It was once called lunar caustic because silver was called luna by the ancient alchemists, who believed that silver was associated with the moon. In contemporary magicks . . .

The touch screen glass was cool under my thumb as I scrolled down the article. I'll read the magickal part later.

Silver nitrate solutions of 10-20 percent can be used to temporarily incapacitate Those Who Walk Between. However, in California, The District of Columbia, and New Hampshire, courts have ruled it cruel and unusual punishment to use silver nitrate this way on vampire citizens. In some states, such as New Mexico, Colorado and Washington, the use of silver nitrate is in legal limbo, awaiting state Supreme Court rulings. Other states, notably Florida and Texas, continue to use weak silver nitrate solutions to pacify aggressive vampire suspects during arrest and questioning. The pharmacology of vampire metabolism and silver nitrate is incompletely understood, and this can lead to idiosyncratic reactions to silver nitrate. There have been reports that some magick users respond atypically to silver nitrate, but as yet these are anecdotal stories. Additional research in this area is required.

See also ST. HUBERT'S KEY

I clicked the link.

SAINT HUBERT'S KEY: St. Hubert's Key is both a Christian and pan–Magickal charm used in the treatment of rabies in both humans and animals (Vampires, of course, cannot contract rabies as the Vampirism virus provides them with immunity). The key was heated, and it was pressed to the area where a person had been bitten by a dog or other animal believed to have rabies. If performed soon after the bite had occurred, the heat had the potential to cauterize and sterilize the wound, killing the rabies virus. Some dog breeders brand their animals with the St. Hubert's key as a preventative measure, but this practice is increasingly seen as animal cruelty, equivalent to ear docking in dogs or declawing in cats.

St. Hubert's key is typically formed from a metal nail that has been removed from a church or other sanctified building. Some St. Hubert's Keys are constructed in the shape of a cross using two nails soldered together. In earlier times the two nails might be tied into place with a thin lock of braided hair taken from a saint. During the middle ages, many St. Hubert's keys of dubious provenance were for sale in every market stall, no doubt constructed from nails picked up from the ground and the hair of the local serving wench. Since the 1920's governments and medical associations have strived to curtail this trade in bogus keys. Keys in use in hospitals and medical practices in the US are required to have appropriate documentation as to their source and authenticity.

I heard the hospital room door open. A muscular Asian man in navy blue scrubs and running shoes walked in, carrying a clipboard. He looked to be around forty years of age. He wore rimless glasses with architectural features and a stethoscope looped around his neck like a mini boa constrictor. I noticed all the hospital staff wore their stethoscopes that way, rather than having the arms of the earpieces rest at the back of the neck as they do on old TV shows.

"Hi, Ms. Murphy, I'm Dr. Chau, I was the chief surgeon who worked on you the other night. I'm overseeing your care." The line between his eyebrows never went away, even when the rest of his face relaxed.

"Hi. The nurse, um . . . Rosemary said I should ask you some things," I said trying to sit up straighter.

"Yes, I bet you have a lot of questions, as do we . . ."

"My understanding is that medical care alone didn't save my life, you guys had to use some kind of magick as well?" I asked.

He cleared his throat. For a moment, Dr. Chau looked as though he was wearing an itchy turtleneck, wanting to squirm with discomfort.

I waited a moment for him to regain his composure.

He sighed, "Yes, surgery alone wasn't enough. We had to use borrow the St. Hubert's Key from the Catholic hospital on an emergency basis."

"What happened, exactly?"

"You wouldn't stop bleeding. Pumping extra plasma into you was like running tomato juice through a colander, your body wouldn't retain it. We figure that something about the revenant's saliva was part of the problem . . ."

"But nobody knows how it might affect a necromancer," I said, half-quoting. Dr. Chau looked startled.

"You've heard that a lot, huh?"

"Just a bit," I said, smiling weakly.

Dr. Chau cleared his throat again and shifted his running-shoed feet on the hard surface of the hospital floor.

"I think the best thing to do after you've had a few days of physio, would be to discuss your long-range recovery goals and plastic surgery to improve the appearance of the affected areas," he said, looking at the papers on his clipboard.

He shifted his stance again. Either he had some pretty serious lower back pain from long hours standing, or he was nervous about something.

"But there is something else you want to talk about first," I said phrasing my guess as a statement.

His brows climbed is forehead. "Yes, that's right," he said.

Briefly, sadness fluttered in my chest. I swatted it away.

"So . . . shoot. Lay it on me. Give it to me straight, doc." Those were all the clichés I could think of, and being a smart-ass certainly helped me avoid feeling my feelings.

"I wonder if you would sign permissions that would allow us to write an article for the *New England Journal of Medicine* . . ."

"About me," I said, flatly.

"Not so much you, per se, but about the surgery, how we managed to save your life, there is really nothing on this in the contemporary literature."

I sighed. "It doesn't really leave much of my confidentiality, being written up as a 'case'," I said.

"We would adhere to the strictest guidelines of patient confidentiality, of course," he said. Beads of sweat stood out on his upper lip. *Man, this conversation made him really nervous. Or I did.*

"Well, it's not exactly like the world is brimming with necromancers. The journal would reference the hospital and city, wouldn't it? From there it's not exactly hard to figure out who the necromancer is."

He opened his mouth, and then closed it, lips pressing into a thin line.

"I'll leave the papers here for you to look at. We can talk about this another time perhaps. Just promise me that you'll think about it." I looked at him and said nothing.

He leant over and placed the clipboard on the bedside table near me. *Curious that he would lean and not simply step closer.*

"I'll be back in a few days, Ms. Murphy, after you're feeling a bit better." He left.

His request pissed me off. Maybe it shouldn't, helping others by contributing information and all that but I was angry. *Haven't I already given enough?* I was also aware that feeling angry was a relief—it beat feeling grief over my mangled chest and shoulder any day.

I was still chewing over all the reasons Dr. Chau was wrong to even ask me in the first place when McCabe and Dougherty entered.

Her face was impassive. He had a worried look and three take-out coffees riding in a cardboard tray.

"Suzi-Q–awake at last!" His cheerful tone of voice was at odds with his facial expression. He lifted one of the paper cups of coffee from the tray and handed it to me. "Your usual. The coffee in hospitals always sucks."

I lifted the cardboard cup to my nose and sniffed it: dark roast with real cream. My mouth watered. I felt a lump start in my throat from this small kindness. My eyes were wet. I smiled at him. Ever the hard-boiled cop, Dougherty pretended he didn't notice. *Thank Gods for that; I was sick of crying, sick of feeling stupid feelings. Ugh.*

Coffee in one hand, McCabe pulled a plastic chair closer to the bedside. Dougherty sat in the armchair, sipping his drink.

McCabe said, "Do you want to talk about your injuries?" Her tone was neutral, her face blank, standard issue peer support techniques from the police department's critical incident stress handbook. I shook my head.

Dougherty shot McCabe a sharp look. "She doesn't have to talk at all if she doesn't want to." His shoulders crept up towards his ears, protective, ready to fight for me.

"Guys," I said quietly, throat rasping, "I'll let you know if I want to talk about what happened. Right now I'd like to think about something else, get focused on work, keep my mind off it."

Dougherty said "Good girl," with a glance of triumph at McCabe.

McCabe rolled her eyes, said nothing, and took a sip of her coffee. I think in Dougherty's mind, McCabe and Dougherty were in a competition to mentor me. Would I choose techniques from McCabe's new human resources-approved policing playbook, or would I go with Dougherty's old-school stuffed feelings and bravado? Clearly, Dougherty thought me not wanting to talk about my injuries was a sign of the latter. *Whatever.*

"What happened with the revenant after I went to the hospital?" I rasped.

McCabe raised her eyebrows as she looked at Dougherty. He said, "I knew that the pencil through the heart wouldn't hold it forever. Your building super was out on the sidewalk in his bathrobe watching all the action. I asked him for some tools, and he was able to find an old snow shovel in the basement. I used that to decapitate the revenant."

I shuddered, imagining the events in my mind's eye. Unbidden, my mind flashed back to the attack—the musty smell of the child-vampire, the pain in my shoulder as she chewed through flesh to the collarbone . . . I squeezed my eyes shut and shook my head like I had water in my ears.

"You ok, Suzanne?" said McCabe.

"Yep," I said, through gritted teeth. "Then what happened?" I asked.

"The criminalists showed up. They took the body and the head away in separate containers. They think the revenant got in through the kitchen window; there was evidence of the lock being tampered with," he said.

"How could she get up there? I'm on the third floor, and the fire escape is on the other side of the building."

Dougherty blew into, then sipped, his coffee. "Well, the best theory that people have so far is that either she flew up to the window, or another vampire did."

McCabe cleared her throat, "Given how limited revenant's mental processes are, it's most likely that a proper, fully developed vampire flew up, jimmied the window, then ferried the girl up to the open window. If a revenant could fly, she would have just broken through the glass. They're not known for finesse."

The wounds on my chest and shoulder still ached from my physio session earlier today. Now my temple was starting to throb-the stress of the case, I guess. I pressed the button on the morphine pump.

"Ok, let's back up just a sec," I said, rubbing my fingers across the knot of tension at the base of my skull. "Vampires can fly?"

McCabe nodded, "It's rare, but some can. It was more common among the original survivors of the plague, the so-called first generation. Since many of the first generation in Europe died during the witch trials, most of the vampires in Europe and the Americas are the second generation or later. The ability is uncommon for them. It's more common for Asian vampires to fly."

"Why's that?" I asked.

"The strain of vampirism that infected Asia was not the same disease as in Europe. I've read that Asian vampirism is likely a mutation of the small pox virus, not the bubonic plague as it was in Europe. It also happened more than a thousand years earlier. And while some East Asian cultures responded as Europeans did, by killing anyone infected by the vampirism mutation, most did not. In China, for example . . ."

Dougherty sighed. "Don't get Wendy started, Suzanne. She's a teacher without a classroom." He grinned at me, then at Wendy. She returned his smile, though her cheeks were slightly pink with embarrassment.

I sipped my cooling coffee and then cleared my throat. "Let me see if I follow you: some big bad vampire— possibly a first generation from Europe, or possibly one with roots in Asia, jimmied my kitchen window, and dropped the revenant inside to lie in wait for me?"

"Yes," said McCabe. Dougherty nodded. "Why me and not one of you?" I asked.

"I'm armed, and trained," said Dougherty, then gestured toward McCabe with his chin. "She's an expert on vampire cultures, and also carries a weapon. You're not armed, and you're the only necromancer we have. If they can take you out, we've lost a good tool."

"Which suggests that we're moving in the right direction," added McCabe, as she threw her empty take-out cup into the trash.

My brows knit together in concentration as I tried to adjust my position in the hospital bed. There was no way to do it without it hurting. *Shit*. Tongue between my teeth, I slid further up and fumbled for the button to raise the head of the bed. I tapped the morphine pump again.

I hissed out a breath, then said, "Getting close, huh? So, what's happened while I was in the coma?"

Dougherty and McCabe exchanged a look I couldn't interpret. Dougherty said, "Remember Duncan Shaw, the coach at Capitol Hill Collegiate? We figured he was doping the students with vamp blood to enhance their performance?"

"Yes, I remember."

"Remember how some things about his background documents, criminal record checks seemed hinky to me?"

"Uh huh," I said.

McCabe broke in. "It turns out he'd had a name change. Before he went to college, he was known as Joseph Geruyter."

"Any relation to our favorite social worker?" I asked. In my mind's eye, I flashed on the images Braydon's ghost showed me.

Dougherty opened his mouth to respond to me, but I held up two fingers.

"Hold on a sec," I said, "I think I just figured out what Braydon's ghost was trying to tell me."

"Really?" said Wendy.

"Can you hand me my notebook?"

McCabe handed it to me, and I paged quickly through my notes. "See," I said, pointing to my notes, "he was trying to show me Neil Geruyter. But who could the mouse be?"

Dougherty cocked his head. "The receptionist," he said.

"What?" McCabe and I asked in unison.

"Remember that day, we were joking about how she looked like a mouse in a Habitrail?" he asked.

"Right!" I said.

"So, Braydon's ghost was communicating to you through your own symbol system?" McCabe asked.

"It would seem so," I said.

"Which means we need to talk to that receptionist," said Dougherty.

McCabe nodded. "It certainly can't hurt," she said.

Dougherty nodded. "Wendy, maybe you can pick her up? I want to follow the paper trail on the brothers. Looks like he's Neil Geruyter's younger brother. Joe Geruyter's juvenile record is sealed, but we've put paperwork in to have it unsealed. It may take a while, but we'll be able to look at those records."

"Did Neil Geruyter have a juvenile record?" I asked.

"Not that my search turned up, but that might mean he was good enough not to get caught for whatever it was he was doing," Dougherty said.

"You think the black hats figured out we're poking around Duncan Shaw a.k.a. Joseph Geruyter and that's why they sicced the revenant on me?"

Dougherty smiled. "Smart girl. That's exactly what I think. And I'll bet you anything Neil Geruyter is involved somehow. With his access to government systems, he might be able to set up alerts whenever certain names have crim. checks run on them."

I nodded.

"That's not all," Wendy said, shifting position on the plastic chair. "After our talk with Mistress Stephanie, I had some of the Vice staff shift from their routines on 12Chan and other sites to more targeted searches and interactions."

"Whaddya mean?" I asked, finishing my coffee.

"You know how we have officers going into chat rooms, setting up stings on pedophiles, right?" she asked.

"Ok," I said.

"I had them change their chat scripts somewhat, using certain kink-related keywords, see what that turned up."

"And that was what?"

"It eventually turned up a screen name . . ."

"It's going to take forever to find the person behind the online identity, if we even can, if he's even anywhere near Seattle," I said, frustrated. The pain in my shoulder and chest was making me cranky.

"Wait for it, Suzi–Q, good news is coming," said

Dougherty. He poured me a glass of water and handed it to me. I sipped.

"We caught a break on this one, Suzanne. One of Vice's techs, Jaz Sarai, has been working a contact for the past fourteen months online. Using a male persona, she's been building trust, grooming him so that he feels comfortable to meet to explore their 'mutual interests in man-boy love'. We happen to know that one of the screen-names her contact uses- Bad Daddy's Mustache- is the same name mentioned in the chat rooms. The IT people worked their magick, and we were able to trace the IP address of our operative's contact and match it to the source IP address when Bad Daddy's Moustache is chatting."

"So, the private communications Sarai was having with her contact and the recent more public chats happening with other officers were all coming from the same place?

"Yes, exactly," McCabe said.

I blew out a slow breath as I absorbed this information, and pushed my bangs out of my eyes. "So now what?" I asked.

"Well, the first thing to do is get this creep to set up a meeting with Sarai, then we'll pick him up, bring him in, question him," said Dougherty.

"We've already got enough on him that an arrest is legit, even if he has no connection to the vampires."

"And we're hoping that there are only so many kinky pedophiles who are also vampire enthusiasts?" I asked.

"God willing," said Dougherty.

I wasn't so sure, but I kept my worries to myself. Something Leopold had said was creeping around the edges of my memory. It was relevant here, but I couldn't quite pull it into my conscious mind . . .

"Suzanne?" McCabe said, brows knitted together. She and Dougherty were both staring at me.

"Huh? What?" I said.

"Where'd you go just now Suzi-Q?" asked Dougherty. "Sorry, I got lost in thought for a sec," I said.

"A sec? More like a full minute," said McCabe, her brow still furrowed. She met Dougherty's eyes and a meaningful glance passed between them. He scowled.

"What?" I said.

"Whaddya mean 'what'?" replied Dougherty.

"I saw the look Wendy just gave you. What's up between you two?"

Dougherty sighed and shifted his weight in his chair. "Wendy thinks you should be removed from the case."

I looked at her. "Is that true?"

McCabe squared her shoulders, then sipped her coffee, buying time to choose her words carefully, no doubt.

"Yes. I think your consult on this case has gotten too dangerous. The fact you're checking out mentally is just one part of the problem."

I felt my face flame hot with anger. Controlling my voice, I said, "And the other parts are . . . ?"

"Well, for one thing, it's clear that you're still in a great deal of pain. Pain frays nerves, it can make people irritable and impatient. That's not good in an investigation like this."

"I see," I said, my brows pinching together. "You think I'm spacey, irritable, and impatient. Is there more?"

McCabe flinched. Whatever it was, she didn't want to say it. I took that as my cue to don my big girl panties and be ready for what she said next.

"Suzanne," she said gently, "You have a rare gift. SPD needs your services. But I think it's wrong for us to use you in this particular case—there is a lot at stake, and it's dangerous."

"C'mon, Wendy, she's worked two other murders with me," Dougherty said.

"They weren't like this, though. Both of those were situations with family members doing the killing, one-offs in each case. It wasn't an organized gang of criminals with the resources and know-how for retaliation against investigators. They've deliberately tried to take out the one person who is both highly valuable and especially vulnerable."

"That's all the more reason to go after these fuckers as hard as we can," said Dougherty.

Wendy sighed, "I agree with you Paul; that's why I don't think Suzanne should be part of this anymore. She's invaluable in working other kinds of cases. I don't think we've even started to use her talents to their full potential yet. But for that to happen, she has to stay alive."

The throbbing in my head was getting worse. *Why the fuck wasn't the goddam morphine working?* I pinched the bridge of my nose between thumb and forefinger. I took my hand away from my face and said, "Wendy, let's back this up a bit. What makes me 'especially vulnerable'?"

Wendy tucked a lock of her flame-red hair behind her ear. "You don't have or even know how to use a gun. You haven't had even the basic hand-to-hand training the cadets get in the academy. You are, um . . . ."

"I think the word you are looking for is 'fat'," I said flatly.

Dougherty smirked at McCabe's discomfort.

McCabe sighed. "I don't think you're fat; I was going to say that you are not in good cardio condition."

"Maybe you were. Whatever. I don't care. So, no gun, can't fight, too fat to outrun anybody, spacey, irritable, impatient—anything else?" I said.

"Isn't that enough?" she asked, eyebrows raised.

I ran my hand through my dirty blond curls and stabbed at the nurse call button with my index finger. *I'm going to slap that Dr. Chau the next time I see him. If I can find someone to blame for this headache, I'll slap them, too. Fuck, she may be right about me being irritable.* The fact that McCabe was offering sensible reasons to exclude me didn't make me feel any better about this. In fact, it made it worse.

I looked at Dougherty. "What do you think, Paul?"

Dougherty scowled, his lips compressing into a thin line. He stuffed his balled-up hands into his jacket pockets.

"I think if most of my left tit were chewed off by a fucking monster, I'd want to get a little payback on the motherfucker responsible," he said.

Harsh as his words and tone were, I could sense his empathy, and it made tears well up in my eyes.

"Don't be nice to me, being pissed off is all that's holding me together," I said, blinking the moisture away.

"See?" he said to McCabe. "She sounds like a cop."

McCabe rolled her eyes at him.

Dougherty said, "Here's my bottom line, Wendy. I think Suzi-Q wants to end this sick shit and put these creeps behind bars. And I think that if along the way some pedo loses a testicle as payback for what happened to her, no one will lose any sleep over that. Most of all, I think we owe her the chance to finish it."

I had reservations about Dougherty's belief that revenge would make me feel better. I wasn't so sure that it would. Furthermore, I wasn't convinced I could do it. But, gods help me, some part of me wanted to try. *This should be my choice.*

I said, "Ok, so what about this: Star makes some protection charms for me, I learn how to use a gun, and I stay somewhere other than my apartment while the case is active?"

Wendy shrugged. "All those things would help, but . . ."

I interrupted her. "There's one other thing."

"What's that?" she asked.

"Something I haven't told you guys about yet, but it's the reason I'm still alive. If I hadn't used it, I would have died on the kitchen floor well before Dougherty got there."

"What did you do?" asked Dougherty, leaning forward in his chair.

I started to tell them about Leopold.

Chapter Thirteen

An hour later, I'd told them everything I knew about Leopold and our psychic link— Leopold's contact with me through dreams, his assistance during the ritual to speak with Braydon's ghost, Leopold's support and advice so I could incapacitate the revenant in my kitchen. I knew that I owed my life to Leopold. I was grateful.

McCabe was frowning, obviously formulating more questions for me. Dougherty was quiet, and his facial expression was flat, emotionless. He gave good cop-face. Shielded that way, he could be thinking anything. My best guess was that Dougherty was pissed at me for not telling anyone about Leopold right away.

McCabe shifted in her chair. Disapproval slunk around her like a bad smell.

She said, "If you think Leopold is trustworthy, you're a fool. He'll keep his word, technically, but find other ways to lie; you can count on it."

I wiggled a little in the hospital bed, trying to sit up straighter without aggravating my chest or shoulder. It didn't work; my wounds started to throb again. I sighed, moved up on the bed, pressed the button on the morphine pump. *Pain be damned, who wants to have an argument while reclining?*

"I bet you guys think that Leopold is just using this situation, using me, to get out of the Den of the Forsaken," I said.

Dougherty nodded curtly, and McCabe made an 'mmm' noise.

"Well, I agree with you, I think he's going to leverage this any way he can."

"So then, why cooperate with him?" asked Dougherty.

I sighed. "What other options do I have? As Wendy has already made clear, I can't compete in physical combat or with weapons. What was I supposed to do, let myself be killed because I shouldn't accept his help?"

Dougherty leant forward in his chair, rubbing a meaty hand over his close-cropped hair. "It didn't start that way, though. You said yourself he helped you get a break in speaking with Braydon's ghost: you should have told us then. I would've got you reassigned at that point and none of this"—he gestured towards my injuries—"would have happened."

Wendy stood up, her arms crossed over her midriff, hands cupping opposite elbows. She started to pace.

"I don't think that would have helped, Paul," she said. "He'd already made contact with her before that, probably her interview with him in the warehouse was enough to forge the link between them."

Dougherty stuffed his hands into the pockets of his jacket. I could see a knot of muscle moving at the hinge of his jaw as he ground his teeth.

"So, you're saying this is my fault, is that it? Because I got her involved in this case in the first place?" His voice was low, quiet, almost a warning growl.

I sat up straighter on the bed, pain in my arm and chest be damned.

"Look, guys, I'm not a victim, ok? Yes, I should have told you about Leopold right away, but let's get one thing clear- no one is forcing me to do this investigation, and I knew when I signed up I could get hurt. Am I more hurt than I thought I'd be? Yes. Chalk that up to my lack of imagination. Whatever, it's done now, so you can both stop with the hair shirt routine, alright? I don't blame either one of you for this."

McCabe stopped pacing and looked at me carefully. "Who do you blame?" she asked.

"Myself, for not anticipating they'd come after me, or come after me so soon. Partly. A little bit, anyway." I sighed. "Mostly I blame the perverted sons of bitches who made a revenant out of a little girl in the first place."

Dougherty moved his shoulder like he was shrugging off a burden. "So that means . . ." he asked, eyebrows raised.

I shifted in the bed, winced from the pain in my injuries.

I said, "I just want to get these guys. If Leopold gets out of the Den and it turns out to be a problem, we can deal with that then. Or Juliet can. I dunno. But I think we need to do whatever it takes to stop these fuckers and worry about Leopold later."

McCabe resumed pacing.

"Has he asked or hinted you should help to get him released?" she asked.

"Not yet," I said. *Why was I lying about this?* Wanting to broker a deal with Juliet through me was almost the first thing Leopold had said. *Exactly how grateful am I to him for helping me save my own life?* I considered correcting myself and coming clean to McCabe and Dougherty. The moment passed. *Think about that later.* "But I haven't communicated with him since this happened," gesturing at my bandages with my chin.

"Any thoughts on why that is?" she asked. "Just some speculation, nothing concrete."

Dougherty sat up a little straighter in his chair. "Do you think the pain meds keep him out, or the stuff they gave you so you'd be in the coma?"

"No, actually I think the opiates might make contact easier than it would otherwise be. I think it might be the silver-based antibiotics they've been giving me."

McCabe asked, "So what's your theory?"

"I think I've got so much silver nitrate in my bloodstream; it blocks him out."

"Why would your blood need to be clean for the psychic link to work? He's not calling out to your blood, he's calling out to your mind," said Dougherty.

McCabe looked thoughtful. "If Suzanne is right, and the silver in her system blocks Leopold's psychic call in some way, I suspect it's because her mind has a relationship to her brain, and her brain is full of blood, and her blood is full of the metabolites of silver nitrates," she said, thinking aloud.

"I don't get you," said Dougherty.

"Ok, try this on for size: Suzanne's mind is tied to her body, right? Because she's more or less a human being."

"Gee, thanks," I said.

Dougherty suppressed a grin.

"Well, I say that because you are not exactly a mundane human being. We may not have a word for your category, but however we think of you, you're grounded in a mostly-human body, right?"

I shrugged. *Ouch. Note to self—no shrugging.*

"I guess what I'm saying is that Leopold might be calling your psychic number, but the silver antibiotics have turned the metaphysical ringer off. You can't hear him calling."

I breathed out slowly. I had not realized I'd been holding my breath.

Dougherty's shoulders relaxed a little. "So, what you're saying is that as long as Suzi-Q is on the meds, he might not be able to get through to her?"

McCabe nodded, "Yes. That is my working theory."

I considered this for a moment.

"Ok, so I guess that buys us some time before we actually have to deal with him asking to be paroled from the Den," I said. "I'm still on twice daily infusions of silver nitrate," pointing to the catheter taped to the inside of my left arm.

"Wait a sec! The whole point of entry into this conversation was that I think you should be off the case," Wendy objected.

"I get it: you want to protect me, and you think the way to do that is to remove me from the case. Dougherty wants me to keep fighting crime and develop resilience and the desire for revenge because that will protect me over the long-term. Both of you want to try to take responsibility for what happened."

Dougherty opened his mouth to say something, but I shook my head at him.

"No Paul, let me finish. I got me into this mess, and now that I'm in it, there's no getting out until the bad guys are locked up. Wendy, they know where I live! They probably know where I work! If they want me, they're going to be able to get me, whether I'm on the case or not."

Reluctantly, McCabe nodded.

"As for you Paul–you think Leopold is trying to use me. I think you're right. I know you're right. But what you don't seem to get is that I am going to use him right back. "

"Seems a dangerous game to play," Dougherty grumbled.

"It's also the only way to play it–the black hats are going to keep coming for me, guys, until they can't."

Wendy nodded, her lips a grim line. Dougherty grimaced but nodded.

"I think we need to work out how to deal with Leopold and with Juliet, and fast, because I won't be on antibiotics forever."

We started to scheme.

*   *   *

The next few days involved developing a routine for my physical recovery. McCabe and Dougherty had promised me immediate updates if the BOLO on LeFarge a.k.a. Joe Gerutyer turned up anything. Ditto if Neil Geruyter could be found.

As part of our scheming, McCabe and Dougherty and I reached a compromise. I promised to stay out of the mundane part of the pedophile sting operation, and they wouldn't make any moves regarding the spooky side of the investigation until we could find a way to encourage Juliet to release Leopold from the Den of the Forsaken.

It wasn't much of a compromise on my side. I don't know much about mundane investigations, and Wendy's team had that well in hand. The face-to-face meeting between one of the undercover officers from Wendy's team and Bad Daddy's Mustache was already set for next week. Nothing a psychic necromancer would be able to help with. I tried to do as I was told by focusing on my physical recovery and my research.

In terms of the first thing, let me just say that everything about hospitals, physical therapy, and the healing process annoyed me.

My injuries throbbed whenever Nurse Rosemary came by to do wound care. When the IV morphine was replaced with Percocet in tablet form, my injuries throbbed at night when I was trying to sleep. It was agony first thing in the morning, too. During the daily physiotherapy sessions, the pain in my injuries was so bad I felt as though dull-edged, white hot soup spoons were digging at my shoulder and breast. The physiotherapist told me that you know it's healing when it hurts. She increased the weight of the dumbbells she made me use. The bitch. I think I hated the physiotherapist.

Dr. Chau came around every couple of days to check on me. He also took my temperature a couple of times on the whole 'sign the release of confidentiality' thing, which would allow the medical team to produce an academic paper based on my surgery and related treatments. They weren't having any luck convincing me. A couple of times

Dr. Chau even tried to talk me into it while Dougherty happened to be visiting me.

I did, at Chau's request, write a letter of thanks to the board at the Catholic hospital that had loaned Seattle General the St. Hubert's Key. I might not be willing to advance Dr. Chau's career, but never let it be said I don't do my part for public relations when I can. At least, when I can remain anonymous.

Chau went so far as to try to pressure Dougherty into pressuring me if you can believe it. I don't think I had ever seen Dougherty grin as broadly as he did while he was watching me refuse to cooperate with Dr. Careerist, MD. Meh.

Signed waiver or no, the hospital insisted on keeping me for another week or so because no one knew exactly what would happen to my wounds; I was still getting the daily infusions of silver nitrate.

If I was more (rather than less) of a regular human being, I might have considered signing–do my bit for the progress of medical and magickal healing and all that. But the fact that I was one of only a handful of necromancers in the country meant there was no way I'd actually have any privacy. Just mentioning the hospital would be enough of a tip-off too. There are no other necromancers in the Pacific Northwest.

My few contracts so far with the SPD had worked out ok for me so far because Dougherty ensured my status as a necromancer was strictly 'need to know'. As far as the police force in general knew, I was a magickal generalist who sometimes consulted on certain cases, one of several garden variety psychics that consulted with the force. Dougherty made certain that the records reflected that and only that. Nothing about me talking to the dead.

Dougherty had warned me before our first case together that if police and military agencies became aware of me, there were only a few outcomes I could expect. Various policing agencies would beg and plead and guilt-trip me so that eventually all I did, all day, every day, was talk to the dead. My life wouldn't be my own. That or some intelligence organization would tuck me away in a basement somewhere so they could use me in research and development. My life wouldn't be worth living.

Two other necromancers in the country had made themselves rich using their gift and achieved a certain amount of notoriety. They also had to spend the bulk of their wealth on personal security. Madame Mogaba, self-styled Necromancer Queen of New Orleans, had only last month rebuffed a kidnapping attempt by some Cubans. They wanted her to speak with the recently-deceased Fidel Castro, and gods know what else. I do not have the money for that kind of security.

As the t-shirt says, it's not paranoia if they really are out to get you.

Even though my hospital stay was punctuated with daily bursts of searing agony from physiotherapy, and worry that somehow my confidentiality could be breached, being in the hospital wasn't all bad. For one thing, I really like Jello. I don't mind daytime game shows, either. I could even nap as much as I wanted.

Dougherty came by for a little while every day just to check on me. McCabe sometimes came with him but was quite deep into her investigations with her tech team so she couldn't come every day. They brought me a replacement pair of hot pink Chucks. Apparently, Dougherty had noticed my old blood-soaked pair in the trash when he'd been cleaning up in my apartment after the revenant attack. It made me cry. They were even the right size!

In terms of my other focus, researching the nature of psychic communications between vampires and humans (or more or less humans), I had some help from Star and her family.

Star, Sarah, and Josh came to visit at least every other day. Josh was learning how to bake and brought samples of his latest experiments for me to try. Most of his creations were pretty tasty. They went some way to improve my morale, particularly when consumed with Jello.

Eventually, I was feeling well enough that I started to get bored. Nurse Rosemary said that is always a sign a person is on the mend. Star brought me my laptop, a basket of magickal scrolls, an Internet rocket stick, and an OCR stylus so the scrolls could be scanned and uploaded to CloudWitch.

Star replenished my 'to scan' pile at every visit, taking any completed items back to the Emporium. After a few days, I had worked my way through all the loose scrolls and had started to work on lightweight paper folios. By the end of that first week, I was using the OCR pen to scan oversized hardbound Books of Shadow.

I'd settled into a nice routine: napping, scanning books, researching things on CloudWitch, reading everything I could find on revenants, ritual magick, and the like. It was almost pleasant.

Until one night, as I was falling asleep, I heard the opening motif of "Clair de Lune.

Chapter Fourteen

I tried to push the sound of the music away, but the psychic pressure of Leopold's presence was too insistent.

~Feeling better, dear girl?~

Yes, much better.

~I am surprised you are alive. I searched and searched. It was like being in a room and smelling the perfume of the person who has just left. There and not there, at the same time. Curious business, that. I assumed it meant you were dead. Were you doing something to keep me away?~

I wasn't, no, but the doctors put me in a coma to help me heal.

~On purpose into a coma?~

Yes.

~Whatever for?~

It's a common medical practice to stabilize people who are really injured. There was some kind of infection.

~From the revenant's bite?~

Yes, the bite wouldn't heal, so they had to treat me with a St. Hubert's Key.

~Ah, yes, St. Hubert's Key. I know of those.~

Anyway, they had me on a lot of different kinds of medication for infection. I'm not certain, but I think something about the medicines kept you out.

~A reasonable supposition.~

I'm not on taking anti-infection medication anymore, just pain pills.

~I am glad we can speak again. I am glad you are not dead.~

I guess I'm your only hope of getting out of the Den any time soon.

~Can a vampire not become fond of a person, dear miss? Perhaps, after one hundred years imprisoned in my own mind, I might actually enjoy a little conversation?~

I shuddered. I didn't want to think too deeply about Leopold's ordeal. I held my mind blank, steady. Leopold seemed to pick up on the psychic equivalent to a dead-eyed stare and changed the subject.

~Be that as it may, the revenant has been killed?~

Yes, Dougherty says that after he had got me out of the apartment, he severed her head from her body, burned the parts in separate fires, and dumped the ash into two different streams.

~Thorough. Everything dies if you cut off its head.~

That should be stitched on a pillow somewhere.

Leopold's psychic presence rippled.

Did you just chuckle?

~I did, indeed, chuckle.~

I felt that.

~I'm not surprised. I understand that there will be more of that as we continue to converse and get familiar with each other. The necromancer I knew before had certain vampires he conversed with this way.~

You mean 'wirelessly'?

~Why would we need wire to speak?~

I'll explain another time. I need to get you some Time/Life year-in-review books or something, Leopold; we have a generation gap.

~Which is?~

I sighed out loud. More like a multi-generation gap.

Another of those changes that have happened since you've been indisposed. I know you will need help figuring out the modern world, but let's actually figure out a way to find the bad guys, get you out of the Den, and we can work on your twenty-first-century skills later.

~As you wish, dear girl.~

So, let me catch you up on what's been happening.

I felt Leopold nod.

The mundane cops are working their informants and checking records from other ongoing investigations of similar crimes. We think the social worker for some of the victims is involved, probably working in cahoots with his brother.

~I have known such men. Usually, a weaker one follows a stronger one and becomes his creature.~

These days, I think we'd say, 'becomes his bitch', but I like your phrasing better.

~Your feelings taste of . . . guilt, I think? What do you have to be guilty about, dear girl?~

I sighed. I did not want to tell Leopold I'd broken my word to him and told McCabe and Dougherty. Of course, trying to not think about an elephant makes a person ruminate on elephants. *Fuck. Cat's outta the bag.*

~Indeed, it is . . . something about you telling somebody about me?~ His presence felt frosty, strained, the psychic equivalent to the coolly-arched brow.

I shifted my position in the hospital bed and thumbed the control to raise the head of the bed up. If I'm going to get chewed out, I should at least be sitting upright.

Dougherty and McCabe were wondering how I survived the revenant attack. Saying 'While she was chewing off most of my left tit, I had a sudden brainstorm to temporarily immobilize her with an HB pencil' was not going to satisfy them.

~I should hope not.~

So, what else could I have said?

Another ripple in the psychic pressure as he chortled, delighted.

~Had you considered perhaps making something up?~

Er, well . . . no.

More ripples of laughter

~Are many of the moderns like you, dear girl?~

What do you mean?

~I mean to say—you are—quite against my better judgment—very charming in your naivety. Pressed for an answer, your first thought was to blurt out the truth.~

Ripples, ripples, until Leopold's psychic pressure in my mind seemed to effervesce like sparkling water.

I fought the urge to pout. No one likes being laughed at.

~Hmm, I caught the feeling of that, but not the wording. It felt like the beginning of a sulk. Come now, let a lonely vampire have his harmless fun.~

That could be cross-stitched on a pillow, too.

I felt the slight relief of pressure I was starting to associate with Leopold shrugging.

~Very well. So, the mundane police know. Does Juliet?~

No.

~Are you certain?~

As I can be, yes.

~Does anyone know I've been building an alliance with you to secure my freedom.~

I think they guess that may be the case, but I've denied it.

~Why is that?~

The truth was, I wasn't certain. I felt—against my will—compassion for Leopold's existence. I wanted to revile him as a monster, but somehow, I had room to consider what it would be like to suffer what he has, the silver knives, the sexual assault, the imprisonment, starvation, loneliness, boredom . . . too much for me to process. I suspect I might want to protect him, even though he'd turned a teenager.

~I felt that, but couldn't make out the exact words. It feels like . . . compassion, pity?~

I took a sip of water from the paper cup on the bedside table.

I think I want to protect you.

~You protect me?~

No ripples. He wasn't laughing now.

I know it doesn't make any sense. I'm not sure I actually can, I'm not exactly a heavy hitter here, magickally or otherwise.

~No, that is not correct. You are not a heavy hitter *yet*, dear girl. Right now, your power is raw, unfocused, gunpowder before it is loaded into the shell. I have tasted your power, it is . . . superb.~

Well then. A compliment. I felt complimented, anyway.

~Perhaps we can salvage the situation.~

How so?

~Perhaps we approach Juliet and let her know I helped you during the revenant attack.~

Ok.

~Then perhaps we further tell her there is much I can teach you that I learned about necromancers of old.~

That will help me load the gunpowder into the shell?

~Yes, just so.~

But why would she risk letting you out? Especially when Dougherty and McCabe have some solid leads.

~Because it seems so far everyone has focused on the human side of these unfortunate incidents.~

And?

~One cannot cater to the various perversities here without, at some point, involving an actual vampire.~

It's true so far, the focus has been the human side, but that's because Juliet wants to handle any supernatural aspects herself. I shuddered at the thought of what that might mean.

~At present, you are involved in the human side of the investigation because you still labor under the notion you are yourself human. I can assure you that you are not. Your proper place is doing the metaphysical work and rooting out whatever vipers Juliet has foolishly clutched to her bosom.~

Ok, I am magick gunpowder, the Great and Terrible Oz, she needs me to help with the other part of the investigation, she just doesn't know it yet. How do you fit in?

~I do not know what an 'Oz' is, but I suspect that does not matter. Yes, you have my point precisely. I am uniquely positioned to help you use your power to find any supernatural co-conspirators. A tutor, if you will.~

If Juliet lets you out, you will load the powder into the shell?

~Indeed.~

And then what, she points me at whomever we think the supernatural co-conspirators are?

~That would be the next step, yes. I hope she can do so wisely, after proper consideration.~

You think she might be hasty?

~Juliet is not known for her patience, nor her planning.~

I have seen her behave impulsively. I was thinking of my first meeting with her, where Juliet had slapped and humiliated Yvonne. I pulled the woven cotton hospital blanket up to my chin. *I wasn't cold, so why was I shivering?*

~You seem to have a fear of Juliet—that is perhaps wise, dear girl.~

I felt myself nodding an assent. I wonder if Leopold could feel that?

~Yes, I felt your nod.~

How is it she became Acolyte of the Western Lands if she's not a planner and can be impulsive? I would have thought she'd need good political skills to rise to the top.

~The Western Lands were not then as desirable a habitation as you may now find it. The truly powerful Acolytes were, in my day at least, in Europe and Asia.~

Is it safe to say that Juliet, in order to gain power at all, had to be in the hinterlands?

~Yes, that is fair. She styles herself after the first generation of European vampires, more old-fashioned in the study and deployment of power. Juliet is still a bully, I assume?~

I have seen that side of her.

~Individuals can always be counted on to be themselves.~

I think these days we'd say that "everywhere you go, there you are. That actually is something that worries me about you, as well.

~Worried how?~

I'll be straight with you, Leopold. What you did, back in the day, with the teenager, turning him so you and your boyfriend would have a young man to use as a sex toy.

~Is that what they told you?~

I was told that you and your boyfriend/co-conspirator grabbed a sixteen-year-old boy and Turned him for sexual purposes.

~It was not as simple as that.~

Ok, so what was it?

~Carlos and I sometimes sought the attentions of young men who needed money.~

You paid him for sex, and for the fun of Turning him?

~Nothing as villainous as that, I'm afraid. You over-estimate me.~

So what was it, then?

~There was something special about him. We took him in. He was a handsome and clever boy; too special to live on the street, starving~

But you were exploiting him.

~That may be, but it did not seem so to us. He was often hungry, beaten by men who hate lovers of men, we wanted to help him.~

Provided he gave you what you wanted. I was surprised by the bitterness welling up in me.

~Everything has a price, dear girl.~

Even safety, even decency?

~In my day, yes. Has it changed so much?~ I felt his sneer, and my cheeks flamed.

Maybe not. But it should. Why did you Turn him?

~He asked us. He had been with us for many months, and then he got ill, started to show symptoms of the consumption.~

He had tuberculosis?

~Is that what they call it now? He preferred to live with us eternally with a just a few symptoms than die coughing blood, gasping for air. Can you blame him?~

I considered that.

Why not just ask Juliet for permission to turn him on compassionate grounds?

~We did ask. She refused. She felt he was too young, too small, and she did not like sickness. She wanted only beautiful specimens.~

So you Turned him anyway.

~I did. We loved him.~

And when she found out, Carlos ran away, and she tortured you were the only one she could get her hands on.

~Something like that~

A wave of sadness and compassion washed over me. *I don't know what to say, other than I am sorry.*

~I think I am through talking, dear girl.~

He disappeared from my mind with a wistful piano tinkle.

Chapter Fifteen

After my physio session the next morning, I watched The Price is Right and ate the hospital lunch. I was putting off talking to McCabe and Dougherty about Leopold's offer, and how and if we could present it to Juliet. At a quarter to one, I couldn't take any more rumination on the subject, so I dialed McCabe's cell.

"Go for McCabe," she answered.

"It's me, Suzanne."

"Developments?"

"Yes, with Leopold." "Are you in danger?"

"Not any more than I was before I talked with him."

I heard her exhale in relief. *Did seeing my number come up make her panic a bit? Fucking cops could be so hard to read.*

"I can be there in about two hours. I'll bring Paul with me; I was meeting him at that time anyway."

"Status update on your side, too?"

"Yes," she said. I heard what must have been a ring clack against the cell phone's mic as she shifted the phone in her hand.

"Suze, hold on a sec," she said, without waiting for me to reply. I could hear her talking to someone else in the room with her, but couldn't make out the words, just heard the sound of her voice.

"Suzanne, I gotta go, but Paul and I will see you at fifteen hundred hours. Krispy Kreme and coffee?"

I smiled. It's the little things that make a girl feel loved.

"Yes, please!"

"See you then."

I spent the next two hours reading *On the Interpretation of Dreams* and using the OCR stylus to scan in pages from some of the larger, heavier, folios. Some of the folios had beautiful illuminations, detailed ink drawings and other elements that could be a bit tricky to scan in using a stylus. Even so, as I worked, I noticed that my arm and shoulder felt stronger. The pain was less severe than it had been, too. As much as I hated to admit it, slowly the physio sessions seemed to be paying off. *I should tell Nurse Rosemary that I might be ready just for regular Tylenol now.*

That thought pleased me: I dislike taking pills, or drugs of any kind, really. I rarely drink alcohol. Thinking back, the last drink I'd had was the Frangelico Juliet gave us that night after the visit to the warehouse. I couldn't recall the alcoholic drink I'd had before that one.

I chalk my avoidance of altered states up to being a necromancer. From what I'd read, necromancy usually started to manifest for people as young adults in their late teens and earlier twenties. It can happen in childhood, though. I'd read a nineteenth-century case study of a girl who was only three when she started to speak with the dead. She ended up killing herself before she was ten. Horrible.

While I'd been scanning the folios, I'd left the TV on as background noise. The broadcast was well into early afternoon talk show fare. I dunno why we still call them talk shows since the people on them are mainly screaming, not talking. *How many histrionic displays does a lady need to see in a day? Zero, that's how many.* I flipped the channel.

Every other channel seemed to be on commercial breaks. You know the kind of commercials they have on during the day: commercials for shitty private trade schools that offer GED upgrades, ads for mini-mall lawyers who specialize in personal injury cases, and menstruation products. Lots of footage of blue-tinted water dribbling onto maxi pads interspersed with shots of young white women twirling in fields of flowers and competing in triathlons. *Ugh. Right, that's realistic.*

On second thought though, maybe that's how menstruation is, normally. *What do I know about normal?* My first period triggered all my latent necromantic abilities, so it was hard for me to separate what is a typical biological function from all the contact with the dead and the personal and family chaos that followed in its wake.

I shuddered. That's not a day I like to think about. There are more than a few of those days, actually. I stabbed at the remote with a stern index finger to shut it off. Outside my hospital room window, I saw low-hanging dark clouds, pregnant with rain. They were just starting to spit.

I suspect that if my necromancy abilities had manifested later in life, I might have been a more typical teenager. But after it manifested at age thirteen, I spent all of my energy trying to cope with it. When the friends I'd made in elementary school started developing crushes, or going to middle school dances, or experimenting with purloined liquor, I was going to mental health clinics with my mum trying to find out what was wrong with me. It took eighteen months before they'd ruled out any psychiatric issues. Most people who see, hear, and feel things no one else does is struggling with mental health problems, not necromancy.

Even after the professionals had determined I was having metaphysical experiences, not mundane crazy ones, people continued to treat me like I was crazy. That's by design. My mum had joined an online support group for friends and family member of those "afflicted" with paranormal abilities. People there had advised my mum we should keep quiet about my abilities. My mum loved me and didn't want anything bad to happen to me, so she made it very clear I was to let people believe I was crazy. She'd heard too many stories from people in the group about attempted kidnappings, hate crimes; you name it. She told me to take advantage of the fact that everyone thought I was nuts.

You might think that keeping my paranormal abilities a secret would be hard. It wasn't. My mum and dad were divorced about six months before I was diagnosed, so even he didn't know I'm a necromancer. He simply believed that I had "some problems" as a teen that somehow resolved when I went to college. He and I were never close after the divorce, so it really wasn't difficult to keep it from him.

So, from thirteen until I left for college, I let people believe I was delusional and having mental health episodes when in reality I was trying to figure out how to work with and manage my abilities. By the time I went away to college, I wasn't disabled by my necromancy anymore. I had learned enough ritual magick to keep it tamped down. In my last year of high school, I had even had a sort of boyfriend, though we never went very far with anything sexual, not much beyond kissing. Mainly we hung around playing video games and writing bad poetry together. He broke it off with me a few months before prom, so I didn't go.

I entered college an ostracized, friendless loner without any experience of the sex, drugs, and rock n' roll that people seem to think is the normal teenage experience. I don't actually think I missed out on all that much. I went to college in Oregon and lived in the dorms. This gave me some distance from my mum and anyone I'd known in high school. I took the opportunity to reinvent myself.

I kept up with ritual magick secretly, in private, but never shared that part of myself with anyone. I studied library science in college, so most of the other students were quiet, bookish young women. I fit in. On campus, our programme was nicknamed "Team Virginity," so I wasn't the only one who still had her v-card. The small number of friends I made at college would have rather talked about indexing systems than be drinking, partying and running around with various lovers, anyway. So would I. Eventually, just before graduation, I threw myself at a shy young man and got rid of my virginity just so I could say I had.

Just as I was finishing that last few pages of the last remaining folio, I glanced at the clock. Two fifty-two. I looked outside. The clouds were no longer spitting; and they were now trying to drown Seattle, one cold splat at a time. If you've never been to the Pacific Northwest, you may not know this about us, but the fact of the matter is that everyone who lives in Seattle is obsessed with the weather. In true Seattleite form, I noted that it had rained at least once a day, every day I'd been out of the coma. *Friggin' rain.*

Dougherty and McCabe walked in, bringing smells of dark coffee and warm sugar with them. "Suzi-Q, are you wearing a bathrobe with cartoon cats on it?" Dougherty asked, teasing.

For a moment, my mind flashed back to poor Bluebell and how I'd found her the night of the revenant attack. My eyes were wet. I sniffed and blinked back the tears. I took a deep, steadying breath.

"Of course," I said, "I'm a cat-lady in training." Even to my ears, my tone sounded brittle. No one was convinced.

McCabe shot Dougherty a dirty look. You know the look I mean, the look men either don't see or pretend they don't see, the look that says something like I can't believe you just said something you should know is so obviously wrong and will hurt her. She looked back at me and rolled her eyes. *The classic one-two punch.*

Dougherty's cheeks got slightly pink, but then his concrete cop-face dropped into place, and he forged forward, conversationally speaking.

"So, you have some news for us, Suzanne?" All business now.

"Yes, I do, and Wendy told me you guys do, too?"

McCabe stepped closer to the hospital bed and handed me the paper cup of coffee. She placed the box of doughnuts on the bedside table, picked up a paper napkin, and retrieved a doughnut with it.

"Doughnut? We'll fill you in as you eat, then you can tell us happened with Leopold," she said.

"Sounds good," I said, taking the napkin-wrapped doughnut from her. I placed it on my leg and opened the flap in the coffee cup lid, took a sip.

"Remember Jonathan LeFarge?" Dougherty asked. I thought for a moment, sipped my coffee again.

"He's the Head of Athletics at U-Dub, right? The one we think was supplying vampire blood to the basketball team at Seattle Collegiate High School?

"And we found out, the brother of Neil Geruyter," put in McCabe.

"Right, you guys told me about that before. Any luck getting Geruyter's juvie records unsealed?" I asked.

"Not yet, but we got something better," said Dougherty. I raised my eyebrows.

McCabe interjected, "My team in Vice compared his home IP address to IPs we know Bad Daddy's Moustache used."

"And they matched?" "Yes," she said.

"So, why wasn't he using a VPN to hide his IP?" I asked

Dougherty took a bite of his doughnut, chewed, and pointed with his chin to McCabe.

McCabe said, "He was using one, sometimes. It seems that the service he used to obtain a proxy IP was a bit flaky. He'd log on to the VPN, and stay hidden, but every once in a while, he'd leave his home computer unattended. It would go into sleep mode. When he next touched the keyboard, his computer would wake up, but the VPN wouldn't auto-connect. It would sometimes take him an hour or two to figure out he was showing his actual IP to the whole Internet."

I sipped my coffee and considered this. "So, basically, he cheaped out, had a membership with a shitty VPN company, and his IP was exposed in error?"

"Yes, exactly," said Dougherty. He had shards of the Krispy Kreme sugar glaze on his shirt and brushed at them absent-mindedly.

"He eventually realized it, I guess?" I asked.

"Yes, he did, and changed to a more stable, more expensive VPN platform, but the records we had were enough to get a warrant for a search."

"Then what?"

"We nailed him!" Dougherty said, his eyes a brilliant blue. He was getting a little adrenalin spike just thinking about it.

"When we served the warrant and searched his place, he said nothing to us, just sat on the porch and made some calls on his cell phone. Unis weren't close enough to hear what he was talking about," said McCabe.

"It had better have been a good defense lawyer," said Dougherty gleefully, "We found 20 terabyte drives full of child porn stored at his house."

"Did the porn have any revenants in it?" I asked.

"My team has just started reviewing the contents earlier today, so I'm not sure yet. Probably there will be some of that, it will take some time to get it all sorted," said McCabe.

"If there is, we'll find it," Dougherty said, "We've been given approval for all the overtime we need."

"When did you guys pick up Jonathan LeFarge aka Doug Geruyter aka Bad Daddy's Moustache?"

"I think the best name for him is 'dipshit'. Simple, easy to remember," Dougherty said smiling. He reached for another doughnut.

"We served him at oh-seven-hundred hours this morning before he left for work," answered McCabe. "So far, he hasn't had much to say, so we're letting him stew in lock up."

"Has he talked to his lawyer?" I asked.

"So, that's an interesting thing," said McCabe, as she sat down and crossed her trousered legs at the knee. "Even though we know he made a bunch of calls this morning, it doesn't seem like any of them were to a lawyer. And we don't know who he called yet because before the unis realized what he was doing, he removed the sim card from his phone and . . . swallowed it."

Dougherty chuckled.

"Which brings me to the best part," he said. "Apparently, there is legal precedent where judges have decided it's ok to search a person's stomach contents when they've swallowed some evidence. The DA is right now trying to figure out if that means we can get authorization to pump his stomach regardless of him consenting, or if we have to wait for him to shit it out. Which means the toilet in his holding cell has been removed, temporarily, and if he wants to shit, he's going to have to go in a box under supervision." Dougherty laughed harder.

McCabe sipped her coffee. "The IT department tells me that stomach acid won't actually destroy the sim card, so we'll know who he called eventually."

"And until then he can just use a litter box!" Dougherty laughed so hard it made me laugh. It wasn't that funny to me, but the fact it was that funny to him was entertaining. Eventually, even McCabe snickered a little.

We finished our coffee and the half-dozen doughnuts they had brought, chatting about some of the details of the ongoing Vice investigation into online pedophiles, how the cases overlapped. Dougherty was jovial throughout. It was good to see him smile. It made me dread having to tell them about Leopold. I was reasonably certain it would take the shine off Dougherty's mood and refresh McCabe's request to have me off the case.

To the sticking place, Suzanne.

"So, do you guys want me to tell you what happened with Leopold last night?"

McCabe and Dougherty both sat a little straighter in their chairs. Cop-face times two was installed.

"Yes, please," said McCabe, while Dougherty nodded.

"So, you know my theory that Leopold wasn't able to talk with me psychically because of the silver–based antibiotics?"

They nodded in unison, eyes watching my expression carefully.

"It would seem that my guess might be right, because last night, my first night without that antibiotic, he made contact."

"And?" Dougherty prompted, shifting in his seat. He licked his lips. *Was he getting nervous*?

"He says that he wants out of the Den." Dougherty shrugged and made a disdainful noise.

McCabe said, "We expected that."

"Here is his reasoning." I paused to finish my last sip of coffee. It was cold now, and my stomach was a bit unsettled. *Too much sugar from the doughnuts*?

I continued, "Leopold says that Juliet doesn't know it yet, but she will likely need my help in finding out who among the vampires has been working with the pedophiles. He thinks it's likely a lot bigger network that she suspects. He also said that Juliet is a weak leader with poor planning, that she can be impulsive."

"Those sound like vampire problems to me," said Dougherty.

McCabe looked at him sternly. "Yes," she said "but vampire problems have a way of becoming human problems, eventually," McCabe cautioned.

"That's fair," assented Dougherty. He shrugged.

"From my perspective, if we can snip this off at the ground, but if we leave the root there, it will just regrow in the future," I said.

"So, what does he propose to do about it?" asked McCabe

"Leopold says that he is uniquely positioned to train me to blend my necromancy abilities with certain ritual magicks, that I have power, but it's not really . . . weaponized yet," I said.

"And let me guess, he can help weaponize you? And all we have to do is convince Juliet to let him outta the box?" Dougherty asked.

Wendy raised her eyebrows. "How so?"

"He said that his co-conspirator many years ago before Juliet put him in the box, was a necromancer. He was also a ritual magick user for most of his human life before he became One Who Walks Between."

"Goddamn it, why are fucking vampires so pretentious!?" exclaimed Dougherty.

McCabe and I looked at him, startled.

"'Den of the Forsaken', 'Acolyte of the Western Lands', 'Those Who Walk Between' . . . would it really be so hard for them to say 'jail', 'queen bitch', and "scary-ass vampires'?"

"We've talked about this before, Paul. It's cultural, you know that," said McCabe.

"Yes, Madame Anthropology, I get it; doesn't mean I have to like it."

McCabe sighed.

"Ok," said McCabe, "but what assurances do we have that he won't just run off once he's free and not help at all?"

"He says he will swear an oath to help."

"So what?" asked Dougherty.

"That's actually a big deal, Paul. He must, as a kind of dead, tell Suzanne the truth to the best of his knowledge. That leaves him room to manipulate his wording to deceive her without outright lying, but vampire lawyers have skill at drafting documents that anticipate any such loopholes," Wendy said.

"He also said he was prepared to do it inside a sacred circle with me, and let Juliet watch so that she can see it being done."

"Really? Interesting . . ." said McCabe.

"Interesting how?" Dougherty asked.

McCabe tucked a strand of her long red hair behind one ear. "He's essentially offering to pledge fealty to Suzanne, to be loyal to her, help her in any way he can. That's some serious magick."

"You make it sound like an offer of marriage or something," I said. That thought made me uncomfortable.

"It's more binding than that, Suzanne: a person can get a divorce; the only way out of such a pledge for Leopold would be to meet the sun . . ."

Dougherty made a scoffing noise and rolled his eyes.

McCabe gave Dougherty the disapproving fisheye, and continued, "for him to destroy himself or if you yourself actually severed the magickal bond."

"He must want out really badly if he's willing to do that," said Dougherty.

"Well, as Wendy said, we already figured out he was desperate." I added, "With what is in CloudWitch and with Star's help, I think I can design a ritual that will bind Leopold to my service."

Dougherty shifted uncomfortably. I don't think he liked this one little bit. He got up and started to gather the used napkins and empty cups from our snack.

McCabe said, "Having a more experienced magick user to help you is a good idea. I think you will also need to consult with a vampire lawyer as well. I think my captain has someone we've used before. I'll get something set up, a Skype consultation or something."

"Ok, when Star comes by later on I'll find out when she can be available for a conference call, and we can coordinate something."

"Ok, and then just email me when she available, and your availability as well?" McCabe asked.

I grinned. "As long as I don't miss The Price is Right, any time works for me. Do you think we could schedule it to conflict with physio?"

Dougherty was seated again after disposing of the trash. He raised one eyebrow. "No dice, missy."

"Can't blame a girl for trying," I said.

Dougherty smirked. "That's a debatable point, but never mind that for now. I think before we contact any lawyers it would be important to find out if Juliet will even agree. Wendy, I think we're going to have to kick this upstairs."

"Meaning?" I asked.

"Meaning Dougherty thinks that Juliet will be more likely to agree to this if the request comes the top," said Wendy.

"Yes, exactly," he said, "we can request an audience with the chief through our captains."

Wendy said, "Yeah, my guess is that given that we've got approval for all the OT we need, they'd agree to almost anything to wrap this up sooner rather than later."

"Yep," Dougherty said, nodding.

"Ok, sounds like we have a plan: Dougherty and I will ask our respective captains for an audience with the chief. You'll continue to research what you need for the ritual, getting some help from Star on the strictly magickal side, as well as insight from Leopold on how magick and necromancy will interact," Wendy said, her eyebrows raised.

"Yep," said Dougherty.

"Yes, even though that means I can't ditch my physio sessions," I said.

Chapter Sixteen

After Dougherty and McCabe had left, I fiddled around a bit with CloudWitch, saving passages that seemed relevant to binding and loyalty spells into a Word document. Eventually, the hospital staff brought me some supper. I was just finishing it when Star arrived, with her step son Josh in tow.

The three of us exchanged some pleasantries about goings-on at the Emporium. Josh was pleased to announce he'd been chosen as Evergreen High's mathelete in the state tourney coming up in January. Eventually, Josh started to play a game on his cell phone, and Star and I got down to brass tacks.

"There is something I could use your help with," I said.

"Ok, shoot," replied Star.

"I'm told that there are binding and loyalty spells that could be used to help ensure that Leopold's promises to me are kept."

"Why is Leopold making promises to you?" she asked.

I filled in Star regarding my conversation with Leopold and the discussion that I'd had earlier with McCabe and Dougherty. Star wore a skeptical expression. Josh was interested enough that he stopped thumbing his phone, and sat still, listening.

"Ok, lemme see if I have this straight. The best information you have is that Leopold, himself a magick user during his life and now his afterlife, used to know a necromancer. Leopold says he has special knowledge of how necromancy and magick interact, and can guide you in ways that no other person- human or vampire- can," Star said.

"What about Madame Mogaba?" asked Josh, not looking up from his phone. He'd gone back to playing his game. His thumbs flew over the controls.

"What?" asked Star. We both looked at Josh quizzically.

"Remember when you came out to me as a necromancer, Suzanne?" he asked. Still no eye contact; he was an expert multi-tasker.

When Josh had turned fourteen last year, Star, Sarah, and I decided that he was old enough to know about my necromantic abilities, old enough to appreciate the safety concerns I had. Old enough to keep my abilities a secret, in other words. Being raised by two lesbian parents, he was well aware of how bigoted people could be. When I came out to Josh, he'd been curious about how many necromancers there were, and how many of us opted for secrecy versus how many opted for notoriety, wealth, and greater security risks. I'd mentioned The Amazing Rolando and Madame Mogaba as examples of necromancers that had chosen the money, fame, and high- risk option. It seemed he'd filed those names away for future reference.

I considered Josh's suggestion. I said, "Well, I guess I could contact her and try to get an audience with her, but it would cost tens, if not hundreds of thousands of dollars. I bet she also has a waiting list for clientele as long as my arm, too."

Josh looked up, nodded. "Yeah, I guess so. I just wish there was a way to fact-check what Leopold has to say against a neutral party."

Star nodded. "I feel the same way, but I bet Suzanne is right, the time and money involved rules it out."

"Plus, Star can help with some of that, right? As a point of reference?" I asked.

Star shifted in her chair and crossed her arms over her round belly. "Yes, in terms of magickal theory. I'm rusty in terms of practice, but the theory part never leaves you," she said.

A few years after Star opened the Emporium she stopped the routine practice of ritual magick. She hadn't said much about her decision other than participating in a community and selling to a community at the same time felt like a bad boundary to her. She'd said she wanted to keep her business decisions clean from any politics in the magickal communities, and the best way to do that was to wear just one hat, the small business owner hat.

She no longer practiced magick in any of the Seattle circles, and apparently being a sole practitioner like me didn't appeal to her. Sarah, Star's wife and Josh's mum were only very slightly spiritual; the family occasionally went out of state for large group gatherings at Beltane and Lughnasadh.

My cell phone rang, McCabe was calling me. I grabbed it off the bedside table and pressed the green telephone icon button.

"Hey, Wendy."

"Hey, Suze. Star with you right now?"

"Yes."

"Can you ask her if tomorrow at fourteen hundred hours is ok for a Skype conference call?"

"Ok," I said into the phone. Looking at Star, I said, "Wendy can set up a meeting via Skype so that a vampire lawyer can help us edit any ritual we write to bind Leopold to me."

"Good idea. When?" she said.

"Tomorrow at two in the afternoon." "Where?"

"You could Skype in from the Emporium, or we could do it together from here," I said.

"Two works for me. Coming here is preferable, more privacy in your hospital room than the Emporium."

I spoke into the phone. "Star says two is fine; we'll Skype in from here on my laptop."

"Great," McCabe said, "I'll email you the particulars."

"Ok. Talk to you later."

"Bye for now."

I pressed the red telephone icon button on my phone and put it back on the bedside table.

"Hey," Josh said, eyes on his cell phone screen, "Is this guy a human lawyer who knows a lot about vampires, or a vampire who is also a lawyer?"

Star looked at me, eyebrow raised. It seems like that was her question, too.

"Wendy said something about him being a lawyer who also happens to be a vampire, and has legal expertise in all kinds of vampiric legal stuff," I said.

"Makes sense," said Star. "It's not like he hasn't had decades to develop his expertise." She smirked.

I grinned. "True enough."

Not looking up from his phone, Josh said: "You guys going to work on your magick stuff now?"

"I guess we better," I said, looking at Star with eyebrows raised.

She nodded.

"Ok, well, I'm going to the hospital cafeteria, get some of the Jello Suzanne keeps talking about," he said.

"Do you need some money?" asked Star.

"Mum Number Two, I am a teenage boy. I'm never going to say no to your money," he said, waggling his eyebrows.

Star smirked and handed him a ten-dollar bill from her purse. "Come back in about an hour, ok."

"Sure. I don't want to have to take the bus home in this rain," he joked.

Star and I got to work crafting a first draft of the ritual.

Chapter Seventeen

The misting rain was illuminated by the yellow halo cast by the parking lot light. Despite the rain, it felt good to be outside in the night, even if it was in the parking lot of a warehouse near Issaquah. Other than the ride home from the hospital earlier today, I'd been cooped up for almost two weeks. It felt like it had been two years. Besides, the light mist was fine and soft, hardly even rain at all, by Seattle standards. I had been so grateful to leave the hospital earlier today; I seriously considered kissing the rain-slick asphalt of the parking lot.

Dougherty and McCabe were standing in the halo of light with me. Dougherty, leaning against the lamp post, was sipping a gas station coffee as we waited. McCabe took a package of Belmont Kools from the inner pocket of her forest green suede jacket, delicately placed one between her lips, and lit it with a practiced snap of her wrist. The stainless-steel Zippo in her hand gleamed like a mirror.

"Since when do you smoke?" asked Dougherty, as he raised his eyebrows.

"I don't, usually," McCabe said, avoiding his gaze. "I only do it when I'm nervous." Dougherty said nothing and took another sip of his coffee.

What could be making McCabe nervous? She wasn't nervous the first time we were at this warehouse. She's not nervous talking to pedophiles or grumpy senior detectives like Dougherty or dominatrices or half-naked butch bois in leather harnesses.

Before I could say anything, Dougherty asked, "This have something to do with that scrawny, red-headed dink up at Juliet's? That kid who's one of her flunkies . . ."

That's right! Jack, her ex-boyfriend. I scowled at Dougherty. I looked at McCabe. "Wendy, his name is Jack, right? We talked a bit about him that night we all went to that greasy spoon."

Blushing, McCabe nodded.

His coffee finished, Dougherty crushed the cup in his hand and looked around the parking lot for a trash can. As he turned his head, I could see a knot of muscle working in his jaw. I think McCabe saw it, too, because she let out a slow breath, straightened her shoulders, and took a defiant drag on her cigarette.

To both of us, she announced, "Yes, his name is Jack. Yes, he works for Juliet, he has ever since he was Turned. She needs him; he's the only one in her entourage who can drive."

"And you figure he'll be on chauffeur duty tonight," I guessed.

Dougherty narrowed his eyes as he looked at McCabe, and then at me. He ran his rough hand over his close-cropped hair, then wiped the moisture on his pants leg.

"Friggin' rain," he said under his breath. "Don't tell me you're afraid of that carrot-topped little doofus," he said, more loudly.

McCabe shook her head. "No, that's not it at all, Paul. It's just . . . weird seeing him after all this time. If he comes tonight, this will be only the second time I've seen him since we broke up." Her voice trailed off, and she drew on her cigarette again. Her eyes welled with tears.

Dougherty shrugged and muttered something about getting something from the car. *Expecting me to comfort her?* But before he could walk away, a black Lincoln Towne car slid into the parking lot and drew close to where we were standing. Through the windshield, I could see Jack's pale narrow face and shock of unruly orange hair.

Jack parked the Towne car and got out of the vehicle. He cast a few quick glances at McCabe but kept his eyes to himself otherwise. Without fanfare, he opened the rear driver's side door.

Bao, moving like liquid silk, emerged from the car. He was wearing the simple black pants and black shirt I had seen him in before, with an unzipped black leather jacket added to the ensemble. As before, his expression was impassive, blank. *I wonder, do vampires get cold? Or do they dress seasonally so they can blend in?* Bao offered his hand to Yvonne for balance as she emerged from the car. Her bulging pregnant belly made the process awkward and ungainly. *Good grief. Imagine being pregnant for decades.* I shuddered.

Yvonne's four-inch spiked heels didn't help matters on the gracefulness front. She teetered on her shoes like her behemoth baby bump threw off her center of gravity. She was impeccably dressed for the occasion in skinny grey jeans and a nubbly long-sleeved red tunic sweater. She had accessorized her outfit with a wide hammered gold cuff bracelet and an Egyptian ankh suspended on a long chain. Her silky black hair spilled down her back. It gleamed raven-blue in the parking lot lights. Her red sweater did nothing to enliven her complexion. She was pale as milk, her cheekbones angular, her eyes hard and glinting.

Jack walked around the tail of the car and opened the other rear door. Bending slightly, he offered his hand to Juliet. This gesture was clearly protocol, as she slipped from the car with feline grace. Juliet wore her warm brown hair in two braids. Her braids were tied off with short pieces of thick yarn. She was dressed in an ankle-length coat constructed of variously-colored square suede patches sewn together. She was shod in butterscotch leather clogs that had been painted with folk art flowers. Her fangs rested delicately against the plump pink cushion of her lower lip. Janis Joplin meets the Queen of Darkness.

Dougherty pushed the door open, as I cringed at the screeching. The warehouse was dark. "Does anyone remember from the last time where the light switches are?" I said.

Yvonne said, "To your left, necromancer."

I pressed the bank of light switch buttons, and the fluorescent tubes above us started to hum and flicker. The light stabilized.

"Suzanne, how much room do you need for your working circle?" Juliet asked.

I looked around. The circle of rock salt and lavender buds I had made the last time I was here was still mostly intact. I stepped toward it and inspected it more closely. It looked like curious mice had investigated the salt crystals and dried flower buds. They had added a few droppings of their own manufacture here and there. Otherwise, the circle was more or less intact.

"The one from the first interview is ok, needs a little maintenance, but I can do that quickly, no problem," I said.

"Jack! Bao! Kindly retrieve Leopold's coffin and bring it here," Juliet commanded.

All the time I'd spent scanning and uploading grimoires and books of shadow into CloudWitch while I was recuperating in the hospital had paid off. I had a pretty good idea how to undo the spell cast on Leopold's coffin back in 1911. Arrogant or no, I wasn't worried that I could break open the previous necromancer's spell. I was worried that my psychic link with Leopold would weaken my hold on the containment circle. Yes, Juliet had reassured me that she, Yvonne, Jack, and Bao would be able to hold Leopold physically, if it came to that . . . but still, I worried.

Normally a garden-variety magick user would cast a circle around the coffin of the vampire to be released. This was to provide some control over the starving and disoriented vampire. Without a magick circle, he might run around crazily, grabbing the first person he found, drinking, murdering, running amok. The point of having him in a magick circle was to keep him under control until he had fed enough to be somewhat rational.

While Jack and Bao went to retrieve Leopold's coffin to the working area, I slid my messenger bag off of my right shoulder. Bending over, I rummaged until I found what I needed: a hand-held whisk broom. I flicked the mouse droppings out of the circle and away from the line of salt and lavender. I whisked an opening in the circle, then started to tidy the edges of the salt line. Tiny, tentative mouse feet had made the line less-than-crisp. *I hate a messy circle.* I left a sizable break in the line so the men could carry the coffin into the center without treading on the salt.

Just as I completed the last of the maintenance, the men returned, each holding one end of a flimsy raw pine box, slightly more than six feet long. It looked a bit spindly and thrown together. They placed it in the center of the working circle, then backed out through the opening, careful not to dislodge the salt.

Dougherty cleared his throat, "How does it keep him contained for all this time-it looks pretty flimsy."

Yvonne and I spoke at the same time, "The magick does it."

Juliet smiled at me.

McCabe looked at Juliet, and then at me. I saw a question form on her face, and I felt my face start to flush. *Never mind that,* I told myself, *focus on what you're doing*.

I took a deep breath while I closed my eyes, centering myself. "Shall they enter the circle, necromancer?" asked Juliet.

Eyes closed, I nodded. I could feel everyone's eyes on me, and the interested spirits just beyond the veil. *Fucking dead people, they're so pushy.* I nudged that thought away and breathed some more.

When I opened my eyes, Yvonne and Bao stood on either side of the coffin inside the "C" of salt and lavender buds. I walked over to the opening in the line and sprinkled more salt to make the "C" an "O." I stood just outside the boundary of my magickal working. The toes of my hot pink Chuck Taylors almost touched the salt.

In my mind's eye, the circle was actually a sphere. I didn't know if Leopold could fly or not. To be cautious, I had decided my casting should be in all three dimensions.

Humming a note from a minor key, I opened myself. As always, at first, I felt nothing. I was an empty meat suit, deaf and hollow. I leave myself when I do a casting, to prepare, or maybe just because I'm afraid.

The bubble of silence burst. My ears roared with the voices of the dead. I flinched from the force of the sound. It made the injuries on my shoulder and chest ache. The healing skin felt hot and tight.

I took a deep breath and blew it out slowly. I focused my attention on the feeling of breath in my body. The wall of sound that enclosed me dulled. It faded into the background like the radio in a car that is driving past you.

"Leopold von Ursler. I come tonight to release you from this Den. You are forsaken no longer."

I heard scrabbling from inside the coffin.

A small puff of dust escaped a crack in the pine.

"Juliet, Acolyte of the Western Lands, is here, and I do her bidding."

The coffin creaked.

"It is her will that you be released from bondage, and harm none."

I heard a dry rasp. *My gods, is that his voice? Is he laughing? Never mind that, focus.*

I felt some force around the coffin give way. It was like two magnets had been held close together, then abruptly shut off. The force was noticeable to me only in its absence. I think Juliet felt it disperse too, as her impassive, cold face showed a micro-second of surprise. She shifted her weight from one foot to the other. *That's her binding-will released.*

I visualized my necromancy as a sinuous tendril of red light. I used it to probe Leopold inside his coffin.

~Suzanne?~

"Yes," I said out loud. *It's rude to have a psychic conversation when others are in the room.*

~There is a spell.~

"I know there is. I know what to do."

~Why do you wait?~

"I'm trying to figure out if you'll lose your shit if I snap the old spell."

~I cannot lose my shit. Vampires have no shit, and even if we did, I have been starving for a century. I'm empty.~

"It's an expression. Never mind. Are you in control?"

~I . . . I'm not sure. I think I am.~

"If I snap the spell and you eat everybody, break the containment sphere, and run amok across the Pacific Northwest, neither of us will ever live it down," I said, whistling past the graveyard.

He chuckled in my mind. I think he was too dry to chuckle with his body.

~There is only one way to know, dear girl.~

"Break the spell, necromancer!" Juliet commanded.

I sighed. I visualized the old necromancer's spell as a dirty band-aid taping the coffin closed. I put every concrete detail I could think of into the visualization- the stickiness of band-aid adhesive on the skin, the peculiar smell of old band-aids—medicinal, sour—the texture of the plastic if you run a fingertip over them. I wrapped the red tendril of my necromancy around the old spell and yanked.

The pine boards of the coffin clattered to the floor, and the nails flew outward, plinking off the inside of the protective sphere as if it were made of glass.

At first what was revealed looked like a pile of tattered rags and dried sticks. There was no part I could look at and say "Oh, that's his hand" or "I think that's his knee." Leopold's psychic presence was gone suddenly from my head, our psychic link severed as abruptly as a neck in a guillotine.

Leopold?

No response. I started to hum "Clair de Lune" in my mind, eyes closed, gathering my energies.

"Leopold?" I said, while mentally focused on the tune in my mind.

Nothing.

"Yvonne, feed him," Juliet said.

Yvonne, ungainly in her advanced pregnancy, knelt on the concrete near what I imagine she supposed was Leopold's head. Bao crouched behind her, balanced on the balls of his feet. Yvonne, kneeling, leant back slightly against Bao, resting against his torso. She rolled up her left sleeve, and slit open her inner forearm with an adamantine fingernail. She'd made a vertical cut along her inner arm, not a horizontal one across her wrist. I think I read somewhere that – in humans at least—it made the blood flow more freely. *Wonder if it's true for vampires, too?*

Yvonne's blood was thick, sluggish, almost black in color. If I hadn't seen her cut herself for the purposes of giving blood, I might have thought she'd spilled a ribbon of molasses down her arm. Yvonne extended her forearm over where she must have imagined Leopold's mouth was. Bao assisted, his thumbs holding the edges of the cut open. *Trying to stop her from healing too quickly?*

Drip. Drip. Drip.

Moments passed as we watched Yvonne allow drops of her blood to fall into Leopold's mouth. Despite Bao's assistance, every few minutes she had to stop and re-open the wound with her thumbnail. Juliet stared at Yvonne, Bao, and the remains of Leopold as if hypnotised. McCabe, eyes unfocused, seemed to have pulled back into her private ruminations. Dougherty shifted from foot to foot, uncomfortable, looking everywhere except the magick circle.

In my mind's ear, I could hear the beginning of "Clair de Lune," as though someone was playing the piano a block away. The rag pile twitched. Neither Yvonne nor Bao moved. Their concentration was immaculate.

The rag pile twitched again. The music in my mind got louder, closer. I could see wavy golden hair growing out of the far end of the rag pile. Gradually the pile of tattered cloth and dried brown sticks started to shift, filling out the cloth. Now I could see a narrow foot extending from a pants leg. Then the other foot. Then hands emerged from the tattered lace of the shirt cuffs.

Over ten minutes, a human-looking body had emerged. It was like watching a film in reverse- instead of shrinking away like the wicked witch—I'm melting! I'm melting!— Leopold was . . . congealing? Reforming? Re-fashioning? *I wonder if vampires had a word for this process- must remember to ask Leopold later.*

Leopold, stretched full length in his ragged Edwardian finery, was still motionless but for occasional twitches. *Nerves firing as the muscles re-animate?* His skin texture and color was reminiscent of beef jerky.

"Put it in his mouth now, see if he will drink, it will be faster," Juliet said.

Yvonne leant over Leopold, pressing her slice wound against Leopold's parted lips.

I glanced at Dougherty- he looked relieved that this was going to hurry up. McCabe had emerged from her mental fortress of solitude; her eyes were fixed on Leopold and his transformation.

I reached out with my mind. *Leopold?*

Nothing.

Almost too fast for my eye to see, Leopold's hand shot up and gripped Yvonne's elbow while his mouth fastened onto her wound in an obscene kiss. He pulled her arm closer, unbalancing the kneeling Yvonne.

I could hear the wet noises Leopold made as he fed on Yvonne's arm, saw his throat working as he swallowed down huge hungry gulps of her blood like it was sticky toffee syrup.

Bao's brows knit together like silken caterpillars. He wrapped his arms around Yvonne from behind, tender, protective.

"Mistress, he takes too much," Bao said, his voice a low growl.

"He takes what he needs, what I offer him," she replied.

Leopold started to gnaw at Yvonne's arm, not just sucking at her wound, but using his sharp fangs to worry the flesh open wider. Leopold's face and hands looked pale and soft now, his wavy blonde hair lustrous.

Yvonne tried to pull away from Leopold, alarm on her face.

"Do not pull away from him, Yvonne. He will pull your arm completely off if he has to, let him drink," Juliet said.

Leopold was looking better by the second. Yvonne's face was creased with worry, but her body was limp, not fighting.

Bao glanced over his shoulder at me, eyes burning with rage.

He's starting to freak out. Oh shit.

"Please," he mouthed to me.

He thinks I can stop Leopold from draining Yvonne.

I took a deep breath, gathered my energies and pushed my will at Leopold as I had before breaking the wards that had bound him.

Leopold!

~Yes, dear girl?~

You're going to drain her, let her go!

I felt my psychic command bounce off of Leopold's unfettered will power.

Without the wards, I cannot compel him! Shit, shit, shit.

~It is true; you cannot command me, not without the bindings.~

Please stop! Juliet will stake you if you kill Yvonne! At the least, she'll put you back in the Den! You don't want to go back in the Den, do you?

I could feel Leopold's sigh.

~ Very well, I do see your point. It is a pity; I love the blood of my own kind, it is a rare treat, especially after a century of starvation.~

Please just stop it.

~As you wish.~

He released Yvonne's elbow. Bao pulled her limp body back against his chest, cradling her while her head rested on his shoulder, eyes closed.

"He does your bidding, necromancer?" asked Juliet.

"No, I can't compel him."

"Why did he stop?" she asked, head tilted in curiosity.

"Um, 'cause I asked him nicely?"

"Truly?" she asked, eyebrows raised.

"And I pointed out that you would likely stake him where he lies if he didn't."

"Very astute," she remarked "Come, now Leopold, do you still need more blood? Tell me truthfully."

Leopold sat up, his fair skin rosy across the cheeks, his eyes sparkling.

"Cack- hwelaugh," he said, eyes widening in surprise. A small cloud of dust floated from his mouth.

~I am not quite healed. Tell her.~

"He says he is not entirely healed yet; he needs more."

"Yes, it seems he is still very dry inside," Juliet said, nodding. "Bao, put Yvonne down, feed him a bit more, just enough so he is well-lubricated," she commanded.

Bao, expression flat, picked Yvonne up in his arms. Her body was still limp, her eyes closed. He brought her over to my edge of the magick circle, laid her tenderly on the concrete.

Against my will, I felt my heart start to pound. My stomach twisted, and my upper lip started to sweat.

~Too close to one of us? Your heart flutters like a trapped bird.~

Yes. You can feel that through the link?

~I can hear it. As can every vampire in the room. It's delicious.~

A shiver ran through me. Four unfettered vampires and maybe a thousand imprisoned ones, all perving on my fear and beating heart.

Gross, Leopold. I don't think I needed to know that.

~Yes, but now you are annoyed. Use that to push away the panic and calm your body.~

Huh. Had never thought of that. I cast my mind back to annoying encounters I have had with presumptuous men— cat calls, idiot remarks, guys coming into the Emporium who tried to make eye contact with my boobs.

~ Yes, that's right. Do you see? You can use anger to chase out fear.~

My body felt calmer. I swallowed my panic and edged away from Yvonne's supine body.

"Bao, what are you waiting for. Feed him!" commanded Juliet.

"Mistress, they are speaking," said Bao.

"I am sure Suzanne will not mind if he talks to her while his mouth is full."

Bao scowled and said nothing more. He walked over to Leopold and offered him a hand to help stand.

Leopold took it and slowly rose to his feet. He tried to draw Bao's wrist to his mouth. Bao took a step back.

"No. Not my arms."

Leopold looked a question at Bao, then stared at the other vampire's groin pointedly.

"Not there either, I am not a lover of men. The neck!" Bao sounded exasperated.

Leopold stepped closer to the shorter vampire, and gently grasped some of Bao's hair, angling Bao's head back. Leopold leant in, and delicately pierced the skin over Bao's jugular vein with his fangs.

Bao stood stoic and statue-still as Leopold drank from him, even when Leopold used his free hand to stroke Bao's cheek.

Leopold!

~Yes, dear girl?~

Why are you pushing your luck?

~You mean fondling Bao as I drink from him?~

Yes, he obviously doesn't like it, what point are you trying to make?

~If one does not use one's power, it becomes a question whether or not one actually has it.~

I wouldn't- we need you now, but what's stopping Juliet from putting you back in the Den once you've outlived your usefulness?

I had the mental impression of a drawn-out sigh.

~Very well, necromancer.~

Leopold retracted his fangs with an audible click, took his hands off Bao, and stepped away from the smaller vampire. He retrieved what once must have been a handsome cambric handkerchief from the breast pocket of his shabby coat. He dabbed at his lips delicately.

McCabe's concentration on Leopold was palpable; her body strung as tight at a bow string about to snap. Dougherty, standing beside her, was also on alert. His eyes noticed every small motion in the room. His hand hovered near his waistline. It looked to me like he wanted to be able to draw if necessary. *I wonder if he has silver bullets. Do they even work on vampires? I'll ask McCabe later.*

"Leopold, speak!" said Juliet.

Leopold shifted his position to face Juliet. With a flourish of his handkerchief, he gave her a courtly bow, saying "Mistress Juliet, I am healed enough for now. Thank you for my release from the Den of the Forsaken."

"Not a release, a reprieve . . . for now. We shall see."

Leopold's mouth pulled down at the corners in a slight frown, but he said nothing.

"And you, necromancer, what can you tell me about his private conversations with you?"

"I'm not sure what you are asking me," I said.

"Is he quite stable?"

"Not sure what you mean by that, but his side of the conversation is coherent, and he responds to reason, if that's what you mean."

Unexpectedly, Juliet smiled, dimples appearing on her plump face. "I suspect you want to say, 'are you, any of you, ever really stable?'." She chuckled to herself.

"ah . . . um . . ."

"Oh, close your mouth girl, you are gaping like a fish. No need to cater to my vanity, I know that your kind thinks us all mad things," she said, gesturing at all the vampires in the warehouse.

I bowed my head in acquiescence.

Juliet clapped her hands sharply. "Enough, we need to return home. Bao, take Yvonne to the car, leave her in Jack's care. Then come back here and clean this up," she said, nodding at the pile of splintered wood.

"Suzanne, after you break your circle and complete your ritual, get your things from Dougherty's car, you will ride back with us. You can communicate with the officers tomorrow if you must. Leopold, when the circle is down, follow me."

She turned on her heel and stalked from the warehouse.

Chapter Eighteen

An hour later I was unpacking my suitcase. The bedroom Juliet assigned me in her home was on the third floor. The window looked out onto inky blackness. There were no lights on at the back of the house, but I knew beyond the window, there was a velvet-deep forest.

The room itself was small but well-appointed. Whoever Juliet's decorator was, they had a thing for Mid-Century Modern. The streamlined dresser on angled legs was made of teak, the grass cloth on the walls authentic, and the linens on the bed at least six hundred thread count. Swank, in other words.

As I was laying out my toothbrush and other toiletries in the adjacent en suite bathroom, my cell phone rang.

"Suzanne Murphy," I said. "Suze, it's me, Star."

"Hey!" I realized I forgot to call her to let her know of my leaving hospital.

"Where are you?"

"I'm at Castle Dracula," I said, placing the packet of floss next to the brush. "The doctors released you?"

"Yep."

"And you've gone straight back to it, huh?"

I sighed. "I know, I know. I just want to get this done and over with."

Star paused. "I know you do, Suzanne, and I respect that. I'm just . . . worried about you."

"Worried-cause-you're-my-surrogate-mom worried, or worried-because-you-did-a-tarot-spread-and-the-omens-were-bad worried?"

Star chuckled. "Column A, column B, what's the difference?"

"I'm probably safer here than anywhere else."

"I know it, but I don't have to like it. I feel shitty that you can't stay here with us."

"You know I would like to, but I don't want to put you guys in danger," I said.

"I know, you are probably safest there, but I wish you were here anyway. Sarah was grumbling for a whole day after she heard you couldn't accept our invite. 'Damn vampires taking our girl away from us. They've never messed with me; I'd give them something to think about'."

Star did a passable impersonation of Sarah that made me smile. Sarah was an interesting woman, passionate and protective of the people she cared about. I was lucky to have such found-family, particularly since my mum retired to Phoenix last year.

I made myself comfortable on the bathroom counter. *Imagine a bathroom big enough that I can sit on the counter. Luxury.*

"So, what is your game plan out there at Castle Dracula?" Star asked.

"Well after the crash course in magicks I got from working on CloudWitch, the plan is I practice some location spells, get some hands-on help from Leopold in how my necromancy can make standard witchy work go sideways, do what we can to prevent that, and try to figure out where Geruyter is."

"And then?"

"And then, after all that, the cops will arrest him and hopefully he goes to jail for a billion years."

"Guys like him make me glad Washington state still has the death penalty."

I paused for a moment. "I'm not sure you really mean that."

"Maybe not, but the whole thing is so gross, I get so angry that these things are happening, and so angry that you were hurt . . ." Her voice broke.

"Star," I said softly, "It's ok. I am doing much better, I'm in the safest place I can be at the moment, and we're going to find a way to stop all this, ok?"

"I know, I know." She sniffed. "Sorry, I don't mean to put this all on you—it's ridiculous, actually—you were the one who was hurt, and I shouldn't make you look after me."

"It's ok, Star, really. I am feeling much better, and mostly I'm mad as hell and want to find a way to fuck this guy up."

Silence from Star's side of the phone call.

I started to wonder if we'd lost cell connection, then she said, "Like black magick fuck him up?"

"No, no, not that, but y'know, work hard at learning the new spells, work hard at modifying them, so my necromancy doesn't bugger them up, and just . . . give the cops his location so that they can nail him."

I let out a breath I didn't realize I'd been holding. My chest felt tight. I think I was actually angrier than I was letting myself feel.

"I'm glad to hear you say that, Suzi-Q."

"How come?"

"I've seen witches go some pretty dark places when they were out for revenge; I'd hate to see that happen to you. And quite frankly, given how much metaphysical juice you have, I wouldn't want to be in the splash zone, if you know what I mean."

"You think I'd be scary?" "Yep."

"How scary?"

"Like 'Now I am become Death, the destroyer of worlds' scary."

"Really?"

"Really."

"I'm actually a bit flattered you think I have that much potential."

Star's tone was stern. "Don't tease; it's not actually funny."

I felt abashed. She was right.

"You're right, that was a bad joke."

"It's ok; I love you anyway."

"I love you, too"

"Take care of yourself in Castle Dracula." "I will."

"Call if you need more scan-ables, or something from my personal library, or something from your apartment."

"The bag you packed for me seems to have everything I need. Not sure about books or supplies. I might have to send somebody else to pick it up, as I think I'm under house arrest here."

"Yeah, I figured"

"Love to Sarah and Josh, ok?"

"Yes, I'll tell them. They love you right back."

"Good! Talk you soon."

After Star rang off, I spent some time thinking about revenge and magicks. How committed was I to doing everything above-board? Could Leopold be trusted to honour my intentions? I thought not.

But my options to learn what I needed to learn were vanishingly thin. Could I talk to Juliet about it, get her to see that staying within lawful measures was better in the long run? Was it actually better? I knew I was going to have a hard time getting to sleep later, with these thoughts ping-ponging through my head.

*   *   *

I spent the next two days sleeping, and the nights in seclusion with books and CloudWitch, continuing my crash course in magicks. Juliet had hoped to do the ritual as soon as Leopold and I had been installed in her home, but Leopold needed time to convalesce. On Hallowe'en, Leopold finally had recovered enough that we could do the ritual. He was still weak and on bed rest, but his ki had healed enough that magick was possible.

As per the agreement we made in the Skype session, Juliet and I called Duane Booker, the vampire contractual expert who'd consulted on the binding ritual. He advised that he was not available until the evening of November second. We agreed on the time, and I spent the evening of November first going out and about with Jack, picking up supplies for the ritual and some human food for me. Castle Dracula had an extensive selection of alcohol and bags of refrigerated plasma, but not much in the way of actual food for living people. We also picked up some clothes for Leopold. The rags he had worn while imprisoned in the Den had been thrown away. Juliet had provided him with a pair of pajamas to wear while convalescing, but Leopold would need proper clothes if we were signing contracts in a business meeting/magick ritual.

At precisely seven p.m. on the designated night, a silver Tesla made its way around the hairpin curve in Juliet's driveway. I was sitting in the dark living room, supplies ready on the coffee table. I was startled from my own thoughts by the movement of the headlight's beams over the creamy yellow walls. I walked over the intercom system mounted on the wall and announced, "Duane Booker has arrived. Please come to the living room." I turned on a few lamps; we would need more light than just the candles we were going to use in the ritual. Or at least I would. Vampire night vision is excellent, but mine, not so much.

By the time I turned around to answer the door, Jack was already opening it for Duane Booker. Booker was a dark-skinned black man with close-cropped hair. He was dressed in a charcoal grey suit with a lavender shirt and an Imperial purple tie. He carried a leather briefcase and had a camel cashmere overcoat draped over his arm. He was wearing the most beautiful oxblood leather brogues I had ever seen. They looked like they cost at least six months of my salary at the Emporium.

Booker noticed my glance at his shoes.

"They are beautiful, aren't they?" he asked, his bass voice so deep it made my breastbone vibrate.

I nodded.

"I had them handmade for me the last time I was in Italy," he said, his dark chocolate eyes meeting mine.

I wasn't afraid to meet a vampire's glance anymore; I now had enough experience with them to realize my necromancy gave me immunity from any hypnosis they might try. I also knew that Booker wouldn't try, as he knew that I was some kind of psychic. Besides, he was a friendly—the SPD was certainly paying him enough in fees to merit a little professional courtesy.

"Where are my manners," he said, extending his hand. "I'm very pleased to meet you in the flesh, Suzanne Murphy."

My pale warm paw disappeared in the grip of his manicured ebony hand. We shook. He was wearing a gold signet ring that glinted when we did so.

"If you don't mind me saying so, Ms. Murphy, you look younger and smaller than you did on Skype," Booker said.

"Trick of the camera, I guess," I said, smiling. "This is Jack Oswald, one of Mistress Juliet's retainers; the others will join us in a moment."

Jack and Booker shook hands as well. Booker's French cuffs sported cufflinks that matched his ring. *This guy is well-kitted out.*

"Allow me to take your coat, Mr. Booker. Would you like a beverage? We have a house cocktail you might like to try," Jack said.

"Why not?" said Booker. "I will try the cocktail."

"Suzanne, anything for you?" Jack asked.

"Coffee, if there is some made," I replied.

"There is. I'll be right back," Jack said.

He walked away holding Booker's overcoat. Juliet passed Jack as she came through the archway, followed by Yvonne and Bao. Yvonne and Bao supported Leopold between them, his arms over their shoulders. Leopold seemed small and frail in the black pants and turtleneck sweater. Jack and I had guessed Leopold's size when we purchased him clothes. We had not gotten it right. Leopold looking fragile wasn't just a side effect of clothes that were too big for him. His gait was slow, uncertain. Nevertheless, his eyes were alert, fever-bright.

"Mr. Booker, I am Juliet, Acolyte of the Western Lands," she said, walking toward him.

"The pleasure is all mine, Madam," he responded, bending to kiss her hand. Juliet allowed it.

The doorbell rang, and I went to answer it. That must be McCabe.

"Hey Wendy," I said, opening the door.

McCabe had a worried look on her face. Nervous about seeing Jack again?

"The lawyer just got here," I said. "They're doing their introductions. Jack's getting drinks. I'm having a coffee. Do you want anything?"

Wendy took off her trench coat and shook the water droplets from it. "No, I'm fine."

We walked into the living room. Everyone was seated in a circle, sipping their drinks. A cup of coffee steamed on an end table. I sipped it while McCabe and Booker were introduced.

"We are all here now, and we have everything we need?" asked Juliet, glancing at McCabe.

McCabe nodded.

Booker cleared his throat and retrieved a sheaf of papers from his briefcase. "The usual thing, as I've mentioned, if for the practitioner and the vampire to perform the ritual, then sign the papers and have them witnessed. The contract is legally binding from the moment the papers are signed, but magickally binding from the moment of oath-taking. Do you understand Ms. Murphy? Mr. von Ursler?"

Leopold and I both nodded.

"Excellent. Please begin your ceremony whenever you are ready," Booker said.

Bao helped Leopold to a straight-backed chair sitting in the center of the circle. My basket of supplies sat on the floor beside it. When Leopold was seated and Bao had returned to his own seat, I retrieved my jar of rock salt and lavender buds, and sprinkled the mixture in a circle four feet in diameter, encircling Leopold and me. Standing behind Leopold, my hands on his thin shoulders, I closed my eyes and breathed deep to center myself. I could feel the energy of the earth under the foundations of the house, the energy of the stream that ran underneath this room at the bottom of the ravine. I heard the opening motif from "Clair de Lune."

Are you ready, Leopold?

~ Yes, dear girl, as always.~

I lit a red candle and placed it on the eastern edge of the sacred circle. "Hail to the guardians of the East, bringers of morning light," I said.

I lit another candle and placed it on the southern part of the circle. "Hail to the guardians of the South, bringers of warmth and growth."

I hailed the two remaining directions and their guardians, marking their places with candles also. I laid three tarot cards on the floor in front of Leopold: my card, The Star, on the left-hand side, the Two of Cups in the center, and Leopold's card, Strength, to the right.

"This company is gathered to witness Leopold von Ursler pledging his loyalty and fealty to Suzanne Murphy."

I felt energy stirring in my belly, and a musical note started to bubble up through my body. I sang the tone, my voice strong and clear as a bell. The circle was cast, sizzling like an electric fence.

"You may begin, Leopold," I said.

I stood behind him, hands on his shoulders, my eyes closed. In my mind's eye, I could see the red thread of my necromancy. I started to wrap the red tendril around Leopold, starting with his left leg.

"I pledge to you my truth," Leopold said.

I visualized wrapping his right leg with my power.

"I pledge to you my aid, whenever I can give it."

I wrapped glowing red energy around Leopold's hips and torso.

"I pledge to you my strength, my will. You are the hand; I am the glove."

I probed the center of Leopold's chest with the tip of the red thread, gently. His heart chakra was open to me.

"I am your servant and vassal. Our spirits are as one."

In my mind's eye, I pressed the glowing red thread through Leopold's chest, piercing him with my magick. When I touched the center of his spirit, my ears filled with the sound of "Clair de Lune," turned up to eleven. All the hair on my body stood on end. I started to tremble.

Leopold placed his hand over mine where it lay on his shoulder. Turning his head, he raised my hand to his lips and delicately pierced the tip of my index finger with one fang. A single drop of rich red blood welled up. It clung, shivering, to my fingertip before dropping onto Leopold's outstretched tongue.

I stopped trembling. I felt strong, certain. I exhaled a shaky breath, thanked the guardians of the directions, and magickally broke the circle, intoning, "It is finished."

The candles snuffed out of their own accord, wisps of smoke curling up towards the vaulted ceiling of Juliet's living room.

I looked at the spectators. McCabe wore a disapproving expression, her mouth a grim line. Jack wasn't paying much attention to the proceeding; he was focused on McCabe, looking at her with such longing that it was painful to observe.

Booker, Juliet, and Yvonne wore identical unreadable expressions— 'vampire neutral', I call it. Bao was looking at his shoes, but was holding Yvonne's hand, rubbing his thumb over Yvonne's knuckles. *Bao must be a closet romantic.*

~Yes, I think that is true.~

Gah- forgot you were there.

~Yes, I think it best you assume I am with you, rather than assuming I am not.~

Not certain how I feel about that.

Leopold chuckled in my mind

Hey, that tickles.

He chuckled harder. ~Rather too late to worry about that, dear girl. Even if we signed nothing, in magick I am yours.~

Well, I guess that means I can just order you to stop it, right?

~Only if I was harming you or was deliberately deceitful. Vexing you is entirely another matter.~

Great, we're the metaphysical Bickersons now, are we?

~I assume that is another popular culture reference?~

I sighed, this time out loud. *Leopold needed to get a Netflix account or something; this was getting ridiculous.*

"Ms. Murphy," Booker said, "Are you ready to sign now?"

I started. The psychic conversation with Leopold had made me momentarily forget about the others in the room. Now that he was my vassal, the communication was stronger, more engrossing . . .

~As is to be expected, dear girl. Mr. Booker is still talking to you, however.~

I shook my head to clear it.

"Yes, I am ready to sign now," I said. I walked to the teak console where Booker had laid out the document and proceeded to read and sign them.

Booker handed me a small Exacto knife. "Sign in blood, also, please."

I pricked the hole Leopold's fang had made in my fingertip, re-opening it, and signed with that. Then Leopold and Booker both signed the documents. McCabe and Juliet witnessed them.

Booker was just packing up his things when McCabe's cell phone rang. She stepped into the hall to take her call.

We said our formal goodbyes to Booker. Yvonne and Bao helped Leopold back to bed.

Juliet and I sat in the living room, sipping our drinks while Jack started tidying up, using a Dustbuster to suck up the rock salt on the carpet. When McCabe entered the room, he switched the small vacuum off when he saw the look on her face.

"What's happened?" I asked, feeling my panic start to rise.

"That was Dougherty," she said.

"Bad news," said Juliet, a statement not a question.

"Yes, he says that Joe Geruyter was found dead in his cell about an hour ago," Wendy said.

"Do they think he killed himself?" I asked. *Lots of people would, given the child pornography and sexual abuse charges he faced.*

"Only if he did it by ramming his own head into the cell bars a few hundred times," Wendy said, voice flat. She gave cop-face almost as good as Dougherty's.

"Murdered, then," Juliet said.

McCabe nodded.

"...and Neil Geruyter is still at large, no one knows where, right?" I asked.

"Yes, still a BOLO out on him, no leads."

"Do you think this social worker has murdered his brother somehow?" Juliet asked.

McCabe said, "It's possible, but really unlikely, I think. I mean, he might have been able to bribe an officer to do it . .. but there are other possibilities."

"Like another prisoner?" I asked.

"Not in this case, he was being held in PC to keep him safe, and city cells don't get too many skinners, so he was alone in his cell," McCabe said.

"Skinners?" ask Juliet.

"Jail talk for 'pedophile'," said McCabe.

Juliet nodded.

"So, if it wasn't Neil hiring someone to kill Joe, and it wasn't another prisoner killing Joe, who could have done it?" I asked.

"Another co-conspirator," said Juliet. Wendy nodded.

"Which means that this pedophile ring might be a lot bigger than we thought?" I asked.

"Yes, bigger, and more powerful, better-connected," Wendy said.

"Oh shit," I said.

Chapter Nineteen

I spent the next few evening researching geo-location spells. If McCabe and Dougherty were going to crack this case, they would need to nab Neil Geruyter. It seemed he was the ring leader and the key. And since the SPD's and state police's respective BOLOs had turned up bupkiss, I figured I might be able to help with a little magick.

The main obstacle I had encountered so far in my research is that all geo-location spells required a personal effect of the missing person. A toothbrush, a hair brush, used Q-tip, any of those would work well. The more intimate the object, the better the spell's accuracy. The crime lab would share items from Neil Geruyter's house on Dougherty's say-so. Getting the ingredients wasn't the issue. The problem was in the nature of geo-location spells themselves. No matter what magickal tradition one worked in—Gardnerian Wicca, Tibetan Buddhism, Voudun, Paolo Mayombe, various eclectic styles—geo-location spells are apparently notorious for how flaky and imprecise they could be, with no opportunity to practice it until perfect.

In most magick spells, a person could cast over and over again until she got it right. With geo-location spells, the magickal practitioner could only cast them once or, very rarely, twice. To even start a second geo spellcasting, a practitioner often had to work in another magickal tradition entirely. I did not yet fully understand why geo-location spells gave you one or just maybe two shots at getting it right.

Given that they are hard to cast, might not work with any precision, and offered no opportunities to fine tune or practice, most magick users didn't bother with them. Even experienced practitioners like Star had not ever cast one successfully. I wanted to learn all I could before I tried it.

I also spent time sitting at Leopold's bedside. Leopold was still recovering. I had expected that once he was strong enough to participate in magick, he would have been right as rain. Juliet told me that he needed not just blood, but also time. Apparently recovering from more than a century of starvation and solitary confinement wasn't an easy thing, even for a minor magickian/ major vampire such as Leopold.

As his strength gradually returned, we talked about magick, and he told me stories from his life before he was Turned. He had been very interested in all kinds of magick and alchemy before in his human life. Indeed, he implied his interest in metaphysics is what had eventually led to his contracting vampirism. I was very curious to hear that story, but he was not yet ready to tell it.

When Leopold was too tired to talk, I would read aloud to him. Mostly articles on twentieth-century history, culture and technology—thank gods for Google and BuzzFeed listicles "Top 10 Atrocities of the 20th Century," "Inventions We Take for Granted that Would Have Amazed your Great-Great Grandfather." Sometimes I read aloud to him from *Harry Potter and the Philosopher's Stone*. He thought the book was hilariously funny, but not at the actual funny parts. Vampires: they are weird.

We also watched movies from various decades. Juliet would often sit with us at those times. She had already seen *Star Wars* and *The Silence of the Lambs*, but apparently she felt they were worth repeated viewings. When we started in on the first season of *Breaking Bad*, she even invited Yvonne, Bao, Jack, and Wendy McCabe to join us, turning Leopold's room into a makeshift theatre.

Bao usually declined as he had seen the entire series before. He preferred to practice with his wooden katana on the side-yard patio for hours every night. The constant rain did not appear to bother him. Yvonne explained that said it kept Bao calm to practice. She didn't seem to mind him spending time alone, which surprised me a little. They always seemed glued at the hip.

Yvonne seemed to enjoy *Breaking Bad* as much as Leopold did. In between episodes, Juliet made Jack run downstairs and make kettle corn for McCabe and me as well as her disgusting house cocktail (two parts whisky, one part Southern Comfort, one part B-positive) for the vampires.

After about a week of bedrest, all the blood he could drink, and hours and hours of television, Leopold announced he was ready to try some magick. He suggested we practice with certain other spells that shared common elements with geo-location spells as a way to work around the problems of my relative inexperience and the finicky nature of what we wanted to achieve.

We scheduled our attempts for the Saturday evening after Hallowe'en.

Chapter Twenty

The night Leopold and I were scheduled to start practicing, I was sitting in my room with Juliet, waiting for Leopold to wake for the evening. Even though he was improving every day, he still needed more rest than the other vampires.

Juliet and I were discussing the upcoming election— new vamps usually voted, but older ones tended not to. Even though Juliet was not newly made, she did her best to keep up with the times. She had voted in every election since Roosevelt. She was not a fan of either candidate but seemed weirdly fond of Vladimir Putin.

"If only there were a way for Putin or someone like him to run in this election," she said.

I raised my eyebrows at this, but before I could reply, felt my cell phone vibrate in my pocket.

I grabbed it and looked at the screen. McCabe was calling. "Hey Wendy."

"Suzanne?"

"Yep," I said.

"We've gone to get Neil Gerutyer. They're holding him at the border. Canadian immigration officers stopped him. Don't know many details yet, but they are holding him for us. Dougherty and I are en route to pick him up and bring him back to Seattle to central booking."

"Ok," I said. I exhaled a breath I didn't know I'd been holding. All my research and planning . . . useless now.

"Dougherty wants to know if you want to come with to pick him up."

I thought for a moment and looked at the magick supplies in my basket. "Well, I was going to do a ritual with Leopold."

"A ritual for what?"

"Building blocks of the geo-location spell. Trying to get some practice."

"Well, it looks like you won't actually have to," she said.

"Looks like it," I said, feeling oddly disappointed. "There are some other things Leo and I could work on, too, tho'."

Silence on McCabe's end of the call. "You still there, Wendy?"

"Yes, still here, just . . . thinking." I could hear the concern in her voice.

"What's bugging you?"

"How secure is Juliet's place, now that the protective detail's been called off?" she queried.

"I'll ask her," I said, and looked at Juliet as she was seated on the couch.

"I can hear what she says," said Juliet, "Vampire powers, remember? Tell Ms. McCabe that I have state of the art alarm systems both mundane and magickal. If an unauthorized person or vampire crosses a threshold, I will know."

I repeated what Juliet said to McCabe.

Silence again from McCabe's end of the call. "Spit it out, Wendy," I said.

"I'd prefer you were with us, but it's your choice," McCabe said.

"Ok, well, it's not like you need me to wrestle Geruyter to the ground and put the cuffs on him. I'll be here, trying to find the bad guys on the vampire side of the equation."

"I understand. You want to be where you can be useful."

"Yes, exactly."

"I get it, but I have a bad feeling about this anyway," said McCabe.

"Noted. I'll call you or Dougherty in a couple of hours to see how the arrests went. We might have some leads on which vampires are the naughty ones by then."

"Ok. Talk to you then."

"See you," I said

"Hey Suzanne," Wendy said quickly. "Yeah?"

"Be careful."

"Yes, I will."

I pressed the red telephone icon on the display of my phone to terminate the call. I put my cell on the coffee table.

"Ms. McCabe is worried for you," said Juliet, a statement, not a question.

"Apparently."

"Does she have a touch of the Gift? Not necromancy, as you do, but perhaps premonition?"

"Not that she's mentioned," I said.

"Possibly she doesn't know herself," said Juliet.

"Could be."

Juliet sighed. *Why did vampires do that? It's not like they actually have to breathe air.* I guess the habit of human body language is indelible. Perhaps only a sigh can say everything and nothing at once.

Juliet said, "I find I am envious of her concern for you."

"Envious how?"

"It has been a long time since someone . . . worried about me." Juliet drew her eyebrows together, and her Cupid 's bow mouth pulled down at the corners.

I felt compassion wash over me. What would that be like, leading alone? Juliet had told me that as vampires aged they lost most of their human desire for closeness, friendship, love; looking at her now, I wondered if that was more a wish than a reality for her.

Juliet scowled when she saw my compassionate glance. She drew herself to her full height and squared her shoulders.

"Never mind that," she said. I nodded.

"Have you gathered everything from Leopold's list?" she asked.

"Yes, I think so: but with a switch in plans, it doesn't actually matter.

"All right, I will go to his quarters and rouse him and, as you say, 'get this party started'" Juliet smirked at her own joke. "Even if you two do no magick tonight, we can certainly watch Walter and Jesse cook up more methamphetamine."

I smiled slightly in response. "I think this is where you want me to say 'Science, bitches!', am I right?

Juliet giggled girlishly, a silver bell.

"I should meet you in Leo's quarters in what, ten minutes or so?" I asked.

"That should be long enough for his necessary toilette," Juliet said.

You mean gulping down another pint or two of blood and then- hopefully- washing his face. I nodded and smiled.

"See you in a few," I said as Juliet glided out of the room.

I checked my email on my phone and busied myself with the organizing supplies I needed in a basket.

Just as my internal clock told me it was time to make my way to Leopold's rooms, Yvonne walked in.

"Suzanne," she said, coldly, staring down the length of her long, narrow, nose. I looked up.

"Yes?"

"Juliet wants you outside; there is something she wants you to see."

"She was just here; she wanted me to meet her in Leopold's rooms."

"Never mind about that. Now she wants you outside on the side-yard patio."

I glanced out at the inky dark night. The window was glazed with rain. "In this?"

"Do not question me, necromancer, I am doing as I am bid." Her shoulders lifted in the subtlest of shrugs.

I sighed, stood up, and grasped the handle of the supplies basket on the coffee table.

"No need for that," Yvonne said, gesturing at the basket with a jerk of her chin, "leave it there."

I raised my eyebrows and said nothing. *Some arguments are not worth having.* I followed Yvonne down the stairs, through the living room, and out onto the patio.

The black November night enveloped us. Juliet's home was far enough up the mountain that there were no streetlights or even nearby neighbours. The only light on the patio spilled out from the living room through the sliding glass doors. I wrapped my arms around myself and shivered. *I should have put on a coat*; my sweater was not enough. I could see my breath. The pelting raindrops were icy pins. I could hear the gurgle of the stream that ran underneath the house, so it wasn't could enough to freeze running water. *Stop being a baby about the cold*, I told myself. *Something was not right. Focus on that, Suzanne.*

"Where is she, Yvonne?"

Yvonne smiled creepily. "She will be here."

That's when I heard it.

"Gnung gnung gnung."

I startled and spun to face the voice I heard.

A small head crested the embankment that led to the stream. The person continued up the embankment, and soon it was clear that it was a slender girl of ten clad in a torn, dirty shift.

"Gnung gnung gnung."

Oh shit. That sound. That's the revenant sound. Oh, fuck oh fuck oh fuck.

I felt Yvonne's hand on my shoulder. I screamed. That brought a low chuckle to Yvonne's throat, her syrup-over-sandpaper voice making the hair on my arms stand.

"Suzanne" Yvonne whispered, "Your fear is so delicious, it is like sugared berries on my tongue."

You know how time can dilate? How under great stress, our minds try to help us by slowing the progress of events, so we have—seemingly—more time to process our thoughts? Time opened its petals, and I was able to piece it together: motive, means, opportunity, just like Dougherty had taught me.

Motive: Yvonne was sick of Juliet's rule here in the Western Lands, Yvonne thought she would make a better Acolyte than Juliet.

Means: As a vampire, Yvonne could take the 'throw-away' children that Geruyter offered her and make revenants. Using the revenants as slaves in the sex trade would give Yvonne cash to finance bribes and other aspects of her coup d'état, as well as providing some blackmail and extortion opportunities later. At least some of the pedophiles and kinksters seeking contact with revenant children would be well-placed, socially and financially. That meant more money, more access to power.

Opportunity: Juliet did not believe any of her henchies would betray her, and thus was blind to anything hinky on Yvonne's part. Yvonne had spotted Juliet's enormous self-satisfaction and exploited it.

"Gnung gnung gnung."

The sound of the revenant child brought me back to here and now. Time resumed its normal pace. I felt the icy rain on my face.

"Yvonne," I said, my voice quavering, "Why have you done this? How could you? Those children—they were innocent. They deserved to be safe and to have a childhood." My voice cracked.

Yvonne's laughter was unexpected, a sharp bark at the edge of the pool of light spilling through the patio doors. "You know nothing," she hissed. She stroked the matted hair of the revenant as the small figure stood next to her. "Those children were not children as someone in your times would think of them. Besides, you moderns are too sentimental about children and childhood. Face the facts—children are a resource to be used. The children we took, they were loved by no one. They were there to be used. They already had been used by, what is called now, the 'social welfare' system. They were loved and protected by no one. If not used by me, then they would be by someone else. You mistake these children for more than what they were, Suzanne. They are a basket of windfallen fruit."

If I can get Yvonne talking, I might be able to delay or forestall whatever fate she had in mind for me.

Yvonne continued to speak while my mind raced. "You are a stupid modern woman. You think there is a line between good and evil, right and wrong. There is not. There is only one eternal divide, between the weak and the strong. Everything is permitted if I am strong enough to take it for myself. So, I have my Bao, I have this sweet thing,"—she caressed the revenant's neck, and the child vampire arched into the gesture like a cat being petted. – "to be serve me. Soon I will have you, if I want it. I have not decided. I am thinking of it, how you moderns say it? In terms of a 'cost-benefit analysis'."

I could see her smirk at her own cleverness; her features beautiful, cold, deranged.

I said nothing. I was focusing on the feeling of my stomach dropping thirty floors. Being in the presence of such calculated cruelty made my reality list suddenly to one side, like a capsizing ship. *Where is my phone? Can I dial 911? Oh shit, I left it on the table in my room.*

Yvonne continued, still stroking the revenant, "I don't know if your mortal brain can absorb this, but I want the Western Lands. I plan to Turn everyone who can assist me with that goal. Hence my consideration of you, sweet Suzanne. You are a useful bargaining tool when I must battle with Juliet for control. She desires you and is intrigued by your abilities. You are worth something to her.

I shouldn't wonder that she plans to keep you in a couple of positions to serve— perhaps as a kind of interrogator for diplomatic use, and most definitely as a servant between her legs."

Yvonne stepped closer to me, her slender, graceful hand outstretched to smooth some hair off my brow. I steeled myself to stop from cringing. Her hand slid down my face and cupped my flaming cheek.

"Ah, a blush-I think you might like to serve her as much as she might wish to receive your service. Our Juliet is very unusual among our kind, you see. She does not feel lust often, but when she does, it is invariably for a plump partridge of a woman such as yourself. I shouldn't wonder that she tumbled the rosy-cheeked milkmaids into haylofts before she was Turned. I have never known her to lie with a man willingly."

I kept my mind half on Yvonne's monologue and half on trying to see what was on or near the patio. There was nothing I could use as a weapon. Shit, this is going to get bad. I tried to stop my heart from battering against my ribcage like a trapped bird.

Yvonne ran her fingertips over my face, lightly. I could hear the revenant's vocalizations.

"Gnung gnung gnung."

I bit back a scream.

Bao walked around the side of the house, carrying a body over his left shoulder. By the time he'd reached the amber circle of light that illuminated the brick patio we had stood on, I could see it was Juliet, and she had part of a wooden katana sticking out of her back.

Chapter Twenty-one

The revenant's sounds got louder, more excited; I think she could scent Juliet's blood. Being vampire, when wounded, Juliet did not bleed freely as a human being would. Instead of bright red rivulets, a viscous mahogany-colored ichor oozed around the edges of her wound.

"Was she any trouble, love?" said Yvonne, one hand smoothing over her prodigious pregnant belly.

Bao shook his head. "No, she never suspected. She allowed me to walk behind where she was seated. I pierced her heart through the back."

Yvonne frowned, raven-wing brows drawing together over the bridge of her nose. "I suppose that means the Eames chair in Leopold's quarters is ruined?"

Bao shifted Juliet's body higher on his shoulder, redistributing her weight. "It cannot be helped; I would have had no better chance."

Yvonne shrugged. "You are very likely right. And what of Leopold?"

"I had almost drained him dry, reclaiming what we had fed him, but then I heard this one scream," Bao said, pointing at me with his chin. " I came to you so we can finish our business with Juliet. Leopold is not going anywhere; he was so drained and dry he looked like parchment and had lost the power of speech."

Yvonne nodded. "To the stream then."

Bao and the revenant started down the embankment toward the stream rushing under the house. I did not move until Yvonne grabbed me by my hair and started dragging me along with her.

I let myself be dragged without protest as I was busy trying to reach out to Leopold with my mind. *Leopold! Help me!*

Nothing but a soft tinkle of the opening phrases of "Clair de Lune." *Shit shit shit. Still there, but barely just. Shit shit shit.*

Yvonne yanked my head backwards using my hair as a handle. "Trying to reach out to him, little necromancer? It will do you no good. If Bao says Leopold is incapacitated, it is hopeless. Soon Juliet will be dead, Leopold will be dead, there will be no one to help you."

Her beautiful blue-green eyes glittered like pitiless marbles, and she grabbed my arm with her free hand and twisted it up behind my back. I heard something pop as something gave way in my shoulder. *Oh fuck, has she dislocated it? Why don't I feel it?* Then I noticed the pounding of my heart and the manic song adrenalin was singing in my blood. *Right. Fight or flight. If I survive the night, my shoulder is going to hurt like a son-of-a-bitch later. Here's hoping I live that long.*

Yvonne frog-marched me over the crest of the embankment and down the slope to the stream's edge. The embankment was much steeper and deeper than it had seemed from its crest, the stream rushing madly along the bottom of this ravine. My Converse sneakers gave me little purchase on the sodden grass and oozing mud. Yvonne was oblivious. She dragged me down the wet slope, her boots squelching through the mud.

Bao and the revenant had laid Juliet's body out on a canvas tarp. The ground below was so saturated with the November rain that the tarp looked like a sheet of paper towel tossed over a spill; dark splotches appeared. The icy rain continued to pelt us, but the three vampires seemed indifferent to that.

How are they going to burn her down to powder in a downpour like this?

As though he'd heard my thought, Bao drew a slender can of lighter fluid from the cargo pocket of his black tactical pants.

"Not yet, my sweet, not quite yet. First, this little one gets to feed!"

"Gnung gnung gnung gnung" shrieked the revenant.

Yvonne released her hold on my hair and my arm. I immediately slipped in the mud and landed on my ass, both feet in the stream.

Yvonne stroked the revenant's dirty face with tenderness, even though the child-sized vampire was slathering at the mouth in anticipation of drinking Juliet's blood and eating her flesh.

Yvonne held the smaller vampire's chin in her hand. "You may drink, you may eat of her flesh, but do not sever her head from her body, or dislocate the katana from her chest. Your punishment will be severe if you do."

The revenant nodded in response.

"Then feast, my pet, feast."

The revenant fell upon her meal. She ripped Juliet's dress down the front and plunged her fangs and fingers into Yvonne's soft white belly. She growled as she ripped and tore Juliet's flesh, careful not to disturb the broken wooden sword sticking out of Yvonne's chest. Bao watched over the revenant as she ate, ready to intervene if the stake started to work its way loose of the tunnel it had made through Juliet's chest when Bao had impaled her.

I managed to stand up on the sodden shoulder of the stream, water squelching around my soaked and frozen feet. I was cold, so cold I was numb everywhere. My nose was running; my teeth were chattering. My sodden hair hung around my face like icy snakes.

"Yvonne," I said, trying to keep my voice, low, calm. *Find out what she wants.*

Yvonne glanced away from her pet's meal. "You are wondering why I have not killed you yet?"

"Yes."

"Like Juliet, I think you could be useful. And profitable. I can think of many individuals who would pay to . . . study you."

"You mean ... do experiments on me."

Yvonne shrugged. She glanced back at the revenant feeding on Juliet under Bao's watchful eye. A smile played over Yvonne's lips as if she was watching a favorite kitten gambol after a laser pointer.

I shivered, not from cold.

"There is an alternative to that," she said.

Dear gods, do I really want to know?

"I could protect you from those who might like to study you, or use you for their own ends."

"What do you get out of it?"

"Access to your powers once they are fully developed. And a few odd jobs along the way."

I definitely did not like the way she'd said 'odd jobs'. I noticed I was trembling, my teeth chattering.

"So, if I agree to develop my powers, and let you wield me as a weapon, you'll let me live?"

"More or less," she said, shrugging.

"What's the more part?" I asked.

"I want to see you deliver the critical blow that will help finish Juliet forever," she said, pointing at the body on the tarp.

The revenant was still drinking from Juliet and eating chunks of Juliet's flesh. I tried not to think about the wet slurping sounds she made as she ate. Juliet's abdomen from bottom of the rib cage to just below the navel was scooped out and hollow. There was much less gore than there would have been if Juliet had been human, but the sight was no less disgusting for all that.

Yvonne clapped her hands. "Enough! Bao, drag her away, she's had enough to eat."

The revenant paused for a moment, absorbing what Yvonne had said, then ravenously took several large rapid bites from Juliet's pelvis. Her cheeks bulged as she chewed. Her mouth was so stuffed that shreds of something pale and gelatinous hung over her chin. *Ah, good grief, is that a fucking ovary hanging out of her mouth?* I shuddered and felt my stomach lurch. *Don't throw up, don't throw up.*

"You know what needs to be done?" asked Yvonne.

"Yes. I must sever her head from her body after she is staked, then burn the parts," Bao said.

"And spread the ashes into two separate bodies of running water. Juliet built her home over a stream for just that reason, you know," Said Yvonne.

"And what, we go on a field trip to chuck the cremated head into the Sammamish?" I snapped. Faking bravado makes me feel better.

Yvonne chuckled. "No need to go that far. Further uphill there is another stream. We will go there."

"Yvonne, what purpose does that have? I mean, I know you could kill me where I stand quicker than it takes to say it, isn't that enough leverage? Do you really have to implicate me in Juliet fully Crossing Over so you can hold it over me? You have all the power here."

"It's not about leverage. Of course, I want you to be loyal to me, and me alone. But I want this because the thought disgusts and horrifies you, it is written all over your face." She smiled broadly.

Sadistic bitch.

"That thought was an obvious one, too, Suzanne." Yvonne, faster than a blur, was holding my hair and dislocated arm again, steering me closer to Juliet's ravaged body. It happened so fast I didn't even have time to scream.

"Look at her," Yvonne purred, "even now if we took the katana stub out of her chest, gave her extra blood, in time she would heal what my pretty pet has done."

Yvonne foot swept me and caught me before I fell on my face in the mud and mahogany ichor. *It looks like a rooibos treacle. Irrelevancies. Isn't that a sign of shock?*

Yvonne was speaking. I wasn't paying attention, though. I was dizzy from the pain in my dislocated shoulder; my numb feet had stopped hurting—always a bad sign of frostbite.

Yvonne tugged on the dislocated arm and shouted "Suzanne!"

I focused my eyes on her face.

"I said get on your knees, you stupid girl," she shrieked.

It took a minute, but I figured out how to kneel in the icy mud near Juliet's head.

"Do you know what I require?"

"That I cut off Juliet's head, so we can burn it, and her headless body."

"Not 'cut', Suzanne." She palmed the back of my head, her bony fingers caught in my tangled, soaked hair. She started to force my head down.

Oh, hell no! She wants me to chew through Juliette's neck. What the fuck!

I took a deep breath but realized that opening my mouth would make it easier for Yvonne to force my teeth into Juliet's throat. *Don't panic don't panic don't panic.*

Until that moment, I had thought I was just playing along, that I didn't really have any intention of beheading Juliet to save my life. But as Yvonne forced my head the final few inches to Juliet's neck, I knew that now I wasn't playing.

I am not brave. I am afraid to die.

I opened my mouth just as my lips brushed the cold velvety skin of Juliet's neck. I bit her, again and again. I did not think about texture or flavor.

Yvonne's laugh was warm honey over fine gravel. I could feel her eyes on me, minutely examining the flex and tension of the muscles of my jaw.

"Look how she works, so methodical! Even in a straight line!" she said.

I felt Bao and the revenant draw closer to observe.

The muscles and tendons of Juliet's neck tasted slightly salty; then I realized that tears were pouring down my face as I gnawed. And it was still fucking raining. I growled.

Yvonne responded by jerking on the injured arm, jostling the shoulder. I screamed.

I felt something flutter in my stomach. For a split second, I thought I was just readying to vomit; then I realized that a sound was building up in my core. I flashed on that night in the warehouse when I used sound to abuse Leopold while he was still trapped in his coffin. The pulse of the sound or musical note or whatever it was throbbed inside me, as I continued to use my teeth to decapitate Juliet.

The sound burst out of me even though Yvonne's hand would not let me up. I had chewed away enough of Juliet's neck meat that I had a bit of breathing room. That room was also enough to release the sound. It came out all at once and flew away as if tied to an arrow, headed where I did not know.

"She tries to speak," said Bao

"So what?" responded Yvonne.

I continued to chew, even though I heard rumbling and cracks in the distance. Vampire hearing being what it is, they could hear something I could not. Yvonne let go of me. The three vampires leapt to their feet, bodies tense and ready for anything. I sat back on my heels.

Now, it's not true to say that I made the unstable stream banks uphill from our position in the ravine rupture. But it'd be a lie to say I had nothing to do with it. Something had happened, and I bet my song was in play somehow. *Good.*

A few moments later I rued that thought, as Juliet's body, Yvonne, Bao, the revenant, and I were swept along in a roiling torrent of icy, muddy water.

Chapter Twenty-two

After what could have been mere seconds, or perhaps an hour, I came up for air. The water was so cold that it almost felt like fire on the few bony parts I have. My wrists and ankles burned and were stiff as concrete. One of my feet was bare. It seems that my left sneaker flew entirely off my foot when the mudslide hit us, taking my sock along with it. I dog paddled, trying to see the vampires in and among the floating debris. The only light came from through the sliding doors of the house, far above us. The faint light spilled over the edge of the ravine; I could make out shapes, but not details. The freezing rain continued.

Numb and breathless, I bobbed in the water, reaching down toward the bottom of the stream with the toe of my remaining Converse. I could just barely touch the stream bed. I dog-paddled toward the closest bank until I could plant sneaker and barefoot on the solid-ish ground. I walked the rest of the way out of the stream, forcing my numb limbs to keep moving as I pulled myself up onto the bank. The chattering of my teeth was loud; I was sure the vampires could hear it.

Vampire senses being what they are, I knew they could see, hear, or even smell my location long before I knew theirs. *Pointless to try to hide.* I scanned the surface of the water for something I could use as a club or a stake. My brain was working triple time trying to find a way out of this. *Don't have a chance in physical combat with vampires. Can I make them mad enough that they'll just kill me quickly?* A wave of shame passed over me about what they had forced me to do. *I deserve to die after something like that.* My thoughts raced in contradictory directions: on the one hand, I was disgusted at my own cowardice, at acquiescing. On the other hand, I wanted to live, despite the fact that some third part of my thought process was aware that was likely a pipe dream. *Never mind all of that. Figure out a way to get the fuck out of here.* I decided to go with Plan C and get the fuck outta here.

As I grew more accustomed to the low light, I could make out some branches with something tangled in them, sticking out of the middle of the stream a few yards way. The revenant, floating face down. One leg and both arms stood out from her body at odd angles. Not actually floating, either—two stout branches had impaled the revenant as she had tumbled downhill with many thousands of gallons of water and mud. She was speared on the branches, body out of the water, head under the surface, face down. At least that means I can't hear that goddamn noise she makes. Given her predicament, I could wade out to her and cut off her head, bringing to final death to her. *I need something sharp.*

My focus on the revenant was so single-pointed, I was startled by a few splashes coming from the other side of the stream. I could barely make out the vague shape of Bao dragging Yvonne up onto the opposite stream bank. He propped her up against a tree, legs spread out in front of her.

"She is not dead, merely pinned. When we draw the wood from her body, she will heal."

At first, I thought he meant the revenant girl, but as I looked more closely, what I thought were shadows cast by the faint light from above were actually black branches protruding from Yvonne's chest, throat, and shoulder. She too was pinned and helpless, her eyes closed. Her rounded pregnant belly seemed incongruously unharmed. *As she was swept away, did Yvonne try to protect her belly? Never mind that right now, Suzanne, think!*

Bao knelt next to her, examining the placement of the branches. He was clearly assessing the best way to pull the branches out of Yvonne. He tenderly brushed the hair away from Yvonne's face as he shouted, "Necromancer, come here. Your mistress needs your assistance."

I don't know if it was watching Bao treat the monster Yvonne with such concern and consideration that did it. It could also have been Bao's matter-of-fact assumption that since they had been successful in forcing me to savage Juliet, I was now their creature. Maybe I was sick of being frightened. Maybe I was curious what would happen if I tried using my song as a weapon.

I felt the now-familiar unsettled, burning sensation in my stomach. I thought about what Yvonne had made me do, what Yvonne had done to the children she'd turned into revenants, I thought about my mangled breast and shoulder. My rage swelled.

I threw my head back and howled a shrill note. Bao clapped his hands over his ears, bent double in pain. Even the two pinned vampires responded. The revenant splashed in the stream, wriggling around on the branches like a worm on a hook. Yvonne's eyes flew open. She could not move other parts of her body. Her nose started to bleed, slowly, that same mahogany ichor that had been in Juliet's body. Her eyes rounded with fear.

I could learn to like that expression on her face.

I stopped for a second to grab a steadying breath, then continued to howl. Bao was shrieking in pain, clutching his ears as he thrashed on the ground. The revenant girl flopped like a suffocating fish.

Teardrops of ichor slid over Yvonne's cheeks, and her nose continued to bleed. Her head popped like an overfed tick.

My ears still ringing with the sound of my own voice, I sat down hard in the mud, exhausted.

Bao was covered in splatter. Brains, ichor, bits of skin and hair covered his face and clothes. He stared at the ragged wet stump that used to support Yvonne's head. I smelled a scent that was a mixture of low tide and poopy baby diaper. *Is that her brains that smell like that?* I gagged. *Don't throw up; you'll have to look at chewed up pieces of Juliet's neck if you do.* That thought didn't help. I retched convulsively until all I could do was dry heave. I did not look at what had been inside my stomach. I wiped my mouth on my waterlogged sweater sleeve.

Bao, still as a statue, stared at Yvonne's remains.

"If it was severed, it could have re-attached itself over time. I would have cared for her, helped her." His voice was mournful. He plucked some greyish chunks of brain from his sleeve, rubbed them between his fingertips. "I do not think this can be healed."

You know how people talk about having out-of-body experiences when they are in car accidents or fall of off buildings? It happens at other times, too. Like when you look in the eyes of a man who loved a sadistic, murderous bitch for over a century, and has now discovered you've popped her head like a rotten grape.

I thought about my mum, about McCabe, Dougherty, Star, Sarah, Josh, all the people I would be leaving behind. I thought about how none of the kids that we tried to save actually were saved. I squeezed my eyes shut and waited for Bao to murder me.

Instead, I heard him say,"Oh!"

I opened my eyes.

He was crouched down near Yvonne's remains. When her head burst, it looked as though something had also happened to her belly. It was splayed open like a nineteenth-century anatomy drawing if the drawing had been made by Jack the Ripper. I think Bao and I had both been so shocked by her head exploding; we hadn't looked to see if my song had other effects.

Bao reached his hand inside the cavity and felt around, a thoughtful look on his face.

Bao couldn't see that a pale blob was inching slowly away from Yvonne, something gooey, gelatinous. It left a trail of mahogany ichor. Yvonne's fetus had escaped the prison of Yvonne's body.

"Hey, look!" I said, pointing at the slime trail and the squirming blob undulating across the grass.

Bao emitted a loud, joyous bark, scooped up the jelly baby, and disappeared at the speed of blur into the deep dark forest.

"Huh," I said. *Not sure what to make of that. Was he going to come back? Don't worry about that, Suzanne, try to find help.*

I started to make my way along the creek bank. I knew that downhill from Juliet's home, the creek was crossed by a bridge. If I could get to that bridge, eventually a car would pass, and surely someone would help me. Besides, given the icy temperature and the fact I was soaking wet and slathered in mud, I needed to keep moving.

As I slowly clambered through the forest, I actually caught a break: for the first time in months, the rain stopped. More time passed. Just as I approached the road and bridge, I noticed that the skies had cleared enough that I could finally see the inverted bowl of the night sky, stars glittering like flecks of mica. In the distance, I could hear the sirens of emergency responders.

Chapter Twenty—Three

Which brings us to now. Where do things sit now?

Leopold survived the near-draining Bao had inflicted on him. Apparently, Jack had returned home after his grocery and plasma run, saw the damage and debris left behind by the torrent of water. He searched the house, room by room. One of the first rooms he checked was Leopold's as we'd all been spending quite a lot of time in there watching shows.

Jack opened a vein when he found Leopold and shared as much blood with him as he could. When Leopold could speak coherently, he described how Bao had staked Juliet and tried to drain Leopold, that I'd reached out to him psychically, but he'd been too weak to help me. Jack called McCabe and Dougherty and told them Juliet and I were missing, but that at least I was still alive. Leopold had told Jack he could still feel my psychic presence, even though he was too weak to reach out to me.

McCabe and Dougherty had returned to Seattle from the Canadian border with Geruyter in shackles. Just as they were finishing the booking paperwork, a uniform told them there had been a 9-1-1 call from someone near Juliet's home, something about a mudslide or flood or avalanche that had messed up one of the palatial homes lower on the mountain that Juliet's. They'd left SPD city cells immediately. They were almost to Juliet's house by the time they heard from Jack that Juliet and I were missing.

The house downstream that had been damaged in the mudslide was unoccupied at the time as the owners were away in Aruba. However, they employed a live-in farrier to care for their horses. The farrier had called 9-1-1. She'd heard some rumbling and saw the mudslide roll in over part of the fields, enveloping fences, damaging the foundation of the main house, and upsetting the horses.

The firefighters were the first to make it to the area. Their truck had gone speeding past me as I stood at the side of the road waving my soggy sweater arms. I don't think they saw me. But the ambulance that followed them about three minutes later did. They stopped, loaded me into the ambulance, and kept on toward the horse farm. I told them about Leopold, and they called that in as well. Central reported to McCabe and Dougherty that I had been picked up by an ambulance, was receiving treatment and was not in any immediate danger.

By the time everyone was on the same page, and Leopold and I had been transported to the hospital, it was almost dawn. Seattle General had only one light-tight ward suitable for a vampire patient as vampires tended not to seek treatment in hospitals. Nevertheless, civil rights laws demand that every hospital has at least one vampire-friendly room. Leopold and I had asked that I share his four-bed hospital room, and no one wanted to argue about it as we were mere moments from sunrise.

Dougherty and McCabe had stayed at Juliet's to search the woods for the revenant girl, Bao, the vampire fetus, and what might remain of Juliet. Because I had not managed to sever her head from her body, her injuries would not be fatal unless Bao had circled back to finish the job.

Later that morning, one of the unis participating in the search found the remains of the revenant girl, still impaled on debris in the stream. Her wet environment had not helped her when the sun came up. In fact, it probably took longer for her to cook into crispy critter status than it otherwise would have. I could not feel sad about that. They decapitated and burned what was left of her, and sprinkled the cremains into two different fast-running streams, just to be safe. It's wise to leave nothing to chance.

Everything dies if you cut off its head.

After a few days, Leopold and I were released from the hospital to continue to convalesce at home. Neither one of us wanted to go back to Juliet's house; my apartment was even less secure. Now that the core group in Juliet's Coven was missing or destroyed, Leopold told us to expect both local vampires and ones from further afield to try to fill the power vacuum. Best to be hidden away when that started to happen.

Jack, Leopold, and I moved into rooms at the Holiday Inn. Leopold wanted the Hilton, but Jack pointed out that Leopold's bank accounts had been dormant for over a century, so he had no access to his fortune at the moment. It would take Booker some time to get all that sorted out. In the meantime, the Holiday Inn was the best Jack, and I could do by pooling our resources and getting a bit of emergency funding from the SPD.

Star, Sarah, and Josh wanted me to move in with them, but I declined. I don't think they understood why I couldn't join them. They had normal lives. I wanted to keep it that way. I'm not sure if that would continue if I moved in. I hope that being a lightning rod for trouble doesn't continue, but I've learned there are no guarantees. Bao could be in any midnight shadow waiting to murder me for killing his lady-love. Not to mention what the vampire fetus might be able to do. It makes me shudder just to think about it.

So, I'm in an in-between place right now. I value the normal-ish life I had as a bookstore clerk and part-time necromancer; I just don't think I can necessarily go back to it.

Dougherty understands that sentiment, a little. He really doesn't approve of Leopold nor Jack, so I haven't seen much of Dougherty. McCabe understands it a lot. She's been spending a certain amount of time with us in the hotel, binge-watching *The Sopranos* and holding Jack's hand. They are definitely an item again.

Given that Leopold hadn't fully bounced back from being released from the Den and a century of starvation before he was near-drained by Bao, he's still not up to full strength. He's my vassal, so he's my responsibility. I take the best care of him I can.

My cuts, bruises, and dislocated shoulder I suffered the night of the flood and mudslide have all healed, as they were just mundane injuries. My shoulder and chest still hurt a lot–given the magickal nature of those wounds, they may not get much better. Dr. Chau informs me that as they are magickal, it's unlikely I'll be able to have reconstructive surgery to rebuild my left breast or do anything about all the scars. It is what it is; I try not to think about it too much. It's not like anybody sees me naked, and it'll be months before tank top season, so I'll worry about my appearance later.

Mainly I keep dreaming about Juliet. No one's found her body. It could be that she is still alive, maybe. Perhaps Bao has her. Or perhaps he did but has since disposed of her. For all I know, he chopped her up and fed her to the jelly baby.

When I dream about Juliet, I am back in the forest, chewing on her neck meat with my blunt human teeth. In my dreams I enjoy it, every chomp is almost ecstatic. Do I actually want to take that last bite? Gods save me from me.

About the Author

Chloe Cocking is a writer of dark urban fantasy and a lover of all things caffeinated. She is almost entirely normal in her non-writing life, so there is no reason to be afraid. She is hard at work on other projects. Want to know details? Sign up for her newsletter or check out her blog *Dark Wine and Shallow Graves*!

You can say "Hi" on Good Reads, or reach out on Twitter @LadyIncisor or check out her author page on Facebook.

www.ingramcontent.com/pod-product-compliance
Lightning Source LLC
Chambersburg PA
CBHW030402030726
47497CB00002B/448